R

Ralph was getting excited. This was something of an achievement, given how drunk he was. It was common at this point in the evening to find him unconscious, slumped over a table with his cheek resting in a puddle of slightly stale beer, or asleep at some random point between the tavern and the bum hut where he and most of the bob-a-days spent their time waiting for work loading and unloading the passing river boats. Ralph was angry though, and his anger was having the effect of, if not exactly sobering him, at least stimulating his brain to a point where he could focus his eyes and his thoughts to a greater degree than might have otherwise have been the case.

"I did get hit by lightning!" he protested loudly. This earned him a sour look from the barman, and he continued in a voice that though for the moment at least was quieter, was not any less heated. "I thought I heard a noise in the garden, 'nd I got out of bed and went to the window," he said thickly, "and there was this big bloody flash, 'nd next thing I'm stood starkers in a field, hugging my bits 'nd wondering what sappened." Ralph paused and gave his captive but somewhat less than captivated audience a pleading look.

1

The young man sitting across from him was trying to keep his expression as blank as a virgin canvas, but though he achieved this credibly well, his eyes still betrayed something of the frustration that he was feeling.

Ralph gulped his beer and put it down. "Enaway, that wos wot sappened" he insisted, daring the stranger to suggest that it might have been otherwise. He drained the beaker and stared into it longingly. "Still haf a scar on my chest y'know." He brightened a little as he said, "wanna see it?"

Jarek did not want to see the scar. He would have gladly traded a year of his life to be able to turn the clock back to a point when the possibility of that question and the events leading up to it could have been avoided. At best he was indifferent to the drunk's problems - real or imagined - and would have happily paid someone to swap seats with him if he had not spent his last few pennies buying a drink to avoid being thrown out.

Ralph continued to rail against the world - this world - and the seemingly discriminate way that it had rough handled him into his present situation. He grew redder in the face as he struggled to find and form words that would do justice to his indignation, but nothing he said seemed to cause more than a slight lifting of an eyebrow. Ralph slapped his palms down angrily on the sticky table, causing the two beakers that were sat upon it to bounce. His being empty bounced higher, and would have toppled onto the floor but for Jarek's quick intervention on his behalf. He glowered at Jarek then lowered his chin on to his hands and sank into a sullen glassy-eyed review of the preceding weeks.

Jarek was doing something similar. He tried to compose a mental catalogue of the many bad things that had happened to him that day, but much of it was blurred snippets, or so frenetic that he was unable to isolate more than a few scraps of the detail. He wondered briefly if he had unwittingly offended a luck weaver or some other kind of magic peddling scoundrel with the ability to ruin what might have been a perfectly good day for him.

"I toljer 'bout how blue the sky was in summer, dint I?" Jarek groaned inwardly. That morning he had been sat in a pub with painted walls and clean sawdust on the floor, cock sure of himself and brimming with a sense of his own worth. Now he was sat in a grubby tavern, the gods knew where, scared to leave for fear of what he might find waiting for him outside. He wanted to go home, wanted to go back to the quiet and safe little town where he had grown up. His auntie's house that had seemed confined and smothering to him only a few hours ago, now filled him with a sense of longing that made his chest ache and his eyes water.

Jarek was considered by some people in his hometown to be a talented graphical humorist. 'Some' was basically his aunt Laurie and a few of her friends who agreed with her more out of politeness than from any particular opinion. One of these friends had told his auntie that someone else had told her that they had heard more than one person say that his work was a bit funny. Believing that to mean funny humorous rather than the other way that they had actually meant it, Jarek decided that it was time to leave home and go and see if he could make a living at it. He left home with a haversack on his back and four pounds and threpence hay-pn'y burning a hole in his pocket. He got as far as the next village and booked himself into a way-man's lodge. Jarek stowed his bag under the bunk in his stall and went down to the barroom and bought himself a drink to celebrate his newly gained independence.

Some people will tell you that a good pub should have plenty of character, but most good landlords will tell you that it is the characters propping the bar up who make the pub good or bad. They entertain themselves at each other's expense rather than the landlord's, and they hardly ever complain about the price of the beer or the state of the toilets. The young man who was sat at the bar showing one of his regulars some sketches was not what you might call a character, but he was a bit of an oddball, which in the landlord's opinion was almost as good.

The sketches were of Lowland trolls getting up to some of the more bizarre things that it was believed that Lowland trolls got up to in private. In truth, very few people knew what Lowland trolls got up to in private, because that would have meant getting private with one of them to find out, which was something that very few people wanted to do because of what they had heard.

Sat on the other side of Jarek was a small time theatrical agent with a big problem. The agent was almost as drunk as Jarek was starting to get. He had gotten drunk intentionally in an effort to dull his senses to a point where he would not feel, or at least would not remember feeling the beating that he was expecting to get that evening when he told his clients that he could not deliver the comedy striptease act that he had promised them. The reason he had been unable to get the promised act was due to his clients being Lowland trolls - a detail that a colleague had failed to mention when putting the job his way!

The agent almost fell off of his stool when he heard the young man who was sitting next to him telling someone that he was a comic strip artist who had done some stuff with Lowland trolls. He had of course only been half listening to the conversation, but it was the half that he wanted to hear that he thought he had heard correctly. He turned slowly in his seat with his most winning smile in place and offered to buy Jarek another drink.

It did not take the theatrical agent long to realise that he had made a mistake, but he figured that Jarek - who was now almost blind drunk - might be persuaded to take the gig on the basis that it would give him a chance to observe the subject of his sketches up close. Several more drinks followed and were then followed by a bit where Jarek slapped his hand down and exclaimed loudly, "by god, I'll do yer show and damn the critics!" after which he slipped off of his stool and knocked himself out on the edge of the bar.

The next few hours were a blurry nightmare for Jarek. He was moving, and on a cart of some description - that much he could tell from all the jostling and creaking - and his hands and feet were tied securely so that he was unable to sit up or move about. His shirt had been pulled up over his head, limiting his view of the world to the shifting dapples of light and shade that played like an out of focus movie on the material.

The first time he was conscious enough to voice any concern, he was greeted with soothing reassurances from the theatrical agent. The second time was answered with a knock on the head that made him think twice about speaking a third time, and so he laid there sobbing silently into his shirt, his mind racing from one blood curdling scenario to the next as he considered what it was that his captor might want with him. Finally, warn out by worrying, he fell asleep.

Jarek was shaken awake a few hours later and trundled from the back of the cart. He might have collapsed but for the cart against his back propping him up. It was dark and the temperature had dropped slightly so that he was shivering with more than just fear. Hands gripped his arms tightly while someone untied his legs, then he was led stumbling up several steps onto a small wooden stage.

Jarek felt the scratch of a coarse rope being tied around his waist. Something slapped lightly against his groin with a sound like a small drum being tapped.

"Give 'em a good show lad," the agent whispered next to his ear. There was a note of nervousness in his voice that was further qualified when he added, "and we might both get out of here in one piece." With that the agent quickly untied the shirt from Jarek's head and dropped it onto the floor next to him. He stepped back and looked at Jarek thoughtfully then picked up the roll of drawings and shoved them into his still bound hands. "Do somethin' suggestive with it," he offered, winking in a way that said, and I think you know what I mean.

Jarek watched him go then stared dumbly down at the rolled up drawings and the inflated bladder that was hanging below it. He looked up at the moth eaten curtain in front of him. There was something he was missing, something that he was not getting or had forgotten. All the pieces were there, but he was shook up quite badly and scared, and more than a little drunk still. He listened to the indecipherable thrum of many excited voices coming from beyond the curtain. Occasionally a voice or a snatch of a conversation would rise out of the surrounding noise, but so fragmented and heavily accented as to make it almost unintelligible.

Jarek wriggled his hands in an effort to get some feeling back into them but only succeeded in giving himself pins and needles. Somewhere beyond the curtain a small band thumped and whined into life, and he jumped slightly and let go of the roll of pictures. He managed to catch the corner of one as the rest spilled untidily onto the floor, and it fell open just as the curtain was pulled back.

The audience - fifty-seven Lowland trolls and one very nervous theatrical agent - leaned forward almost as a body to get a better look at the picture that was hanging limply from

Jarek's fingers. The picture - a bold work in pastel and graphite - showed two trolls getting complicated with an elf.

"That ain't natural," a troll exclaimed loudly as the band withered into silence.

"It's proper disgustin' if yer ask me," someone else put in.

A troll sitting near to the front appreciated the technique if not the subject matter and was gracious enough to say so. This was met with a stony silence that slid seamlessly into a painfully stretched out moment, which in turn was followed by the bit where the stretched out moment snaps back to its proper length, catching everyone by surprise.

Jarek gave a little shriek, grabbed what he could of his belongings from the stage and made a run for it. It was pitch black away from the lit camp and he stumbled several times as he ran blindly over the uneven terrain. Behind him the night was filled with the expletives of the angry trolls and the clatter and clash of them fighting their way through a tangle of upturned chairs and discarded musical instruments to give chase.

If Jarek had hoped that the dark would conceal his escape, a jingling tambourine skimming passed his head put pay to that. Desperate and more afraid than he had ever been before in his short life, he hunkered down and squeezed the last of his failing strength into his aching legs. He ran on in a staggering half sprinting fashion for ten minutes or so, but could not keep it up, and gradually slowed to a stumble that was little more than a fast walking pace.

Having seen Jarek off, most of the trolls returned to the camp laughing and joking, and it was only a few young hotheads who continued the pursuit, and they were more interested in tormenting Jarek than actually catching him and risking getting hurt.

Jarek staggered babbling like a Murd touched fool into the path of a mounted patrol. They would have taken him as such had his pleas not been accompanied by the whoops and growls of the few trolls who were still following him, coming from the trees that edged the dirt road. He begged and pleaded with the riders to rescue him and was eventually taken up by one of them.

The riders took him as far as the nearest town and left him outside the tavern in which he was now sat. Unfortunately, the nearest town was little more than a third of a mile along the road from where they had found him, and he was terrified that the trolls might have followed and be out there still, searching the streets for him.

"Enway, I woke up wif a spitting headache ina field, 'nd it was full ov..." Ralph slurred on in that lazy way that only another drunk could ever hope to fully understand. He had his forehead cradled in his upturned hands and was unaware that Jarek had just gotten up and left, preferring at that moment to risk the possibility of bumping into a mob of angry Lowland trolls than listen to one more minute of his drunken prattling.

Ralph looked up as someone at the next table sniggered. "Well thas jus f... thas jus marverous!" he blustered as he looked back to the vacant seat across from his own. He was mollified somewhat when he noticed that the stranger's abandoned beaker was still half full. He reached out slowly to get it, but the beaker was yanked from his grasping fingers within a hair's breadth of their goal, and he was left staring blankly at a damp ring on the table where it had sat. "Thas was mine!" he protested, turning blearily to face a familiar expanse of belly in a beer stained apron.

"Tain't." The barman corrected economically. He leaned forward menacingly, bringing his brick square face to within a few inches of Ralph's. "Now you pack in scarin' off me payin' clientele Chambers or else."

Ralph did not ask what 'or else' was; or else always referred to something bad, and so he slowly lowered his head and settled into a quiet sulk.

Either the world had gone mad or Ralph had. Given that this world was considerably bigger than he was, he felt it wiser and safer to assume that the insanity was his own. The only time that it seemed to make any real sense to him was when he was in a drunken haze, as he was now.

Ralph looked up at the bar miserably as the stranger's drink was poured into the budget barrel, then sank his head onto his hands again. His thoughts trickled like the reclaimed ale, taking him back across the preceding days, weeks and months that had brought him - with a good deal of self help - to this sorry state. He reached the point where his life had taken the sudden unexpected turn that had put his feet on this path, then hit the play button...

...Ralph came to with a start. He struggled up onto his knees, but was immediately overwhelmed by a pounding in his head that robbed him of everything but his awareness of it. He sagged onto his side with a groan and curled up into a foetal position with his arms wrapped tightly around his head. Ralph stayed that way for some time, alternating between violent bouts of shivering and tiny convulsions that made him whimper and grip his head even tighter. Finally, overcome with bone aching weariness, he succumbed to the need to rest and was soon asleep.

Ralph slept through the night and most of the next morning, oblivious to the cool night air that robbed him of body heat, or the new sprung sun that went some way to replacing it again. What finally caused him to stir was something landing on his face. Ralph mumbled a curse and brushed it away, but it returned a moment later, more irritating and insistent than before.

Ralph rolled onto his side, smacked his gummed lips together then for no ready reason that he could identify, came fully awake with a start and sat up. He stared ahead dumbly for a few minutes, unaware of the trickle of blood on his cheek from a tiny bite, then took a deep shuddering breath and got awkwardly to his feet. He was stiff from having slept on the cold hard ground, and his stomach spasmed when he tried to stand up straight. He leaned forward and gripped his knees until it passed. It was then that he noticed, or at least realised the fact that he was naked but for a few tattered and singed pieces of cloth that were all that remained of his pyjamas. He was also coated in a white talcum like powder, and this caused him to sneeze loudly, which in turn caused his head to hurt again.

The bits of cloth - a mixture of manmade fibres and cotton - were being held in place by static, and a few of the heavier scraps fell away as he watched, surrendering to the weaker but more enduring pull of gravity. Ralph caught a piece that was about the size of a small flannel and used it to wipe away some of the white dust. He inspected the cloth closely then sniffed it cautiously. It smelled of burned bacon and something unpleasant that he could not identify.

Ralph started wiping more of the dust off, then yelped as he dragged the cloth across a burn on his chest that had become caked in the stuff. He looked down, surprised, then carefully probed the burn with his fingers. It was sore and weeping where he had rubbed it, but it was not as bad as it looked. Ralph looked at it again and frowned as he considered the possibility that it might leave a scar. He gritted his teeth and wiped the burn a little more carefully, removing more of the dirt. Two vivid lines curled down into a dark ruddy patch about the size of a child's hand. It looked - Ralph decided - like a clumsy cave drawing of a horned animal's head.

Most of Ralph's attention up until that point had been taken up with his own poor physical condition, but that was not entirely to the exclusion of his present surroundings. He stopped fiddling with the burn on his chest and stared across a rolling expanse of giant yellow flowers, the furthest edge of which was a dark smudge of rocky foothills clinging to the horizon. The sky above it was clear and bright, with a few thin wisps of cloud that were moving lazily across the sun, except that it was not the Sun. Ralph could not have said exactly how he knew that it was not the Sun. It was not a considered conclusion. The Sun - this sun - was perhaps a little smaller, but that might have been a trick of perspective. It also appeared a little brighter and ever so slightly lilac, and this threw a sympathetic wash across the sky that seemed wrong to his Earth-honed senses.

There were other things once he started to take more notice. Ralph could not tell a nettle from a sprig of mint, but the waist high plants around him with their large yellow flowers were of a kind that he had never seen before. The greatest sense of otherliness was within himself though.

Ralph shook his head and instantly regretted it. He tried to fill in the gap between standing at the window in his bedroom and being here - wherever here was - but there was nothing beyond the bright flash. If he could have remembered, he would have remembered among other things, sitting on a settee in a small study with no floor or ceiling, sipping tea with Mrs God while she explained to him that her husband was always too busy, and that he sometimes forgot that she was a supreme being with her own needs and interests, and that he - Ralph - seemed like the kind of lower order life form who might understand her. He would have remembered her being startled, then annoyed by the sound of a door being slammed somewhere beyond the room, and a deep voice that rumbled like heavy thunder, complaining that

Lucy and Gabe were sore losers, and that he - God - was never going bowling with them again. He would have remembered his own sudden awkwardness, then alarm as Mrs God gave him a quick peck on the cheek and pushed him off of the settee.

There were other things that Ralph would have remembered, smaller and bigger things: the neighbour's cat taking a shit on his lawn, the nearness of her filling his senses - Mrs God that is, not the cat - the caress of her lips, her breath electric on his cheek, the heady smell of her following him as he toppled from the settee and dropped back into time and space, a single fading word like the twang of a bowstring being released, pursuing him into the next surreal moment: "sorreeeeeee!"

Ralph would have pinched himself to make sure that he was not dreaming as he stood there staring, but the pain from the burn was real enough to make that particular test unnecessary. Whatever and wherever this place was, he was fairly confident that it was real and - and this was the real stomach twister - it was not Earth.

Ralph placed his hands over his exposed groin and turned around slowly. Behind him the ground rose up in a series of exposed weather worn rocky steps and grassy humps to maybe twice his height, blocking his view in that direction.

At the top, a small lichen covered stone obelisk was stood pointing up at the sky like a crooked finger due to a break part way down, where the frost had worked upon it over several hard winters, leaving the top half balanced at an odd angle.

Ralph looked from the pointing obelisk to the sky and a small misshapen moon that was hung there, blue and hazy. "What the!" he exclaimed under his breath.

"What the, what?" a helium pitched voice inquired unexpectedly.

Ralph jumped slightly and turned around, but there was no one there. "Who said that?" he asked in alarm.

"What, who; two questions and neither one of them with an answer that's likely to please you very much," the disembodied voice trilled. "Maybe you'd be better off staying ignorant, eh?"

Ralph felt suddenly very exposed. He ripped a large leaf from the stem of one of the flowers to cover up the greatest source of his embarrassment.

"Ouch! What do you think you're doing? That smarted rather a lot you know!"

'Smarted rather a lot'? Ralph thought it an odd sought of comment, but then, he was standing naked in a field full of large yellow flowers underneath a slightly lilac sun; what was there that was not odd about this situation! He shrugged, then realising that a modicum of concern might be called for, asked what had smarted.

"You go and pull a leaf off and have the gall to ask me what smarted!" the tiny voice snapped back at him.

There's no need to be nasty," Ralph said, colouring slightly. "How was I to know that you were alive? I mean, you're a flower, for fu..."

"Oh, and don't flowers have feelings?" the voice asked. "Don't we breathe? If you prick us, don't we bleed... sap?" Ralph's uncertainty made him slow to answer, so it added, "don't the fact that I'm holding a bloody conversation with you, give you a bit of a clue?"

Under more normal circumstances Ralph might have reached out and stroked the flower and said something consolatory like, 'there, there', but that would not have been normal under any circumstances. He stamped his foot in frustration, which in itself was not a very normal thing for a grown man to do either.

"Hey, mind where you're sticking them great clodhoppers!" another voice protested from somewhere down in the grass between the flowers.

Ralph looked down in horror and confusion and took a step backwards. "Now what!" he cried in alarm, then said, "I mean, sorry." He took another step backwards, which raised yet another pain-racked cry, and then more cries as he started to hop from foot to foot in an effort to avoid the plants and their roots.

Ralph was soon dancing around on his tiptoes to an accompaniment of squeals and screeches that were starting to sound suspiciously like laughter, but he was running out of steam very quickly, and he finally collapsed to his knees with his heart thumping loudly in his chest. The effect this had was as confusing as it was unexpected. It was as if someone had pushed a button marked, 'push for amplified canned laughter and raucous heckles'.

The noise bombarded him from every direction, worrying away at his unraveling sanity like a cat pawing at a ball of wool. "Leave me alone!" he shouted angrily, his voice rising in pitch so that it almost matched that of his unseen tormentors. He grabbed hold of a flower and wrapped his hands around its stem as though it were a throat and started shaking it. "Leave me alone!" he cried again, almost sobbing.

The laughter swelled until it felt as though it was coming from inside his head, then stopped suddenly as the sound of what he took to be the wailing of a distressed animal came to him from somewhere beyond the rise. It was only as the sound trickled away that Ralph realised that the melancholy cry was that of a horn being blown. The horn was blown a second time much closer, startling Ralph's unseen tormentors into a frenzy of tiny flapping insect wings that filled the air like scraps of tinfoil being scattered by a leaf blower.

Ralph swiped what he took for a bug away from his face and watched fascinated as it spiralled to the ground and crashed silently near his feet. His fascination turned to incredulity when it stood up on two legs, gave him a filthy little look over its bony little shoulder and limped off into the undergrowth. "Sorry," he mumbled at its departing back. "I wouldn't go wastin' an apology on that little bugger," someone behind him said.

Ralph struck the pose of a man waiting for the bite of the executioner's axe. When nothing happened, he turned around carefully and found himself staring across a shiny fuzz ringed desert with a pointed ear sticking up on either side of it. He lowered his gaze slightly to meet the eyes of its owner. The man - Ralph assumed that he was a man - was a head shorter than he was, and built accordingly so that he looked scaled down rather than short. However reduced in size the little man might have appeared on that first brief inspection, Ralph found nothing of the same in the cold eyes that were looking up at him appraisingly.

The elf did not try to hide his curiosity as he looked Ralph up and down. Humans were rare in these parts, and this was the first one that he had ever seen in the flesh, or rather, with its flesh in it. Once when he was a child, a travelling curio peddler had passed through his village with an almost complete skin that he claimed was from a human, but seeing one intact as it were, well, he had to admit that he was a little disappointed. Ralph for his part was not at all disappointed with the elf. Of course he did not yet know that the man in front of him was an elf.

The elf had a broad triangular face that was dominated by piercing green eyes that seemed too big and far too direct in their appraisal of him. It/he was dressed simply, if somewhat garishly, in a bright red travel coat and deep blue knee length shorts. The elf was barefooted but for a simple toe ring on the biggest toe of each foot, and ankle bracelets with a profusion of small charms and beads hanging from them. Under other circumstances Ralph might have laughed at its almost comical appearance. Standing there having to endure the full brunt of the elf's intense scrutiny, he had rarely felt less like laughing.

The elf looked down at the ground, lifted one of its bare feet and put it down again firmly. There was a pitiful squeal which was cut off abruptly with a quick twist of the heel.

Ralph stared in horror at a few prettily twinkling shreds of gossamer thin wing that were poking out from underneath the elf's foot. "Did you have to do that!" he asked angrily. "They were only teasing me."

"Only teasing you!" the elf said incredulously. "Of course they were teasing you! Fairies like to play with their food before they eat it."

Ralph started to say that there was no such thing as fairies just as a fairy that had been hiding in the grass nearby made a run for it. He shut his mouth on what he was going to say, and instead said, "so you're?"

"Northan," the elf offered with a quizzical lift of one eyebrow.

"No," Ralph said, "I mean, your a..."

"Elf?" the elf offered.

Ralph pursed his lips and nodded. "Of course you are! What else would you be!"

"You're not from around these parts?" the elf asked in a tone that implied that an answer was not absolutely necessary.

"Is this Nottingham?" Ralph asked him.

The elf shook his head. "No."

"England?" Ralph asked hopefully.

Again the elf shook his head.

"Earth?"

"Never heard of the place," the elf told him.

Ralph sat down heavily in the patchy grass between the flowers, put his elbows on his knees and dropped his head into his hands. "No, I'm not from around these parts then," he mumbled miserably at the ground.

The elf looked at the shallow body shaped hole behind Ralph. It was scorched around the edges, and there was a thin crackling of fused earth lining it, some of which had been disturbed and had fallen away like pieces of blackened eggshell. "Magic's happened here," he said, adding, "might be an illogical immigrant, like when the other humans first immigrated here?"

Ralph was about to ask what he meant, then realised that he was being discussed rather than addressed. "There's another one of you behind me, isn't there?" he said, looking up slowly. The elf shook his head. "No; there's definitely only one of me," he assured Ralph.

Ralph relaxed a little.

The elf nodded his head at the place behind Ralph where there was not another one of him and said, "that one's my brother in law, Gem'." He added, "and there's only one of him as well."

"Hey-up," Gemfelt greeted cheerfully as he stepped into view.

Ralph stood up quickly and took a step backwards, stumbling slightly as his foot went into the hole behind him. His head started to swim again but he did his best to ignore it.

Gemfelt pulled a square of cloth out of his breast pocket and wiped a bead of sweat from his forehead. "I reckon he's a bit left of alright, if you get my drift. Probably got him sen lost, and what with the fairies playing with him... Well, no surprise if he's gone a bit soft in the head," he offered by way of a more likely explanation.

Northan huffed. "Look at the hole." All three of them did. "That's magical work, or I'm a Lowland's uncle," he insisted. "And where there's magic, there's usually a wizard's hand in it somewhere."

"What do we know of wizards around here?" Gemfelt asked, grinning at his brother in law. "You and my sister'd have 'em blamed fer every clumsy-arsed thing that's ever happened if you could. You sort of get to wondering if even they could be that industrious!"

The discussion carried on for a few minutes with Ralph stood there looking back and forth between the two elves, trying to get a handle on what they were talking about. "Look," he said, exasperated. "I've been struck by lightning and teased by fairies. Now I'm being talked about as if I wasn't here! I think the least I'm entitled to, is an explanation!"

"Why?" Northan asked, breaking off from his discussion.

Ralph was flabbergasted. "Why!" he repeated in astonishment. "Why! Why, because..."

Gemfelt and Northan were both looking at him expectantly.

"Because..." Ralph made small circular motions in the air, trying to urge them to see something that should have been obvious to them, even if the reason had momentarily slipped his own mind. "Just because!" he concluded weakly.

"That's about what I thought," Northan said dryly as he turned back to Gemfelt and continued his conversation. "It was never like this when the GDC still had some teeth. I mean, you hear about some odd stuff goin' on in the cities, but..."

Gemfelt started to laugh. "You hear about a lot of things happening in the cities out here, but I doubt above a quarter of it has much truth in it. And as fer your Council having teeth! If that bunch of old porridge suckers had had teeth to start with, they wouldn't've needed to go begging the wizards for their help in the first place!"

"Hello!" Ralph interrupted again. "You could at least tell me where on Earth I am?"

Northan bit back on his reply to his brother in law and turned to Ralph again. "I thought we'd already got that one sorted out," he answered in a somewhat irritated manner. "Wherever your Earth is, this place isn't." He turned to face Gemfelt again. "We should take him with us. Gertru will be interested in him, and she might know something as'll help him. Whether the wizards had anything to do with it or not, if he did come from the same place they did, then it's them he'll need to see if he wants to get back there."

"Gerty knows too much about everything," Gemfelt interjected, adding, "and everyone." He gave Ralph a sly wink. "Mind, I'm sure she'll be happy to do somethin' for you."

Gemfelt and Northan had a stride that needed a complicated equation to make it fit their inside leg measurements. Ralph on the other hand did not, and he was forced to do an odd sort of stagger-jog to try and keep up with them. It was not long before he was stumbling along behind them, wheezing like a blunt saw going through a rotten log.

Gemfelt to Northan's disgust slowed down and allowed Ralph to catch up with him. The look of gratitude that he received was pitiful, and he could not shake the feeling as the human caught up and staggered along at his side, that their help was only putting off something that was inevitable. Life away from the cities and towns was hard enough for those who were born to it, but if what the human had said was true, he was not even born to this world.

Gemfelt passed the time while they walked, telling Ralph a little about his world. What Ralph learned from the elf was that he was on a continent that most people seemed to agree was called Derrian, and that Derrian was the smallest of three continents on a world that the Derrianites at least, called Quathliom. What Gemfelt found less easy to explain, or rather, what Ralph found less easy to understand, was the political and national divisions on the continent. A country being a country seemed to depend on three things: a desire to be independent, the ability to be independent, and the willingness of others to let you get away with being independent. Derrian could lay claim to - among others - a couple of portable countries, two countries that existed in the same place because their respective peoples got on very well but could not agree about where they lived, a divided country that was separated by an impassable mountain range, a group of allotments, smallholdings and farms that had gotten together and formed a commonwealth, dozens of ships and barges that had declared independence for tax purposes, three subterranean nations, two mountain ranges, the rim of an active volcano, one hundred and sixty two islands of various sizes, a forest, a footprint - don't ask - and even the sky above their heads, which was divided vertically as well as horizontally into no less than twelve different realms.

Ralph examined Gemfelt as closely as politeness would allow as the elf continued to speak. Northan kept a little way ahead of them, preferring to remain apart despite having been the one to volunteer their help. It was impossible to believe, yet impossible to deny that they were what they claimed to be. He knew of course that their pointed ears could have been done with latex and a bit of makeup, but the rest?

The morning saw them through the vast rolling expanse of yellow flowers, and into less even scrubland. This proved to be an even bigger trial for poor old Ralph who was tired beyond belief. Every stone felt like a tiny dagger under his bruised and cut feet as he staggered along, driven on by the fear of being left behind to face this alien world alone.

They came across a steep banked stream around midday. It cut across their path, providing Ralph with a rare opportunity to sit down and rest for a few minutes. On the far side of the stream was the beginning of what might have been a forest or just a wood.

Ralph stared at the trees blankly, too wrapped up in his own pain and fatigue to realise or care that a few of them were of a kind that were native to Earth, their ancestors having been carried there as seeds by the first feathery settlers from Earth to spread their wings and their dung over their new world.

Ralph stretched his legs out, expecting that the elves would stop and rest for a little while before crossing the stream. His misery over his various aches was joined by consternation when the elves did not stop, and they were soon across the stream and lost among the trees on the far side.

"Would fifteen minutes've killed them!" he complained to himself as he struggled to his feet. He limped over to the edge and stared down into the silt heavy water, tumbling over its hidden bed as it raced towards the sea, several miles away, drawn on by an ebbing tide that had reduced the water level by several feet, making the steep banks muddy and treacherous underfoot. Ralph contemplated the slippery sides with understandable trepidation. He took no comfort from the ease with which the fleet-footed elves had managed to cross.

Northan and Gemfelt had reappeared and were watching him from the far side with a mixture of exasperation and amused expectation on their faces. Ralph gave them a sour look, but there was nothing for it if he did not want to be left behind, and so he placed the ball of his heel behind an exposed root to give him some purchase, and testing it, put the whole of his weight onto it. The root was thin, but it held for a moment, and he placed his other foot alongside it. Ralph turned sideways and was about to slide his left foot a little further down the bank, when the root snapped, and he shot forward like a surfer riding an oil slick.

Ralph stayed upright for a few seconds, then landed on his back with a jar to the back that knocked the wind from his lungs. He slid down the bank quickly, gained some purchase with his feet almost at the water's edge, then shot forward flailing like a windmill in a hurricane and toppled head first into the freezing water with a splash.

Ralph surfaced like a breaching whale almost before his feet touched the muddy bottom of the stream. He stood there dripping dirty water and shivering violently. The elves had of course found the whole thing from start to finish highly entertaining, and were doing nothing to hide it from him. Ralph glared at them indignantly, his fists clenched tight, as much from anger as from the shock of the sudden cold that was rapidly sapping the heat from his weary body. When despite his obvious lack of amusement, they continued to laugh at his expense, he managed to chatter something short and to the point, to the effect that they should both get lost.

Northan shrugged and said that they would give it a go, but that it would be difficult given that, unlike Ralph, they knew exactly where they were. That said, he and his brother in law turned away and went back into the forest.

Ralph felt very vulnerable standing there alone in the middle of the stream with nothing but his skin between himself, the seeping cold, and anything else this strange world wanted to throw at him. "Erm, hello," he called out uncertainly. "When I said g'get lost, I didn't really m'mean g'go. It was just a figure of speech." He splashed his way across to the other side and dragged himself out of the water. "Hello?" he called again, then more anxiously, "HELLO," as he started to scramble and claw his way up the far bank. Fortunately despite it being slippery still, he found more reliable footing and was able to make the top without any further mishap.

Ralph stood up at the top of the bank caked in mud. He hugged himself and eyed the trees warily as he caught his breath and waited for the shivering to subside a little. Nothing short of a charging bull would have persuaded him to go in to those trees on his own, and the elves might easily have been half a mile or more away without him slowing them down. Ralph was not particularly concerned about getting lost among the trees - getting lost would have required him knowing where he was in the first place! He just reasoned that it was probably safer to stay in the open where he could at least see danger coming his way.

"Are you coming or staying?" Gemfelt called to him from the trees.

Ralph almost jumped out of the only thing that he was wearing: his skin. He turned slightly and found the elf leaning against a tree with a broad grin on his face. Ralph re-sheathed his glare and closed his mouth tightly around a reply that would certainly have pushed Gemfelt and Northan's already stretched patience to breaking point. He nodded instead and quickly fell in behind the elf.

"This must be pretty hard for you," Gemfelt asked over his shoulder.

Ralph opened his mouth, but again bit back on his reply. It was - he realised - a rhetorical question, born from the same concern that had brought the elves to his aid when they might easily have spared themselves the trouble. Ralph wondered if he would have done as much for a complete stranger. The lack of a clear answer to that question troubled him slightly.

Ralph stumbled into Gemfelt when he slowed without warning to step over a branch that was lying across the path. He pulled back quickly as though recoiling from a striking snake, and would have fallen backwards, but for Gemfelt quickly grabbing hold of his arm to steady him. Ralph pulled his arm away as soon as the elf let go and mumbled something that only just passed for a thank you.

Gemfelt and Northan frightened him. The elves could not have seemed more alien to him if they had turned up in a spaceship brandishing ray guns. It was much more than the pointed ears and the lack of a few inches in height; it was a difference that projected itself in a multitude of far more subtle ways.

For all that there were many similarities between himself and the elves, they were each products of a different world and a very different evolutionary path. Ralph belonged to a specie that had risen to the top of the food chain by default, having outlasted all other contenders for the crown. They were so dominant and so aggressive that their overwhelming presence robbed other species of the chance to evolve. The elves and the dwarves, though very different in appearance to each other, were ethnic subgroups of a modern hominid form, whereas the trolls had diverged much earlier during their evolution, then evolved into two separate species that were as alike to each other as they were to the elves and dwarves, with whom the only thing they had in common was a primitive rodent ancestor. Gnomes and goblins on the other hand, despite looking as though they might be related to the dwarves, were actually descended from a kind of sloth. In short, Northan and Gemfelt were products of a world that had produced several advanced species, that had not only managed to survive everything that it could throw at them, but each other.

"We'd better get a wriggle on if we want to get home before it gets dark," Gemfelt told Ralph.

"Your home," Ralph corrected miserably.

"Yer right," Gemfelt agreed, "but it's my home where you'll get yer sen a bed and a warm meal tonight."

Gemfelt changed the subject and started telling Ralph about the fairies; why they had teased him and what would have happened to him if he and Northan had not turned up when they had. Ralph's blood went cold at the idea that he might have wondered around for hours or even days being tormented by the fairies, until at last he no longer had the strength or will to fight them off.

Gemfelt felt no sense of responsibility for Ralph's wellbeing, but it did not go to say that he did not care what happened to the human. He knew that Ralph had a dangerous journey ahead of him, but nothing he faced would be half as dangerous as his own ignorance, so he shifted the conversation from fairies to whatever else he could think of that might help him live a little bit longer.

Ralph was easily bored by long conversations, especially long conversations that started to sound like they were lectures. His mind would start to wander at such times, so that while outwardly he might appear attentive, inwardly he would be groaning and praying for the person who was speaking to get to the point and shut up. Gemfelt was in the middle of explaining the difference between two leaves, but though Ralph was looking at him, the only thing that was keeping him alert was the occasional nettle-like plant brushing against his exposed skin!

The terrain changed little by little as they walked. Coarse grass and nettles gave way to large clumps of low thorny bushes. In places they were so dense that they would have been impassable were it not for the occasional well used animal run. Ralph found the narrower tracks harrowing. No matter which way he turned, something managed to snag, sting or stab him, so that his exposed skin was soon a mess of bloody little puncture wounds, scratches and vivid welt marks.

Ralph could not imagine what he must have looked like when they finally reached the elven village. Unfortunately for Ralph there was a group of young elves playing a ball game in the clearing who were more than happy to tell him. He slapped his hands to his groin a little too quickly and instantly regretted it. "Haven't they got some woodcraft or something to go and do?" he hissed between clenched teeth. He gave Gemfelt a pleading look, then glanced downwards by way of emphasis.

Gemfelt said, "ah," and nodded his understanding, but he had nothing about his person that he could, or was willing to offer Ralph to cover up his embarrassment.

Northan had walked ahead of them most of the way. He did not stop when they reached the clearing. He nodded at the teenagers in passing, ignoring their questions about Ralph, and hurried on. Gemfelt on the other hand was happy to chat to them, leaving Ralph with the dilemma of whether to follow Northan into the village or stay with Gemfelt and endure the scrutinisation of the understandably curious teenagers.

A small group of onlookers had already started to gather at the edge of the village, and Northan after a brief conversation, went into a house with one of them. He emerged again a few minutes later and came back across the clearing with a pair of trousers in his hand. "Here," he said, throwing them to Ralph. "They'll be tight, but beggars can't be choosers, as they say, and we can't have you walkin' around the village scaring the women."

Ralph who was by then knelt in the grass quietly seething with his arms folded strategically across his lap, took the trousers and - under the impolite stares of the teenagers - struggled to squeeze himself into them. He fastened the last button with difficulty and grunted as he got to his feet.

Tight was an understatement! The trousers garrotted his lower half, pushing his slight paunch and love handles upwards in a way that was gross. He looked down at himself and decided that there were possibly more embarrassing things than being naked in public. His one small salvation was that the material that the trousers were made from had a little elasticity in them, otherwise it might have been more than the last shreds of his dignity that was being crushed.

Ralph waddled along stiffly behind Gemfelt and Northan as they entered the village. He died a tiny death each time they walked passed someone who had not yet had the opportunity to stare at him or make a comment. "I guess there isn't a lot of entertainment around here!" he grumbled. "Not much," Gemfelt admitted. He grinned at Ralph and added, "today's been better'n most."

Elves have been portrayed as everything from impish childlike figures in green tights and long curly-toed boots, to lithe bodied sinister warriors with immaculate hair, smouldering forest green eyes and chisel sharp chins. The reality - this reality at least - did not fit with any of Ralph's preconceptions, and the same was true of their homes and how they lived.

The village was a hotchpotch of large wattle and daub igloos, each one of which had painted in a way that was obviously intended to make it stand out from its neighbour; but in doing so, the elves had only succeeded in achieving a garish kind of uniformity, in which riotous colours clashed in a way that made nothing stand out but the eyeballs of any unprepared visitors. What pathways and common areas Ralph saw, seemed to owe no more to design than might be achieved by spilling a plateful of spaghetti onto the floor and seeing how it falls.

Twice Ralph was forced to climb a ladder and cross a raised walkway where two buildings butted up against one another, and it occurred to him as he looked at Gemfelt and Northan with their gaudy mismatched clothes, that the village with its gaudy mismatched houses and its apparent lack of thought in the way that it was laid out, said a lot about the elves; Ralph was just not sure what.

Ralph looked around himself coyly, hoping against hope that he would spot a beautiful elven princess loitering under a Willow tree in soft focus somewhere. What he actually saw was a lot of scruffy androgynous looking kids, a few mangy looking pets that were not quite dogs, and the occasional scurrying rat that was definitely a rat. The one or two women that he did see were closer to his own height and build than their menfolk, and though not exactly ugly, they lacked - the obvious aside - anything of what Ralph thought of as being a feminine attribute.

Northan stopped at one of the houses and nodded at the door. "Here we are then," he said with excessive cheerfulness. He excused himself for a moment and went in alone to tell his wife about their unexpected visitor, then returned a minute later looking a lot less happy. "Gertru will see you," he told Ralph and stepped to one side so that he could go in.

It was dark inside and the look of amusement on Gemfelt's face did nothing to reassure Ralph.

"Please," Northan said impatiently. There was something of the quality of pleading in his voice as he added, "Gertru doesn't like to be kept waiting."

Ralph felt the hairs on the back of his neck rise, but to refuse would have called for an explanation that he knew would be offensive to his rescuers.

Gemfelt patted Ralph on the shoulder. "I'll leave you to it then," he said winking, then turned and left.

Ralph paused for a moment to let his eyes adjust, but there was no light beyond what came in from the doorway behind him, and his own body was blocking a good deal of that.

"Get yer sen over here, human," a vaguely female voice beckoned impatiently from within the inky darkness. "Let's get a look at yer."

Ralph walked forward hesitantly. He stubbed his toe on something slightly yielding that growled at him before scurrying out of the way.

"Don't bear him any mind; he's a harmless old rug," the voice that emanated from the darkness at the far side of the room reassured.

Ralph squinted and said, "can't you turn the light on?"

"How do you turn light on?" Northan asked from behind him, then shrugged; it did not matter.

"Come on then, sweet-cheeks," Gertru coaxed. She remembered her manners and said, "you must be hungry." She looked at her husband. "Be a sweety, Northy, 'nd nip round to Cassi's."

Northan was about to say that they must have something cold that they could give the human, but he realised that Gertru would already know that, and he turned unhappily and left to do as she had asked.

Ralph stood there in the dark wondering what he should do, and feeling more than a little uncomfortable in the short silence that followed Northan's departure.

"Over here then, sweet cheeks," Gertru said again, sounding impatient.

There was the click and rasp of a flint and steel being struck together. A tiny universe blossomed for a second in the darkness at the far side of the room and died. A few of those pinprick suns collided with an oil soaked wick, and a small flame sputtered angrily into life at its end, creating a gentle pool of warm light.

Sprawling within that gentle wash of light on a floor cushion was probably the least gentle looking women Ralph had ever seen.

"We're semi-noc's," Gertru told him, "so we don't need much light." She smiled at Ralph and tapped a large floor cushion next to her own. "If yer an illogical immigrant as Northy seems to think, then you'd not know that. Come and sit yer sen here then," she said, again tapping the large floor cushion.

Ralph did as she said. He walked over and sat down slowly next to her, fancying as he did that he heard a snap like that made by a mouse trap being sprung.

Even in the kind flicker of the lamplight, the kindest thing that Ralph could say about Gertru, was that she was striking. He took in the hard eyes that were looking him over with something more than curiosity, and the thick square jaw upon which her smile seemed almost feral, and added a postscript to his original assessment: striking in a brutish blunt force kind of way. Ralph could sense the loutish bully lurking behind the smile and the sticky sweet tones that she was using with him, and it unmanned him slightly, made him nervous and uncertain.

Ralph met her eyes and immediately lowered his own. The lingering look that she gave him was unsettling and the setting was far too private and intimate for comfort. As he looked down his eyes came to rest on her ample bosom by chance rather than any design, and he quickly shifted his gaze again so that she would not misconstrue it as being anything more than that. He looked at a patterned bowl, a pull at the edge of a rug, the dog that was not quite a dog that was eyeing him coldly from a still dark corner; he tried to look anywhere except directly at her.

Gertru was looking Ralph over with nothing like the same shyness. There was a nervous excitement about her that suggested that she had far more than a casual interest in him. "I must say, but yer a good looking specimen of yer kind." This was said with a playful punch to his arm. "Not as I've seen so many of your folk, and I've travelled more'n most folk've in my village."

Ralph was not used to women who were - as his mother would say - not backward in being forward. Another time, other circumstances; a different woman and specie for example, and he might have been flattered by her interest. As it was, he found himself staring at the door, willing Northan to walk back through it. "Look," he said, starting to get a little flustered. "I'm sorry, but I just want to know how to get home."

Gertru was not the least embarrassed at having her advances rejected. "It's more'n likely the wizards," she told him, bringing at least part of her attention back to Ralph's problems, "but if it isn't them, it'll still be a wizard you'll need to see to get yer home." She sniffed disapprovingly and added, "there're rules about importing illogical immigrants, but that's wizards for you; give 'em a rule 'nd they'll break it."

"And I'd find a wizard where?" Ralph asked her after a moment, when it seemed that she would not continue.

"What? Oh, Brace, deary," Gertru answered distractedly, recalling herself from an entirely different train of thought. "They've a city called Brace. You'll not swing a pointy stick there without scratching a few of their scrawny necks."

"Just a wild guess," Ralph ventured, "but you don't seem to like wizards very much?"

"Not a quarter as much as I'd like you, sweet cheeks," Gertru said, brightening a little.

Ralph's relief at Northan's return was palpable, but any hope he nurtured in those first few seconds, that Gertru would stop trying to flirt with him now that he was back, quickly evaporated. Ralph was flabbergasted; the woman had the subtlety of a Las Vegas billboard fastened to the front end of a charging bull, yet her husband seemed oblivious to what was happening right under his nose!

"Here," Northan said, holding a bowl out to Ralph. Gertru stopped pouting at Ralph long enough to scowl at her husband.

Ralph looked from one to the other, unable to hide his consternation. He put his hand out to take the bowl then changed his mind, preferring the uncertainty of what lay beyond her door to the certainty of knowing what she hoped to get in return for her generosity. "Thanks," he said, declining the food, "but I should get going."

Northan and Gertru watched Ralph fumble with the latch and hurry out.

"That was a bit rude," Northan said as the door slowly swung shut behind him.

"Yes," Gertru agreed. "I'm a bit disappointed." She turned and smiled down at her husband. "You'll never disappoint me like that, will you, Northy?"

Northan shook his head. "I'll not do that, dearest," he answered nervously.

Gertru's eyes turned cold as she considered him. The smile was still there, but it held no kindness. "Why did yer bring him here?" she asked, changing the subject.

Northan seemed to shrink into himself. "I thought as you'd want to see him, my love," he told her. "I thought as you'd be interested in knowing about him."

"Yer think I didn't already know about him!" Gertru hissed at her husband. "What if the wizards are watchin' him?" She reached out quickly as though to strike her husband, then at the last moment seemed to change her mind, and instead stroked his cheek as one might do a pet.

Northan flinched but she did not appear to notice. "Are you going to teach me a lesson, my love?" he asked in a nervous whisper.

Gertru's cold smile softened a little. "Maybe a small one; later maybe." She leaned down and kissed his cheek lightly. "You know I wouldn't have to if you'd just use yer head once in a while."

"I know, dear," Northan answered miserably.

Gemfelt knew something of Gertru's nature. Northan believed that it was because Gertru was his sister. Gemfelt always laughed whenever he said as much, but did not have the heart to tell him that it was because she had one thing on her mind most of the time, and he just happened to know what that was. Her habits and tastes were legendary, yet it seemed to him that Northan was almost oblivious to what was going on right under his nose! He did not consider that his brother in law might not have been as ignorant of his sister's philandering as he seemed to be, or that there were things about his sister that he did not know, things that he would have found less amusing had he suspected.

Gemfelt felt a small stab of conscience when Northan came running after him on what was very obviously a bogus errand. It also occurred to him that this human who had never known elves, would leave his village thinking that they were all like his gullible brother in law and overly promiscuous sister. Concerned that they would all be tarred with the same brush, he hurried Northan along on his errand, then on an impulse, went after him when he left, just in case.

Just in case happened a few seconds after he reached Northan's house. He was hovering at the front door, trying to think of a plausible way to extricate the human from his sister's clutches, when Ralph backed out and almost hit him with the door. Gemfelt took hold of Ralph's unresisting arm and quickly hurried him away.

Ralph was too distracted to raise any objection or question where he was being taken, but as soon as they were around the corner, he pulled free of the elf's grip and stopped. "You can throw a mat at my place tonight," Gemfelt told him. He saw the look of horror on Ralph's face and burst out laughing. "Trust me, my Cassi's tastes are not as exotic as my sister's," he reassured.

As it transpired, Gemfelt's wife could not have been more different to Gertru, and at first at least, more indifferent to her husband's unexpected guest. Her indifference was rooted in her disappointment at not getting her husband to herself on his first night home. She was also unsure how to behave around a human, or what to expect from him, and this presented itself in a way that came across as rudeness. It was not long before her usual good nature reasserted itself though.

Ralph had been deconstructed, reconstructed, some stuff in the middle that he could not quite remember, terrorised by fairies and marched barefoot and naked through freezing water, thorn bushes and a mixture of nettles and their Quathliom equivalent. He was so far beyond sore that he could not sensibly express himself when Cassi asked him how he was. Cassi frowned deeply then turned on her husband and berated him for coming into the house caked in road dirt. Gemfelt was about to object at her rough handling of him in front of his guest, but she gave him a meaningful look and nodded in Ralph's direction.

The bathhouse was in fact four separate bathhouses, allowing for a disposition of sexes and ages according to the elven concept of propriety. These were sat around a smaller building that took fresh water from a nearby river and heated it up, before feeding it to each of the baths through clay pipes. Cold water was fed to each through a second pipe and regulated by the bath attendants, who also controlled the recycling of the water, keeping the water relatively clean.

Whatever reservations Ralph might have had about sharing a bath with other naked men, were forgotten the moment he lowered himself into the warm water. The bath was a circular pit with a submerged step around its side for people to sit on. There were only a handful of elves using the bath when they got there, but it might easily have accommodated thirty or so sitting around the sides, and there was plenty of room for him to sprawl.

Ralph closed his eyes and savoured the warm water as it moved sluggishly over his skin, easing the dull ache in his limbs, and the soreness from his many cuts and abrasions. He would have stayed there, would have probably fallen asleep where he was sat given half a chance, but Gemfelt was washing and was showing every intention of getting out soon.

Ralph groaned inwardly at the thought of having to get out, but there was nothing for it, and he reluctantly followed suit. He finished washing himself down, then climbed out and took a clean towel from the bathhouse attendant. Ralph dried himself off as much as the humid air in the bathhouse would allow. Unfortunately that was not very much, and his skin was still damp as he started to pull the snug fitting trousers back on. Gemfelt watched him struggling and found it almost as amusing the second time around.

There was a meal ready for them when they returned to the house.

Cassi greeted her husband more gently than she had dismissed him, then rising from what she was doing at the hearth, picked up a small pile of neatly folded clothes and passed them to Ralph. "They're some of my old things," she told him, adding, "they'll fit you a sight better'n a man's clothes will."

Ralph bridled slightly at her suggestion that he was not built like a man, but then it occurred to him that by her measure of such things, he was not.

The gift of the clothes would have been no small thing on Ralph's own world where clothes were mostly cheap and quite easily come by. That these clothes had been laboured over by someone in the village - possibly even by Cassi herself - was not lost on him, and he thanked her awkwardly for the gift.

Cassi dismissed his thanks just as awkwardly. "Away with yer. You can get yer sen changed in there, and you'll find an old pair of sandals on the floor. You can have 'em if they fit."

Ralph changed quickly. The clothes - a simple long sleeved woollen top and a pair of three quarter length trousers - were a much better fit than the pair of trousers that Northan had given him, and he was able to sit down comfortably in them. There was also a kind of hooded poncho that was wrapped into a tight roll, that would if need be, double as a small shelter if he huddled down inside it and pulled the hood forward. This had been treated with some kind of wax to make it almost waterproof. Elves normally went barefoot, so the sandals were a concession to need rather than style, but they fit well enough and were at least serviceable.

Clean and dressed more respectably, Ralph sat down on a floor cushion to eat. Cassi gave him a bowl of soup, and there was a plate of unleavened bread on the floor between them. Ralph shifted the thick soup around with his spoon, trying to identify the lumps. He was a vegetarian, and it was a relief to find that the meal contained no meat. The realisation that he did not know what the vegetables were, was mostly academic when his next meal was as uncertain as the rest of his future. Ralph polished off a second bowl with the last of the bread as his hosts watched in mild amusement.

Ralph had not realised how hungry he was. He felt as if he had not eaten for days. In a very real sense, Ralph had never eaten, or at least his body had never eaten. The body that he was occupying was a copy of the original, taken from the moment when the bolt of lightning had hit him and recreated from the soil and rock of the world upon which he now found himself. If he had thought about it, he might have wondered how he and the elves were able to communicate with each other, or how the atmosphere and gravity of another world so perfectly matched the requirements of his body.

Ralph would have fallen asleep after the meal if his hosts had let him, but they saw it as only fair that he should satisfy their curiosity about himself and his world. Their fascination over commonplace items like taps and toasters tickled Ralph, but he was no less fascinated by many of the things that they saw as being commonplace, and so somewhere between taxis, televisions and tower blocks, he learned more about Derrian, and - more importantly - about the wizards.

It is important at this point to understand that history is glimpsed through accounts that are generally biased and often inaccurate. For this reason, and because the truth is fantastic enough without any embellishments, it is better to relate the events as they happened rather than as they were told to Ralph by Gemfelt and Cassi...

A would be alchemist by the name of Jeremiah Dipple had been trying to turn a turnip into gold. That detail alone spoke volumes about the mental stability of the man, which ironically, was not the reason why he was residing in an asylum at the time. The actual reason was that he had been bequeathed a moderately large estate by a distant uncle, who just so happened to have relatives who felt that they had a greater claim to it than he did.

The experiment with the turnip was a bit of nonsense really, and it would have come to nothing under normal circumstances. Normal is of course a relative thing, and it is sometimes quite difficult to quantify or qualify. It often looks different from different angles, and different under different conditions and circumstances. Jeremiah Dipple had his own ideas about what normal was, and he could see nothing remotely abnormal in what he was doing with the turnip. His keepers in general had a different view on the matter, but they saw no great harm in throwing him the odd vegetable now and again to keep him quiet.

At almost exactly the same time that Dipple was doing his little bit of nonsense with the turnip, one end of an Impossible Vortex was whipping around the general vicinity of the asylum. Normally, apart from a brief upsurge in alien abductions and creative writing, Impossible Vortices tend to just come and go without anyone noticing them. This one sort of did, and did not.

It is possible that the impossible vortex was drawn towards Bracebridge because of certain resonances caused by the wildly abstract thinking of some of the residents of the asylum, but it is just as likely that it settled there because it liked Lincolnshire potatoes, which was one of the other things that the place was known for. It is difficult to find scraps of sense in a nonsensical event, and often quite pointless to try. Whatever the cause of the vortex, the town and its outlying farms and villages, along with everything immediately above and below it, were dropped bang smack in to the middle of a place called Derrian.

Now a student of local history might wonder why the disappearance of an entire town and its surrounding neighbourhood in Lincolnshire went unnoticed in 1801, or considering that it was Bracebridge, they might not have. For anyone who cared to know, the answer was of course that it did not disappear. The impossible vortex happened without anyone noticing it, because it did not actually happen, and Jeremiah Dipple was left staring glumly at a turnip that refused point blank to be anything but a turnip. That did not however stop what did not happen from happening, otherwise it could not have happened, which it both did and did not, depending upon your point of view. It was a classic case of effect without the cause and effect.

Dipple did and did not wake up on a very different world. The Dipple who did, had a headache and a turnip shaped lump of gold in his lap. He also had the dawning realisation that wherever he now was, he was quite literally a changed man. What that meant and its many ramifications would take decades to unravel.

Dipple was not the only one to be changed going through the vortex; they all had to some degree, and in many different ways. For some it was little things, new skills and talents that would barely cause an eyebrow to be lifted, but there were others; midwives who could ease the pain of a delivering mother and her child with a comforting word or touch, healers who could see off an affliction or ailment with a wag of a finger and a disapproving look, nurses who could send someone from the world content and unafraid, bee charmers, diviners, truth sayers, farmers who brought a new meaning to being green fingered, sculptors who could see into the heart of a material and discover its inner shape, artisans and tradesmen whose creations were no longer restrained by physical law. For a few like Dipple who had been at the heart of the vortex - i.e, the asylum - and most attuned to it - e.i.e, slightly unhinged - the changes were much more dramatic. Many of the inmates found that they were able to manipulate energy, matter and even the fabric of space and time itself.

A meeting was held at the guildhall to discuss this worrying development, and to try to decide what they should do about it. Amongst the many suggestions that were put forward, was the suggestion they should bring back trial by fire and water. Another was that they should burn anyone suspected of being insane or of an evil persuasion at the stake. An old woman who was standing at the back grew alarmed at such talk and pointed out that the town was going to get pretty empty if they burned everyone in Bracebridge who seemed a little odd at the moment.

Her comment was met with loud disapproval and the meeting had to be called to order, but there were a number of people there who agreed with her, and one observed that people in glass houses should not throw stones, especially if the people you were throwing stones at could throw lightning bolts back at you or - as someone else put it - melt your face off. This proved to be a compelling argument.

Jeremiah, after his initial surprise when the door to his cell opened when he asked it to, took the rest in his stride. He had during his three years of incarceration, come to the opinion that reality was whatever you wanted to make of it. During his stay in the asylum, he had taken shelter in any number of constructed realities to try and escape the one that he could not. This new one only differed from the others in the level of detail.

Jeremiah poked his head out and looked down the corridor, expecting to see a cloggy - as they called their warders - coming to reprimand him and shove him back into his cell. The corridor was empty and quiet but for the faint moaning of an inmate in one of the cells further along. Jeremiah took a deep breath and ventured out. He stopped along the way to slide back the bolts on a couple of the cell doors, encouraging their occupants to do the same for others, then left by the quickest route possible. This involved dissolving two walls - something that he felt he might never tire of doing.

It was a chance meeting with one of Jeremiah's old students whilst he was strolling along enjoying his first day of liberty in a very long time, that changed not only his destiny, but more importantly, that of Bracebridge. The former student - a respected landowner and barrister - invited Dipple to come and dine with him at the inn that he was staying at whilst in town. Jeremiah was hungry for intelligent company as much as for food, and gratefully accepted the offer.

As they ate their lunch together, the conversation inevitably turned to the current state of affairs in Bracebridge. Jeremiah was almost entirely ignorant of the events that were related to him by his former student, prompting his host to ask where he had been all week. Jeremiah was suitably vague with his answer, and cautious when prompted for his opinion about - as it was put to him - all these occult comings and goings, but he was not as used to drink as he had once been, and became progressively less cautious as the meal progressed.

It was not long before Jeremiah had attracted the attention of some of the other patrons. As a former schoolmaster and accomplished orator, he had a natural unaffected charm that people found attractive, and one or two put good manners aside and turned their chairs around so that they could share in the discussion. What had started out as a private conversation between two old acquaintances, quickly took on all the earmarks of a small assembly as more and more people lingered to listen or contribute.

Emboldened by the general agreement of many of those who were listening, Jeremiah went on to suggest that today's science had once been considered hocus-pocus - indeed still was by some - and that that would ever be the case where the unenlightened few were allowed to hold sway over the masses. He even went on to suggest that the devil could not have swayed so many god-fearing men and women from the path of righteousness, and that if the devil's hand was to be seen anywhere, it was in the hearts of the ignorant and the intolerant. Magic - he told them - was a God given gift that if used wisely, would bring about a new era in which disease and poverty would become things of the past.

Some of those who were listening to Jeremiah talking, grew nervous and hopeful when he started to suggest that the newly found powers that many of them were concealing, were not the devils handiwork as the church was claiming, but were in fact God-given gifts that might one day be seen as being as natural to their day-to-day lives as breathing. Nervous or not, they were all moved by what he had to say, and it was soon apparent to many of those sat there as they surreptitiously gauged each others reactions to Jeremiah's words, that they were not so alone as they had believed. Their spirits lifted briefly by the idea that they had God on their side, his words struck them with the force of a bugler's call to arms, and they responded to it with creditable enthusiasm.

Things sometimes have a way of gathering momentum from the things that they come into contact with. That was pretty much the way it was for Jeremiah Dipple. His doting former student was as influential as he was wealthy, and it was this influence that provided Jeremiah with the opportunity to speak at a privately held meeting. The meeting was attended by some of his former student's most trusted friends and acquaintances; among them a magistrate, three aldermen and a man of the cloth.

When the yoke of authority starts to chafe the necks of those who must wear it, they can often become querulous and indifferent to it, especially when the authority in question are themselves running around like a lot of headless chickens, while their lout of a bailiff/gamekeeper and his two equally corrupt and totally inept part time constables are left to do as they will. From there it needs only the smallest of sparks to set off a rather large powder keg.

The last line of defence against the possibility of insurrection was the threat of eternal damnation in the fiery pits of hell, but when people who have been blindly loyal to the church, and the higher power for which it is ostensibly the sole representative, start to believe that they have already been abandoned by their god, threats from the pulpit start to sound a little hollow.

Even the most indignant of Bracebridge's leaders could not fail to see that the tide was swiftly turning against them, and that riding the crest of the wave was a rather charismatic former schoolmaster who had gained the support of some very influential people.

Rather than have their impotence exposed by trying to reinstate a few ancient and barbaric laws that they could never hope to enforce, they announced their intention to set up a committee whose purpose it would be to better understand what was happening to Bracebridge's population, and to try and interpret God's will in this before making any decision upon the criminalisation of magic.

Thus it was that they tried to invite the wolf in. They stroked him ever so gently on the head and offered him a juicy position on their committee. The wolf - namely, Jeremiah Dipple - had no aspirations in that direction and quickly declined their offer, choosing instead to go back to teaching.

There were many things that Jeremiah might have chosen to teach, but it seemed to him that Bracebridge's general ignorance of their new talents presented him with the greatest opportunity, and so it was that he set up Derrian's first school for the study and teaching of magic.

Rather ironically, he made the decision to set his new school up in a small annex of the asylum. In the beginning his students were mostly former male inmates, who lacking anywhere better to go and being so conditioned to a life within the building's walls, would have sat there watching paint dry with rapt attention rather than set foot outside.

Jeremiah drew the line when it came to educating women though. He was - pardon the pun - old school when it came to the education of the fairer sex. "If God had wanted women to be taught like men," he had once been heard to say when pressed on the subject, "he would have made them in his own image; and anyway, all that flouncing and girly stuff is far too distracting."

More and more people started turning up at Dipple's classes who were not former inmates as the weeks progressed. Most of them came looking for answers to important questions, like, "how do I make this damned flame at the end of my fingertip go out!" and "is my wife really a witch, and if so, why can't I have her burned at the stake?"

Soon the classes were too big for Jeremiah to manage on his own, and he had to appoint another teacher to help him out, then another as yet more of the towns people turned to his school in an attempt to understand and learn to control what was happening to them. In little more than a month he had a school rather than a schoolroom, then a college.

As the self appointed dean of Bracebridge's foremost - only - establishment for the education of young men with a magical inclination, he came to be considered by many, Derrian's foremost expert in this relatively new field. His status was recognised formally with the granting of the title, Superus doctorem autem omnes omnia rebus arcanum et magicum, which was later shortened to Darm to save on time and ink.

Repetition can make many things seem normal given long enough, and life as odd as it was at first for the town's people, eventually settled into patterns that became more and more familiar to them. There were of course the things that did not change: farmers milked their cows, wives churned the milk and made the cheese, shop keepers' assistants were up before the birds filling shelves and taking in the deliveries. The town was a rural town, and like all rural towns of its time, it had always been a little insular anyway. The outside world as it now was, soon became as unimportant to a lot of its residents as the one before it had been.

There were of course some people who were more curious about their new world; entrepreneurial types and would-be adventurers, and there were those who were simply less terrified of what they might find out there, than they were of the town itself with all its lunatic wizards and witches, and the possibility of waking up a different shape in the morning.

This led to a trickling exodus over the next few years that spawned a number of small satellite communities or fed a bit of much needed variety into the stagnating gene pools of already established ones. New villages and settlements started springing up all over the place within the borough; and so it was that the human tide started to creep outwards into what was still very much an alien world.

During this time they encountered a few of the natives as it were, leading to the realisation that their new world was already somebody else's old world. That they had not encountered them before was owing to the remoteness of where their town had materialised.

Imagine their surprise when they first encountered an aboriginal race of highly intelligent humanoids that were not actually human, then imagine their further surprise when they discovered that they had more than one such race as a neighbour. To make matters worse, these natives were not acting like natives were meant to. They did not show the slightest interest in bits of coloured glass and bone combs, and - and this was the really frustrating bit for them - the natives flat out refused to be submissive or subservient! Not surprisingly, not all of those early encounters with Derrian's indigenous population went well.

What with the Darwinists banging on about monkeys and pigeons, and people walking around in the street openly using occult powers without being dragged down into the burning pits of hell, this new blow all but destroyed the church's grip on the community, leading to one Anglican vicar hanging himself, and another being arrested for defrocking himself in a public place.

As Bracebridge grew in prominence, it started to attract traders and opportunists from Derrian's aboriginal population - magic of the kind that the human wizards and witches possessed was a rare commodity that could be converted into hard currency. Most of that currency circulated within the city itself, creating a sense of wealth, or at least creating a sense of the opportunities that existed for attaining wealth, and this latter attracted even more people to Bracebridge. Soon the Bracians - Bracebridge was familiarly shortened to Brace and was eventually renamed as such - were soon able to boast that they had the most cosmopolitan population to be found anywhere in Derrian.

Jeremiah Dipple's advice was often sought by the powers that be throughout this transitional period, and he received a good deal of the acclaim for Bracebridge's growth and increasing prosperity. Although he willingly accepted the praise that was being heaped upon him, he never quite understood what if anything he had done to deserve it. If he had lived long enough to see Brace grow into a nation state, he would have been at a complete loss to find the mechanism by which it had done so, or what his part in it had been. Sadly a midair collision with a bird broke his concentration while he was trying to set a new record for levitation, and he did not get to see this happen.

Brace was like a living creature in many ways. The people living in it rubbed along together like life carrying blood cells, all of them going about their self-interested lives, yet serving something that few of them had the breadth of vision to perceive in its entirety, and in turn finding within it the structure that they needed for their continued wellbeing. Even those who set themselves against the status quo fulfilled a purpose by creating eddies and ripples, generating new possibilities and growth where things might otherwise have begun to stagnate.

A healthy community like a healthy organism, will often develop a shared sense of identity, even a personality of a kind. It gets known for a thing and labeled accordingly. When this happens the credit rarely goes to the whole. Calling a town or village a farming or mining community for instance, takes no account of the butchers, the bakers, the candlestick makers, their partners, children or pets etc. Brace - fairly or not - came to be known as 'The city of the Wizards', and likewise, this took no account of the other ninety percent of the population who were not wizards.

This understandably upset some of Brace's residents who felt that they contributed as much as the wizards to the greatness of the city, but the fact was that the wizards were central to a good deal of the prosperity, and to its growing reputation. It was difficult to think of Brace without thinking of it as being in some way their city.

It was a good place to be a wizard in the early days, but it was also a good place to be a witch or a practitioner of any of the many other kinds of magic, and it was a good place to just live an ordinary life and raise a family. Brace was cosmopolitan, progressive and remarkably tolerant of difference. It might then seem odd that anyone would actually hate the wizards.

The wizards themselves were largely ignorant or indifferent to how others felt about them in those days, and the few who did take more than a passing interest in public opinion, were more amused than concerned by what they heard. What in the end very nearly proved to be the undoing of the human wizards in Brace, was their own good intentions and naivety, rather than the machinations of others.

Nature does not like long periods of stability; things stop trying to evolve, they start to live longer, use up more than they put back into the system. There are a number of mechanisms that stop this happening too often: dependent predators, natural disaster, pestilence and disease, war, and if all else fails, a tendency to go and do something really really stupid.

The elves and the Lowlands shared a long border, and a long history of not getting on very well. The border mostly ran through land that neither nation cared enough about to dispute ownership of, and this created a kind of neutral zone where very few people lived. The few who for one reason or another did live there, lived by their own rules, scratching whatever existence they could out of the land. For some that was hunting - animals or fugitives, depending what was more profitable at the time - while others planted whatever they could grow, and bred lakas and goats, which they took to the border towns and sold or bartered for whatever they needed.

The border towns were typically small, but they where a lifeline to these people, and the trade that passed through them was brisk enough to make even the elves and Lowlands temporarily forget their differences. It was this trickling trade through the border towns that ultimately proved to be the greatest aid in preserving the peace along the border, and ironically, of all the things that might have caused the two nations to finally come to blows with one and other, it was a stupid drunken fistfight between two Lowland trolls outside a tavern in one of those small border towns.

The fight was finished almost before it had started, with only a few punches being exchanged before the two drunken combatants were separated by a couple of elves, who arguably should have known better than to get involved. As they parted, one of the Lowland trolls pulled his arm back to take a parting swing at the other fellow, and his elbow struck one of the elves on the side of the head. The elf landed on an empty chair, and the two Lowlands who were in fact friends, staggered away arguing still, and were never seen again. Unfortunately the elf suffered a major haemorrhage before his travelling companion reached him, and he died in the chair amid the hubbub of the tavern's patrons who were busy righting tables and chairs, and complaining about their spilled ale.

The path between a pub brawl in a border town in the back end of nowhere, and the international incident that it quickly became, is easier to follow than it is to fully understand. Normally a public beating and the payment of a blood-wit to the victim's family would have put an end to the matter, but the troll who had struck the fatal blow was travelling through the town with his friend, and the two were gone before the consequences of the attack were fully apparent. An attempt was made to find the assailant, but the incident itself though unfortunate, was unexceptional, and the response to it was at best sluggish and halfhearted.

Representatives were sent by the grandparents of the dead elf to arrange the transportation of the body, and to see if they could do more than the town's enforcer had to catch the killer of their grandchild. One of the dangers of representing a powerful and/or influential family in this way, is that it is easy to assume that you are an extension of its influence rather than simply acting within its sphere. This sort of conceit can lead to a level of tactlessness that is seldom tolerated for very long outside of that sphere. These representatives had not been chosen for their tact and diplomacy, and it was not long before backs were up and accusations were flying from both sides of cover-ups and the use of strong-arm tactics.

Things escalated at an alarming rate. Tensions that had bubbled away like trapped wind, reached a point where they could no longer be contained. Border patrols that had on occasion in the past reined up alongside each other to complain about the weather and share a nip of 'something to warm yer bits up me old mate,' before riding on, barely managed a nod in passing, or kept apart and eyed each other warily.

Tensions grew further as more soldiers were moved to the border amid fears that things might escalate. This was chiefly done with the intention of keeping their own respective peoples from doing anything stupid, but there was also a growing sense of preparation on both sides, and their presence on the border did far more harm than good.

Hastily assembled units of irregulars started to arrive almost daily, under equipped and under provisioned, and often very poorly led. Most of them were conscripts from the estates of wealthy families who were worried that the trouble would reach them if it was not dealt with quickly, but there were others as well: groups of friends, clubs, would be adventurers, gangs of rogues who came looking for easy pickings, and there were the old soldiers who had never quite adjusted to a life as a civilian.

In those days the Lowland troll nation was much larger, and it occupied territory well beyond what later came to be known as The Barrens. It was governed by district and province through a system that was as old and corrupt as anything that the elves could lay claim to, and on both sides of the border, alliances were being made and broken quicker than the ink could dry on the paper, as each geared up for a war that was beginning to seem more and more inevitable.

Brace had hoped to be left out of it, but there were rumours that human wizards and witches were being hired by both sides in the growing conflict to cause mischief. The elves and the Lowlands were both quick to deny any wrong doing on their own parts, and just as quick to point fingers at each other and at Brace.

Brace of course strongly refuted the accusation that they were behind the actions of the relatively few renegade humans who were actually involved, and they even made several attempts to find a peaceful solution to the escalating conflict, but the hatred between the elves and Lowland trolls had been simmering below the surface unchecked for far too long, and it was soon apparent that it was a matter of when rather than if there would be a war. When the war finally began, it was with such sudden and overwhelming brutality, that no one could doubt that the centuries of rubbing along together had come at a shocking price.

People from other lands and races who had lived and made their livings among the trolls and elves for many years, started to flee with their families and belongings before the borders could be closed, and the tales that they brought out with them were not only of the brutality and cruelty that they had witnessed, but darker tales of necromancy being used to raise corpses from among the slain to take up arms, as though being killed once had not been enough for them.

Each new report found Jeremiah Dipple more and more perplexed and exhausted. He wrestled day and night with the problem of what to do. He hated violence in any form, hated that people could so easily cast aside their general goodness and decency and become such brutal creatures, as though those other things had never been anything more than a thin veneer. Jeremiah would have given his left hand to stop the horror that he was hearing about, but his greater concern was that the violence would escalate and reach into the lives of his own people.

Innocence, decency and compassion were among the first things to be lost during the war. People did things to each other, and behaved towards each other in ways that they would have found abhorrent if they had been onlookers and not participants.

There is a saying that time heals all things. It does not. Given enough time most things can heal, be forgotten, or at least become more bearable, but the war machine was merciless; it rumbled on day by day, week by week, month after month, churning through one, two, even three generations of the same family, taking away that most cherished of all commodities: life with all of its possibilities.

Soldiers on both sides who had on the most part been reluctant participants to begin with, grew more so, and became more and more surly and resistant to being ordered around, especially when those orders put them in harm's way. Soon it became necessary to hire mercenaries to fill out the back ranks and to put the tips of their spears at the backs of soldiers who might otherwise have refused to advance.

Mercenaries, camp wives, horses, food, bladed weapons, WMD's - weapons of magical destruction - all could be bought at prices that would have been considered criminal, if these things were not being used to perpetrate and perpetuate even greater crimes.

Of the six countries sharing some part of their own borders with one or the other of those two warring nations, only two actively deterred their people from trying to profit from the war, and even then not as wholeheartedly as they might have done. Several auction houses even conducted sales in which representatives from both sides were forced to bid against each other for the supplies and weapons that they needed.

It seemed to Brace's aldermen, as it did to the wizards themselves, that the fighting would spread, and that Brace would at some point be drawn unwillingly into the conflict. Brace at that time was still relatively small in terms of population, and could not have assembled much of an army to defend its borders if the need arose. Troubled by this seemingly insoluble problem, the council arrived at what was entered into its records as its first unanimous decision. That decision was to make the wizard's responsible for the defence of Brace.

It was a masterful piece of buck passing, sugar coated appealingly with a promotion for Jeremiah Dipple, who was given the even loftier title still, of, Dominus autem omnes omnia magicum et quae ut quod praesidium autem quod gentem, which was shortened to Dameg to save time and ink.

Poor old Jeremiah. How could he refuse, when all eyes were already fixed on him for a solution! He tried - not as hard as he might have done admittedly. It went along the lines of, 'no no no! I really couldn't; could I?'

74

Day after day Jeremiah listened to new reports and bits of gossip about the fighting and the many plots and deceptions that were fuelling it. It seemed to him that Derrian was standing on the edge of a precipice, being dragged in by the elves and Lowlands, who were now wholly bent on destroying each other at any cost.

Jeremiah was despite his various failings, essentially a man of peace, and the idea of bringing the formidable powers of his wizards to bear against any of Derrian's people was as abhorrent to him as the bloodshed itself. Weighing heavily against his pacifist beliefs was the need to do something soon, or risk the decision being put into the hands of someone who might have fewer qualms about using force. It was in this hard pressed frame of mind that he brought his most senior advisors and wizards together to try to find the peaceful solution that had so far evaded him.

There were surprisingly few suggestions made given the very individual natures of each of those who were present at the meeting, and when a course of action was decided upon, it was even more surprising that there was very little objection made to it.

And so it was that two days later on a night that was suitably overcast and foreboding, a group of wizards met in private on a rooftop, and did a thing that would throw the elves and Lowland trolls into such a state of turmoil, that fighting would become the furthest thing from their minds.

The next morning the elves and Lowland trolls woke up to find that they were not the same people who had gone to sleep the night before. Physically they were unchanged, but they were dogged by a powerful sense of difference within that left many of them staring into reflective surfaces at faces that they did not recognise as being their own. It was only later over the weeks and months that followed that they realised the full extent of what had been done to them.

What the wizards had done was create a spell that altered the way that they interpreted their own emotional responses to external stimuli. It also affected the parts of their brains associated with inherited behaviour, and it was this that ultimately had the greatest long term impact on the Lowland trolls and the elves, changing each as a people by accentuating certain characteristic traits.

Jeremiah had only intended to distract the elves and trolls from their madness long enough to get them around the negotiating table again without any more blood being spilt. He had not expected them to thank him - not straight away anyway - but he was shocked and dismayed at the outcry that his well intended actions caused.

Some of the anger he understood and had even expected; one man's misery is another man's good fortune, as they say, and many sizeable fortunes were being made from the war. When it ended unexpectedly, people who had speculated against the likelihood of a much longer war, suddenly found themselves with warehouses full of military equipment that nobody wanted to buy.

Jeremiah had not been naive on that score. He had known that their actions would not meet with overwhelming approval, but he could not understand - greed aside - why Derrian's various peoples could not see that the war would have eventually spilled across all of their borders if it had been allowed to continue.

As powerful as the human wizards were believed to be, nobody had suspected that their powers were quite so far reaching. Suddenly nobody was safe, or at least no longer had the illusion that they were safe. It was more than that though; it was the way that it had happened. People had quite literally had their minds changed by the wizards, and they had been powerless to stop it happening.

Jeremiah upon hearing that some of Brace's neighbours were getting quite nervous, drafted a letter to each, reassuring them at some length that he and his wizards had only done as much as was necessary to stop the fighting, and that they could have done so much more if they had wanted to. Not surprisingly, this did not have quite the effect that he had intended.

Brace's council had changed very little over the years, and was poorly equipped to deal with the problems of running a growing city, especially one in the midst of a major crisis. It fell apart quietly, passing more and more of the responsibility and administrative control to the wizards, until almost without anybody realising, the wizards were running the whole show. This effectively - or ineffectively, depending upon your point of view - put Jeremiah in charge.

The next few years saw a rapid decline in Brace's fortunes as Derrian turned its back on the city and cut off all diplomatic and trade ties with it. Steps were also taken to ensure that these measures were not circumvented by anyone who might try to seize the opportunity of gaining a more exclusive arrangement with Brace.

All things are the sum of their parts, whatever the poets might say to the contrary. A person is ten trillion or so cells, and ten times that number of interdependent organisms and freeloading parasites. What makes a person special is the level of organisation and cooperation required to keep it all together and working. A city has a much more fragile bond with its organic parts than a living creature has with its various bits, but it is still the same in many respects, and should under the right conditions survive a good deal longer. People are however more self-serving and arbitrary than the cells in their bodies, and their loyalties are a lot less certain. If the same were true of cells, life would never have evolved beyond a single cell form.

Faced with a collapsing economy, crippling sanctions and almost universal disapproval beyond their borders, it seemed to quite a few of Brace's population that the city's future was as bleak as it had once been bright. People of all the races who had once been proud to live there and call Brace their home, started to consider what had once been unthinkable to them; that they might find a better life for themselves and their families elsewhere.

Although Brace itself had been ostracised, humans were still tolerated in the wider world beyond its borders - even by the Lowlands and elves - and were allowed to come and go as they wished. Consequently, quite a few people left in search of a better life out from underneath the shadow that the wizards' actions had cast over the city.

It felt to Jeremiah that he was witnessing a slow bleed as he received daily reports about the comings, and especially, the goings of people across the Bracian border, but in that he did not do his city or its people justice. The city was far more resilient than he gave it credit for, and though many people did leave, a great many more stayed - not just humans - and their resolve became a fiercely stubborn pride in what they could achieve despite, rather than because of Derrian.

One year passed into two, three, then ten and more. Jeremiah meant on so many occasions during that time to reverse the spell that had caused all the trouble, but each time he suggested it to his council, he was met with such overwhelming indecision or objection that he could not bring himself to act on the matter. Some argued that the trolls and elves were still only diverted from their barbaric war. Others suggested that removing the spell would be seen as weakness and a lack of resolve at a time when Brace needed to appear strong. A few pointed out that they had acted once in desperation, and look what that had gotten them! Jeremiah could not argue with any degree of conviction against any of these points, especially when they all so perfectly reflected his own mixed feelings.

The one thing that they did all manage to agree on, was how open the city was to attack. It was not something that they had considered to any great degree until then, but the world outside had turned decidedly chilly since their intervention in the war, and though no military action had so far been taken against the city and its outlying settlements, they could not be certain that it never would.

As a result of this, a huge building project was undertaken to strengthen Brace's defences, beginning with a high wall that would completely encircle the city. This was done at a pace that no army of ordinary stoneworkers could have dreamed possible, and within a few months the city boasted a wall that would protect them from everything but an aerial attack. As impressive as the wall and the city's other defences undoubtedly were, ultimately it was a fear of the wizards themselves that proved to be the greatest deterrent to an attack.

It was decades before the wizards openly ventured beyond their city. The same could not be said of the witches, who during that time had started to insinuate themselves into many of Derrian's communities, making themselves indispensable as midwives and healers, and they and others became the ears and eyes for the wizards, so that the wizards never really lost touch with what was happening in the world beyond their own borders.

Decade followed decade, and as new generations of Lowland trolls and elves came, old ones passed, until soon only a rapidly diminishing few could remember what they had been like before the wizards had interfered with them. The elves and Lowlands were who and what they were now, and no more wanted messing around with than their grandparents and great-grandparents had in the first place, and so it was that life returned to normal, which is not quite the same thing as being the same.

The Lowland trolls had suffered the most and lost the most because of the war, and the spell that had so effectively ended the war, also removed the possibility of them getting back what they had lost to the elves. The Lowlands would have disputed the notion that they had lost anything of any great value, but huge areas of rich arable land had necessarily been conceded to the elves during the fighting, and they had retreated into an area of land that accounted for a third of their former territory, known as The Barrens.

Much of the Barrens was harsh and unforgiving, and necessity and the altered natures of the Lowlands forced them into a nomadic existence. What cities and towns they had built in that desolate place before the war, quickly fell into ruin and were abandoned in preference of a life under canvas, forever on the move.

The wizards were not at all idle in their isolation. They built their city upwards into the sky, and down into the ground, until Brace had become massive beyond the limits of any conventional building methods. More than that though, the wizards had started to grow in themselves and in their mastery and understanding of their gift.

What finally made the wizards take more than a passing interest in the things that were happening beyond their walls, was the unannounced arrival of a small but persistent delegation. The delegation was from a group of individuals calling themselves the Greater Derrian committee. This group was later to be known as the Greater Derrian Council, or GDC for short.

The GDC were at that time a hotchpotch collection of minor statesmen and dignitaries who had been tasked with the duty of ensuring Derrian's greater good through joint initiatives. Unofficially the GDC was also a back door through which communication could be maintained between nations who were not officially on very good terms with each other. That they had not approached Brace before in this capacity, showed just how far from grace Brace had fallen!

Jeremiah could not decide if their visit heralded a turning point in Brace's chilly relationship with its neighbours, or if it was simply desperation that had driven them to come to him. He suspected that it was both, and so he sat smiling encouragingly, and waited for the delegate who was speaking to get to the point.

"The Velvet fist are particularly violent and..."

"I am aware of some of their activities," Jeremiah said, interrupting him. The Velvet fist had made the mistake of threatening the families of a couple of minor officials when they were refused a license to open a gambling house in the city. It was a mistake that they were not likely to make a second time.

"Then you know that they are mostly human, and..."

"I know that they are not Bracian," Jeremiah pointed out, interrupting the delegate again. "I think that maybe you invited the snake in?" He raised his hand to forestall the objection.

The delegate thought about lying, but realised that there was little point. "Their organisation has been used by certain parties on occasion to do, certain jobs," he admitted.

Jeremiah harrumphed at that. He could well imagine the type of jobs that they would have been used for. He let the delegate squirm under his gaze for a moment as though considering his request, though in truth, the decision had already been made. He thought about his people; they had been paying for his mistake for far too long, and there were impatient murmurings from the lower ranks of his order. The last thing he needed - the last thing anyone needed - was an outpouring of idealistic young wizards bumbling around Derrian trying to save its people from themselves! Jeremiah knew from bitter experience where that road led to. "We will help you," he told the delegate after a few moments. He smiled wolfishly. "Now, let's discuss what it will cost you."

Jeremiah had grown cautious and more calculating over his many unnaturally extended years of life, and he had learned to exercise the kind of wisdom that can only be found on the wrong side of a gargantuan cock-up. He was also by his measure of such things, a fair man, and so in the spirit of fairness, he issued a warning to the Velvet hand to the effect that if they did not cease their criminal activities immediately, they would be dealt with in the harshest manner. Jeremiah wrestled with his conscience when it came to the matter of how to deal with those who chose not to heed his warning. In the end he left it to the people he sent to carry out his vague threat, to interpret its meaning.

It came as something of a revelation to Jeremiah as his agents continued to hunt down the remaining members of the Velvet hand, just how much support Brace and its wizards still had in Derrian. There were many people - not just humans - who had deep rooted connections with Brace, and for them as well as for many others, the city and its wizards were something that they shared in common, something that connected them to each other no matter how far they scattered through Derrian.

The wizards withdrew from Derrian's affairs again for a while afterwards, but it was only to take stock of the situation that they now found themselves in. During the next few years, the wizards rose quickly in status and reputation, and it was they in preference to the GDC that governments and leaders started to turn to to moderate or mediate in difficult diplomatic situations, the unspoken implication being that there was an alternative to sitting down and discussing things reasonably. Not surprisingly, it was many years before Derrian saw another conflict on anything like the same scale as the one between the elves and the Lowland trolls, and this was largely and justly accredited to the wizards.

Sleep sneaked up on Ralph like a velvet-shoed assassin. His head dropped forward slowly, came up with a start, then drooped again until his head came to rest on his chest. Cassi stopped Gemfelt mid flow as the human started to snore.

Gemfelt grinned and got up quietly. "I reckon he's got the right idea," he said, taking his wife's hand and pulling her to her feet.

Cassi released his hand and punched him gently on the arm. "He might," she told him, "but you can think again." She waited just long enough for him to get the wrong idea then added, "you can wash and I'll dry."

Ralph was woken the next morning with a gentle shake of the shoulder, and opened his eyes to find Gemfelt smiling down at him. He looked past the elf and stared at the low wattle and daub ceiling as the events of the previous day came rushing back. Ralph teetered for a second at the edge of something that was only marginally more insane than what was happening to him, then let out a low moan and said, "you're an elf."

"Last time I looked," Gemfelt answered as he went back to his cushion.

"I thought for a moment that it was all a bad dream." Ralph shot the elf an apologetic smile and added, "no offence."

"None taken, human." Gemfelt said as he held out a bowl for Ralph to take. "Eat now," he told him. "You've a long walk ahead of you, and no way of knowing where or when your next meal'll come."

Ralph sat up with a groan and took the bowl. The hot bath and good night's sleep had done a lot to revive his spirits, but the long march to the village had been hard on muscles that were not accustomed to vigorous exercise, and that and the many scabbed up cuts and grazes on his lower body were enough to make him start feeling sorry for himself all over again. The thought of having to undertake an even longer journey on his own might have reduced him to tears if Gemfelt had not been sat there looking at him.

Ralph stared absently at the steaming ochre coloured contents of the bowl, then thinking on the wisdom of Gemfelt's words, blew on it gently and raised it to his lips. It was hot and slimy and clung to his teeth and tongue like wallpaper paste as it went down, but it was not unpleasant. "What is this?" he asked, taking another mouthful.

"Tomato porridge," Gemfelt told him.

Ralph paused for a moment with the bowl at his lips, then shrugged and carried on eating.

Ralph said goodbye to Cassi shortly after breakfast. Cassi punched him lightly on the shoulder. "You look after yer sen now, d'you hear."

Ralph was touched by the real concern in her voice and eyes, and on an impulse, gave her a hug. It was like trying to hug a young tree, both in the firmness of her body and the stiffness of her response to the unaccustomed physical contact with a human.

Cassi patted Ralph on the back a couple of times and took hold of his shoulders and pushed him back to arm's length. "Well then," she said awkwardly, "there's a thing."

"Come on then," Gemfelt urged. "No point putting it off any longer."

"I'm sorry if I offended Cassi," Ralph said once they were outside and out of earshot.

Gemfelt shook his head. "You didn't offend her," he reassured. "You just took her aback a little, is all." He gripped Ralph's upper arm companionably and laughed. "It's not every day she gets cuddled by an illogical immigrant."

Ralph was an alien. Seen in this light, it was easy to understand her reaction.

Gemfelt took Ralph to the edge of the village and walked across the clearing with him. He might have taken him further, but short of taking him all the way to Brace, just how far would have been enough to ensure the human's survival? In the end, he thought sadly, some things had to fold out as they would.

"How many miles is it to Brace?" Ralph asked when they reached the trees.

Gemfelt shrugged and asked him what a mile was. Ralph opened his mouth to answer, paused thoughtfully, then said that he did not know.

Gemfelt took a small haversack from his shoulder and passed it to Ralph. "I wish I could do more for you," he said, "but there's enough food fer a week if yer careful, and water fer a day or so. You'll likely find a stream before it runs out, but mind how much you drink. Just remember what I said about the berries though."

Ralph tried to remember what Gemfelt had said about the berries, but Gemfelt had said a lot of things about a lot of things on the way to the village, and Ralph had been too preoccupied to take much notice.

The haversack was very light for something that was meant to keep him alive for a week, but Ralph had no illusions about his own lack of fitness, and he knew that he would soon be thankful for that as much as for its contents. He put the sack on his shoulder and stuck his hand out.

Gemfelt looked at it then said, "Oh, right, I've seen that in an illustrated book about humans." He took the offered hand and held it, but the book had not said what to do with it once he had it, and it was Ralph who provided the up and down motion of a handshake. Gemfelt said, "ah," then, "anyway, it's been nice knowing you."

Ralph shuddered a little. There was a finality to a statement like that that he did not like very much. "Is that how elves say goodbye?" he asked.

Gemfelt gave a noncommittal shrug. "It's close enough."

There was little more that either of them could say after that. There were a lot of pointless noises that Ralph might have made in an effort to delay his departure a bit longer, but Gemfelt would not have played along for very long, and so he turned reluctantly and walked away, better clothed and better fed than he would have been without the help of the elves.

Derrian! It bobbed away on the surface of Ralph's thoughts like a lump of polystyrene in a sloshing water bucket, refusing to sink in. So many things looked the same as they did on Earth but felt utterly different to him, or were alien in an oddly familiar sort of way. He was desperate to get a handle on it, on what was happening to him, but it was like trying to grip a custard door handle. Many of his decisions were mistakes, and his mistakes were only compounded further by his ignorance, not only of Derrian, but of how to survive without a satnav or a supermarket nearby.

Ralph - unsurprisingly - was lost within a few hours of entering the forest. He would have given up and gone back to the village, except that he did not know where the village was, and so he plodded on, working on the assumption that if he kept going in as straight a line as possible, he would eventually come out on the other side of the forest. This of course took no account of the trees themselves making it impossible to walk more than ten feet in a straight line.

Ralph stumbled through what he took to be a dried up riverbed during the afternoon of his third day. It was overgrown and tangled with roots, but there was a path of sorts along the far side, and it seemed to him as good a direction as any to go. He continued along it for maybe three miles, where it stopped at the edge of a steep bank of fallen rock and earth from an old landslide. Ralph paused briefly to let his eyes adjust, and to survey the vast clearing beyond, which stretched out like a welling teardrop, hemmed at its furthest end by low hills. It seemed as he stood there, that the trees surrounding the clearing were held back as though by some invisible wall, but that was just fancy and a trick of the distance.

A stiff breeze ruffled the seed heavy heads of the tall grass that covered the clearing from edge to edge, causing a ripple to roll across it like a wind-stirred swell across water. This was followed by another and another, each in quick succession, giving the illusion that he was staring across a vast lake.

Several large boulders sat proud of the tall grass like small islets, completing the illusion of a lake, and it was on the nearest of these that Ralph set his bearings as he climbed down into the long grass. The grass was surprisingly thin given its height, and it bent aside with ease, hissing loudly as it rubbed against his clothes, or when the breeze lifted enough to stir it. For a moment everything felt, if not exactly right, at least okay with the world - this world. Ralph allowed himself to enjoy the moment; the caress of the grass, tickling almost at times, the strange sun overhead warming his skin, the loud shout that destroyed the moment and stopped him in his tracks...

Ralph turned around sharply and caught a glimpse of something large and hairy back along the path that he had trodden down. He started to hurry, then when the creature dropped onto all fours and started running towards him, he likewise started to run.

Ralph did not dare look back for fear that he would trip in the grass. As it was, he had to high step to avoid catching his feet, and this slowed him down considerably. The creature that was chasing him was not so impaired, and it was a matter of a few seconds before Ralph could hear the hiss of its swift passage through the grass above his own.

Nifnaff could scarcely believe his eyes. The human was walking right into a resting group of young dragons! The place was littered with the creatures, their partially deflated lift sacks jutting from the grass like small islands. He tried to shout a warning, but the human took fright and started to run towards the nearest dragon. For a pinch he would have left the man to suffer the consequences of his stupidity, but it was not in his nature, so he dropped onto all fours and tried to catch up with him.

The nearest dragons upon hearing the commotion, started to stir from their rest, their huge floatation sacks filling quickly as specially adapted organs generated the necessary gas to inflate them and lift them clear of the ground. Nifnaff shouted again, even louder this time, but the human put his head down and ran even faster!

The bearlike creature roared at Ralph again. It was a deep and resonant sound that would have stunned a jungle into nervous silence. He dared to look over his shoulder quickly, but it was all blurred motion and grass. A part of him remembered the small primate from which he was descended, remembered its almost daily fight for survival against stronger, faster and much fiercer creatures than itself, and knew what it had known, that fear was almost as great an enemy to the hunted as the hunter itself.

Ralph dug deeply into adrenalin fuelled reserves and pulled out a little more. He did not need to look back again to know that the creature was now almost upon him. The sound of its feet drumming rhythmically on the ground and the hiss of dry grass being ploughed aside were enough. Out of time, he turned to face his attacker within reach of the rock like a mouse that feels the cat's claws upon its back.

Nifnaff watched as the human turned to face him, completely unaware of the cavernous mouth that was opening up behind it. He slid to a stop and reached out to grab the human, but as he did, the man took a step backwards and stumbled into the dragon's open mouth!

Ralph stared up from his back at the roof of a cavernous mouth, without actually realising that that was what he was staring up at, or that the warm and giving thing that he was lying on was a tongue. The bearlike creature that had been chasing him was pacing backwards and forwards just outside. It glared at him, obviously irritated by this turn of events, and its irritation and reluctance to come in after him, caused Ralph to hope that he might yet get out of this situation in one piece. So minded, he started easing himself further and further backwards into the dragon's mouth.

The creature snarled at Ralph, its wide lipless mouth drawing back to display more teeth than a group photo for an election poster. It shook its head in something approximating disgust, turned to leave, took two steps, then turned back again, and with an almighty howl of rage, dived in after Ralph. Ralph screamed in surprise as the creature grabbed his right ankle with one of its feet. He scrabbled and clawed desperately in an effort to pull free, but the creature's grip was like an iron manacle around his ankle.

Nifnaff spared the human a look that was fairly dripping with disgust, then joined his hands together and punched upwards with incredible force into the roof of the dragon's mouth. There was a meaty thud that caused the world to shake around them both, then he was off at a three limbed gallop with Ralph bouncing along behind him.

Ralph hit his head several times on exposed rocks and stones as Nifnaff dragged him towards the cover of the trees. Just before the thick green canopy blotted out the last of the sky, he glimpsed the underside of an impossibly wide jaw drifting lazily overhead. A large plate sized eye stared down at him disdainfully as the dragon veered away at the last possible moment to avoid getting tangled up in the trees. Ralph turned his head as far as he could to see, but the creature was too big and too close for him to get any clear impression beyond its incredible size. He squirmed, and tried to kick the bear-like creature that was towing him along. He missed, struck his head on a rock and passed out.

Ralph was still on his back when he regained consciousness. Overhead dappled light caused by the interplay between light, leaf and breeze danced confusingly in front of his eyes, momentarily confounding his attempts to focus his eyes. He tried desperately to believe that he had just woken up from a crazy dream underneath one of the trees in the recreation park near his house, and he might have succeeded - for a little while at least - but for several quite distinct points of pain, not least of which was the back of his head.

Ralph groaned loudly then rolled onto his side and threw up. He stayed there for a couple of minutes, his face pale and set but for a flicker at the corner of his right eye that punctuated the rhythmic thump thump thump within his aching skull. He had a nagging sense of urgency, some significant thing that wriggled away as he tried to grasp it; then it struck him like a lunging cobra, and he sat up quickly - too quickly - and scrabbled backwards along the ground until he fetched up hard between the exposed roots of a tree.

Nifnaff had started to build a small fire while the human was still unconscious, but it was a skill that he had not fully mastered and he was not having much luck with it. He sighed in exasperation as another glowing ember faded. Never one to be beaten, he struck another shower of sparks into the little pile of tinder that he had made and blew it gently. This time it caught and a tiny flame sprang up and spread in the tuft of dry shavings. Nifnaff fed it carefully until he was certain that it would not gutter this time, then started arranging thin twigs over it. He cupped his huge hands around it protectively and blew on it again, then added more twigs and shavings, and finally bigger branches. Nifnaff sat back on his haunches and surveyed his handiwork as flames started to lick the branches, stripping them of their moisture noisily.

There is something mesmerising about a fire. It was something that Nifnaff had only come to appreciate properly during his exile in the lowlands. He often wondered why it fascinated him so, why when he needed no great amount of light or heat, he found comfort in both. Ralph's sudden movement destroyed the moment, but he kept his slight irritation from showing on his face as he turned to look at him.

Ralph felt fixed to the spot by the creature's large unsettling blue/grey eyes. "Don't eat me!" he pleaded. Nifnaff turned back to the fire and frowned down at it. "No offence, human," he said in a low rumbling voice without looking up, "but you are not to my taste. I prefer my food from the ground and the bough, not the bone." He was silent for a moment as he contemplated the dancing flames once more then added, "if the dragon had been as choosy as me, it would have saved us both a lot of trouble."

Ralph had not expected such a fearsome looking creature to be able to speak. That it had done so in such a precise and intelligent manner was at least as much of a surprise to him as its assurance that he was not about to be eaten by it. He watched the creature as it sat staring into the fire - Ralph could not yet think of Nifnaff as a he.

Nifnaff was taller sat down than Ralph was standing up, and so heavily muscled that he managed to look squat despite his great height. His entire body with the exception of his face and the flats of his feet and hands was covered in short slab-grey fur that did nothing to hide the rippling strength beneath it.

Ralph looked at Nifnaff's massive hands more closely. There was something odd about them that at first escaped him, then he realised that where a little finger might have been, was a second slightly smaller opposing thumb. Nifnaff's feet were similarly constructed, though with their digits slightly shorter and a little less dexterous. Ralph knew from painful experience that the creature could use its feet to grip still. He rubbed his bruised ankle and thought that maybe he had been lucky not to have been more badly injured.

He turned his attention to the creature's face again. It had large deeply set thoughtful eyes that brooded beneath heavy brow ridges, and a nose and jaw that jutted like an apes, yet wider and squarer, and more solidly boned than any ape that Ralph knew of. Ralph was overawed by the creature. No great ape on Earth had ever been so huge or so powerfully built. Nifnaff looked back at him, the look intelligent and appraising, and unsettling. There were too many contradictions, too many things about the creature that Ralph could not marry together.

"What dragon?" Ralph asked, recalling the creature's words.

"Remember that big scaly thing that you were trying to choke to death with your body?" Nifnaff prompted.

Ralph thought about it for a moment; the creature shouting and running after him, falling backwards into a slightly soggy cave, the monstrously big thing that had fixed him with a big baleful eye as it floated over their heads. "I thought," he started to say, then fell into an embarrassed silence.

"That I was going to eat you," Nifnaff said, finishing for him. "I know."

"I'm not from around here," Ralph said sulkily. He added, "it'll be a miracle if I get to Brace, let alone find a wizard who can send me home."

"I am going there," Nifnaff said without thinking. He saw the sudden hope and pleading in the human's eyes and sighed.

Ralph got up and moved towards the fire. "Do you mind?" he asked, then knelt down and extended his hands towards the flames. "My name's Ralph," he said.

Nifnaff did not feel inclined to give his name to a stranger, but not to do so would have seemed impolite when the man had offered his own. "I am Nifnaff," he said grudgingly.

Ralph was nervous about being so close to such a massive and so obviously powerful creature without several inches of toughened glass or thick bars between them. "If you don't mind me asking," he said hesitating slightly, "but what are you?"

Nifnaff was taken aback a little by the question and by its directness. "What am I?" he repeated as he studied the human's face for any indication that he was being insulted. "I am a Mountain troll, of course," he replied. "What else could I be?"

Several answers sprang to Ralph's mind, none of which he cared to offer. The question however was a rhetorical one and no answer was expected. "A Mountain troll," Ralph repeated, still none the wiser for having been told.

"What kind of human does not know what a Mountain troll looks like?" Nifnaff asked suspiciously.

"The kind that gets sucked out of his bedroom on one world and finds himself in the middle of a nightmare on another," Ralph answered bitterly.

Nifnaff said, "oh," but what he meant was, oh?

It quickly became apparent to Ralph after they broke camp the following morning, that Nifnaff's navigational skills were little better than his own. Nifnaff had no illusions on that score either, but having his shortcomings witnessed as they were by this human only increased his frustration, and he became more and more irritable as the day progressed. His mood did not improve any the next day either, or the one that followed it. This was compounded by Ralph himself, who despite his best efforts, could not hope to keep up with the troll, and he constantly had to ask Nifnaff to wait for him or slow down a little.

The following day they came across a well trodden path. Ralph asked Nifnaff if it was going the right direction. Nifnaff stiffened slightly, then shrugged his broad shoulders as an impulse passed. "It goes somewhere, which means so are we, which is more than we have been doing so far," was all the answer he would offer. Ralph accepted this for the small improvement to their situation that it was.

Tree bark and leaf mulch gradually gave way to shrubs and springy moss, then finally open meadow. Nifnaff became a little more certain of their direction once he was out of the forest, and might have made up some of the time that he had lost were it not for Ralph slowing him down still.

Nifnaff was crotchety. Not having much else to judge him by, Ralph assumed this to be his natural demeanour. He was also impatient, driven and tireless; qualities that Ralph might have admired but for the hardship that it was causing him personally.

Nifnaff's reason for going to Brace was every bit as urgent as Ralph's. Ralph was an inconvenience that he regretted more and more with every minute, hour and day that traveling at the human's slower pace added to his journey. It was not Ralph's fault - not entirely Ralph's fault. Humans were slower, lazier creatures than his own kind, and this one was less than exceptional, even when measured against his low opinion of the species. He was also incompetent and devoid of any skill or ability that might have offset his inadequacies. And there was the rub; Nifnaff knew that Ralph could not make it without him. To leave him, knowing this, would have been little better than killing him, so he endured each additional delay as well as he could, and silently cursed the day that their paths had crossed.

Days rolled into weeks, then a month and more with little to distinguish one from the next. During this time Ralph grew more accustomed to the exertion and to Nifnaff's moods, and he found a pace that he could sustain without having to stop every other hour for a rest. Even then it was not enough for the tireless Mountain troll.

The Bracian border was a ten mile wide belt of land hemmed in by two canals. The land between the canals had been given over to a single crop; a type of linseed that the wizards had modified. Nifnaff knew of the border, though he had never seen it before with his own eyes. Beyond the border was a much different landscape than any they had travelled through so far, and one that might have been more familiar to Ralph had he not grown up surrounded by concrete and tarmac like so much of Earth's population. Great swatches of rich arable land divided by hedgerows and dry walling supported a variety of food and textile crops that were as diverse in kind as the people who used their end products. Here and there the patchwork of fields gave way to lakes and ponds, or were cut through by watercourses, many of which were manmade. Patches of woodland sprouted from the fields like hairy birthmarks, vestiges of a time when the forest had covered much more of the land than it did now.

Eight major roads, each with a narrow canal running along one side and trees lining the other, radiated outwards from the city like the spokes of a bicycle wheel. These boulevards separated the land between the city and the inner canal into eight equal wedges. Smaller lanes and paths sprouted from these main roads like capillary blood vessels, connecting the various towns, villages and hamlets to each other, and via the boulevards, to the city itself.

The settlements and communities surrounding the city grew more widely spread apart the further away from the city you went, but closer in, within the great outer wall, they were so densely packed together that the only thing that separated them was a name, and the stubborn insistence of the people who lived within each to be identified with it. It was there within the walled suburbs that most Bracians lived and worked, tucked between the great outer wall and the much lower inner wall.

Within that inner wall was the wizard's enclave, with its impossibly high towers and elevated walkways and viewing platforms. Three of those towers were so big that viewed from the ground, their tips appeared to scratch the bellies of the clouds as they passed overhead. Nestled among them, small and underwhelming, was the old asylum/college.

Ralph was city born and bred. He was used to horizons that he could bump his head on, not sweeping vistas that confounded a person's sense of scale and distance. As he stared across the vast sea of blue linseed he could not tell one mile from ten. And what a blue! It hurt his eyes just looking at it, and he found himself having to squint.

Nifnaff was affected by the linseed at least as much as Ralph was, but for different reasons. This was Brace, a place that was so distant from the mountains of his birth that it should not figure at all in the lives of his people, yet there were as many tales of it and its wizards told at the hearths of his people as there were of their own great deed-doers. It was also the heartland of Derrian magic. Nifnaff did not trust things that he could not see or touch. That wizard magic was more powerful than any other form of magic on their world, only meant that there was more for him to mistrust. It was therefore a good indication of the level of Nifnaff's desperation, that he was travelling towards Brace and not in the opposite direction.

Ralph sensed Nifnaff's apprehension and mistook it for fear. He tucked himself in as close behind the big Mountain troll as he could, and prayed that he would never meet the thing that could bother a creature as powerful as his travelling companion. This of course blocked his view ahead, and it was several seconds before he realised that the linseed in front of Nifnaff was uprooting itself and moving out of their way. "Why is it doing that?" he asked. He was looking back over his shoulder and was watching the plants creeping in behind him on their spindly roots and digging themselves back into the soil again.

"I would imagine that they do not want to get trodden on," Nifnaff told him.

Ralph frowned. Nifnaff could be infuriatingly literal when it suited him. "I meant, why is it able to move?"

"It is called Fast flax." Nifnaff would have left it there but for the certainty that Ralph would not. "They say that the wizards tried to make a linseed plant that could avoid getting damaged and harvest itself," he explained. "Self-preservation and self-sacrifice are two very different qualities though, and when the first harvest came, they discovered that the linseed had chosen self-preservation over self-sacrifice."

Nifnaff grinned at the thought of a bunch of doddery old wizards puffing and panting around a field trying to round up their froward creations. Ralph watched him. It was a heartwarming glimpse of a side to his travelling companion that he did not often get to see. He wondered at it; wondered whether under other circumstances they might have been friends.

Although it was true that the wizards had altered the linseed, it was not true that their magical meddling had backfired on them; rather, that they had found a use for the linseed that they had not planned for. As it turned out, the modified linseed proved to be an excellent natural repellent against fairies. This was welcome news for Brace's long suffering farming communities, for whom fairies were an all too common problem.

Ralph made a couple of half-hearted lunges at the linseed to see just how difficult it was to catch. The linseed plants dodged each of his attempts with embarrassing ease. Some people would have been satisfied with that, but for Ralph it became something of a sport, then a challenge, a competition, and finally a matter of pride that he should not be beaten by a lot of spindly, brainless plants!

Nifnaff plodded on in dignified silence just ahead, doing his best to ignore what the human was doing, but he was becoming more and more irritated with him. The wizards were a part of his world and Ralph was not. Vandalising their property was not just disrespectful, it was foolish and potentially even dangerous. "Stop that now," he growled when he could take no more of his silliness.

Ralph was getting to his feet after a failed attempt to dive on a few straggling plants. He dusted himself off and stared sheepishly at the troll, fully appreciative of just how much effort it must have taken to grit so many teeth in one go. "Sorry," he mumbled distractedly, his attention only partly on Nifnaff. "You know how it is."

Nifnaff did not know how it was and had no particular desire to find out. He turned his back on Ralph and started walking again.

They reached the inner ring canal just before mid afternoon and crossed the bridge. Like the first bridge, it was a simple wood and metal platform that could be swung aside to allow sail barges and boats to pass without having to drop their masts. Ralph being Ralph had to give it a go when he reached the other side. He leaned into the bar and pushed experimentally, and was surprised to find that it not only moved easily, but that it swung back afterwards on its own volition.

Ralph had made a comment at the first bridge to the effect that he had expected something a bit grander, given everything that he had heard about the wizards. Nifnaff had no particular opinion on the matter, but felt a slight inclination to defend the wizards against the judgment of an outsider. He told Ralph that nothing about the wizards was what it seemed to be, and he found on much later reflection that this was the truth.

Beyond the bridge was one of the eight tree lined boulevards with its canal running alongside it. It was the first properly constructed road that Ralph had seen in Derrian. Up until that point it had been dirt, grass and rock, relieved by the occasional compacted animal path or well trodden lane with rock that had become exposed, forming a natural hardcore. The sight of the precisely cobbled road filled him with a growing sense of expectation.

The trees lining the road were fruit bearing and so laden that Ralph wondered that their branches did not snap under the weight. Some of the fruit was of a kind that he was not familiar with, while others were more recognisable, but unusual in that they hung side by side on the same bough as the other fruits. The closest Ralph had ever come to being green fingered was when the lid on a green felt tipped pen came off in his pocket, but even he knew that oranges and lemons did not grow on the same tree, or apples and pears.

Ralph plucked a pear as he passed a tree and bit into it. The flesh of the fruit was ripe and sweet, and the juice dripped down his chin so that he had to bend to avoid getting it down his shirt. "You should try one," he told Nifnaff as he tossed the core onto the grass verge. This earned him a look of disapproval from his hairy companion, and it struck him then, as it had while they were crossing the field of flax, that Nifnaff had a very healthy respect for the wizards and their property. Whether he liked or admired them was not so apparent.

They saw a few people in the fields while they walked, but they were distant and busy, and none of them showed any inclination to come over and pass the time of day with them, and it was several days before they had their first encounter with other people.

A man - the first human that Ralph had seen so far in Derrian - was walking towards them at the head of a team of mules that were pulling five heavy wagons that were linked together, forming a train. He nodded a greeting at Ralph and Nifnaff as they drew close and shouted back to his brakemen on their wagons to stop, then passed the lead rein to a boy and stepped forward and offered Ralph and Nifnaff his hand in turn. Ralph shook his hand enthusiastically. Nifnaff did so with noticeably less enthusiasm. He could not quite put his tomato sized fingertip on it, but he felt that there was something about the man that seemed a little, vague.

Tumble Wilkins had been waiting almost a week for this encounter and was now running late with his other business as a result. He did not let his irritation show however. As a matter of fact, he was rather relieved. He had started to believe that this encounter would never take place. He smiled just enough and made just the right amount of small-talk to gain Ralph's trust. It was easy. Tumble rarely had trouble getting people to like or trust him. It was a gift that stopped just short of being actual magic. It did not work on everyone of course, not completely, and the Mountain troll was one such, but Ralph was easy - embarrassingly easy. Ralph wanted to trust Tumble. Tumble was human, and for a man who was lost and adrift on an alien world, that was a very strong incentive.

Tumble listened to Ralph, encouraged him to confide in him about the reason for his journey. He sympathised just enough to be believable, then suggested a hostel where the bed sheets were a little less lively, and gave Ralph the name of a friend who would be able to help them to get an interview with a wizard. He even suggested leaving the main road that they were on a little further along and making for one of the smaller gates into the city where - he assured them - the guards were for a small consideration, more welcoming of strangers than those at the main gate. This information was imparted with a conspiratorial grin and punctuated with an occasional wink, all of which was directed at Ralph, while Nifnaff glared down at them both silently. His task done, Tumble bade them farewell and turned his attention to his mules. "Let's get them watered before we get going again," he told his lead driver, "and have someone recheck the tackle. Some of it looks a little loose,"

"He seemed a decent sort," Ralph said as they started walking again. He turned and waved farewell again, but Tumble Wilkins was not looking.

Nifnaff huffed but held his opinion to himself. On the face of things the encounter was not out of the ordinary, and he had no reason to be suspicious, but he was. Lacking any knowledge of the place beyond what he had heard in stories, Nifnaff relented to Ralph's insistence that they should take Tumble's advice, and so they left the boulevard a little further along.

Nifnaff spotted a line of dark dots in the distance a few days later. The dots stayed just that for a week more without appearing to get any closer, then one evening as the light was draining out of the sky, they resolved into a row of great brooding standing stones, jutting up from the ground like enormous blackened teeth. Ralph threw his bag onto the floor at the base of one of them and tried to recall the point when they had started to seem closer, but there was not one that he could bring to mind. He would have been dismayed to discover that it was a little less than three miles as the crow flies from where they had first spotted them a week earlier - a journey of no more than an hour at a dawdle. He would have been even more dismayed to know the reason why it had taken them so long, and who was responsible.

A couple of centuries earlier, a wizard with a penchant for strong ale had been staggering home from a pub one night. Zigzagging and stumbling about in the poorly lit street, it occurred to him, that he was travelling a great deal further than the distance between point A (the pub) and point B (his house). Sooner or later this occurs to most drunks, but whereas most drunks forget their more abstract musings before the first stab of a hangover furrows their cold sweaty brows, this drunk made a point of taking notes. Most of these notes, having been dropped by him on the floor near the hearth when he got home, ended up being used to make paper twists for the fire the following morning by his long suffering maid, but fortunately a couple were missed, and these later became the basis for what the wizard called his third law of inebriate motion, the first two laws of which glowed beautifully for a few moments as the fire was lit.

Ralph and Nifnaff had unknowingly walked through one of the wizard's earlier attempts to put his theory to the test. He had been drunk at the time and upon sobering up, had forgotten where he had left the device. Any local could have told them to avoid that place, and though Tumble Wilkins was not a local, he was well enough acquainted with the area and its history to know what would happen when he suggested that they go that way.

Tumble had watched them leave the road, then sent a runner back to the city with a coded message, safe in the knowledge that it would get there with a week to spare. That done, he had his crew finish watering the mules then got the train rolling again. He stood for a moment as the wagons trundled passed, casting a critical eye over each. "Check that axle when we stop next, Bill," he called to one of the drivers. "Looks a bit dry." The driver leaned over the side and looked down at the wheel then nodded.

Tumble waited until the last wagon was alongside him, then jumped up and made his way forward, climbing from wagon to wagon until he was able to take his seat between the driver and the brakeman on the lead wagon. He put his feet up, pulled his hat forward so that it was over his eyes, and contemplated the next part of his mission.

Ralph sat down heavily at the base of one of the standing stones and leaned against it. He sat there for a moment with his eyes closed savouring its coolness against his back, then leaned forward with a grunt and took his sandals off. "Someone really needs to invent a bus service on this planet," he said as he started massaging the ache from his feet. "They'd make a fortune."

Nifnaff was impatient to be moving again and told Ralph so in his usual brusque manner. Ralph was having none of it this time though. He was exhausted and flat refused to move, even when Nifnaff grudgingly offered to carry him. Nifnaff briefly considered leaving Ralph behind when he still refused to budge, but it seemed churlish to part company with him now, when they were so close to the end of their journey together. "Rest then," he snapped irritably, relenting, "but we will start again early."

Ralph and Nifnaff supplemented their rations with some of the fruit that they had picked from the trees along the way. They ate in silence, each caught up in their own private thoughts as they watched Murd drag the last of the light over the horizon like the train of a wedding dress.

Nifnaff was a creature shaped by high mountains and dark caves; he no more needed the heat or light of a fire than a fish needed an armchair, and he needed no light to see that Ralph was staring intently in his direction.

Ralph moved slightly, getting himself more comfortable, then asked, "Are you awake?"

Nifnaff grunted something that might have been a yes.

"What will you do when you get to the city?"

"Say goodbye," Nifnaff answered more brusquely than he intended. He took a few sips from his flask, corked it and threw it to Ralph. "Then hopefully go home."

There was a shuffling noise and a weary sigh, and Ralph guessed that the troll had rolled onto his side with the intention of going to sleep and ending the conversation. Nifnaff did not sleep though. He stared through the darkness to another place and time, where but for a foolish and impulsive act, his life would have been very different now.

The standing stones were identical, each one forty feet high and set broad to its neighbours. There was enough room between them for two carts to pass each other without scraping their wheels, and it was difficult to see what possible purpose they might serve. Nifnaff thought that they might be collapsed like a row of dominoes if there was an attack, but there would have been large gaps beneath still because of how each would settle against the next, but then Nifnaff thought that maybe he was missing the point of the of stones. Maybe there was no purpose, or maybe it was simply a statement. Maybe the wizards were saying: look at the resources and effort we can invest in something this pointless; imagine what we could do if it really mattered.

Born beneath rock, the monolith towering over Nifnaff brought him some small degree of comfort, and he fell asleep quite soon despite his tumbling thoughts. Ralph took no such comfort from the stones. Their massiveness seemed to hang over him like a pending judgment, and he squirmed restlessly through the night until finally in the early hours, he sat up and nodded off intermittently until Nifnaff's loud snoring and the occasional bird clearing it's throat loudly in preparation for the dawn chorus made even that impossible.

Ralph stared miserably into the velvet blackness, and he worried. Would the wizards help him? Wizards! The word conjured up images of old men with long white beards, and sleeves that you could drive a lorry up, but nothing so far had exactly fitted with his preconceptions. People who could conjure up lightning and rearrange matter with a thought, who could alter the way people think and behave! How far removed from ordinary humanity were they? Could they even be called human anymore? Ralph knew that compared to the least of them, he must seem less than a child, and he had intended to march right into their city and demand that he be sent back home! How ridiculous that now seemed with their city so close.

Murd poked its vibrant face just above the horizon like a child playing peekaboo above the back of a settee. Nifnaff stirred from his sleep and lay staring at it for a few minutes as he came fully awake, then sat up, stretched, farted and yawned, in that order. Ralph laughed, earning himself an icy glare from the troll.

Ralph stood up stiffly, and hugging himself, started rubbing his arms in an effort to generate some warmth in them. No matter how many nights he spent under the stars, he felt sure that he would never actually come to enjoy it. He was born to a cot and raised to a bed; hard turf and inconveniently placed pebbles might suit creatures like Nifnaff, but it was no way for a civilised human to spend his nights. "When I get back home, I'm going to bed for a month," he told Nifnaff.

Nifnaff tilted his head as he was prone to do when mildly curious. "And that is what you are eager to get home for?" he asked.

Ralph grinned. "That and a few other things."

Nifnaff started repacking his travel bag. "What other things?" he asked without looking up.

Ralph thought about it for a moment, but drew a blank. "It's bloody cold," he complained, changing the subject.

Nifnaff raised an eyebrow. He could have come up with a dozen things right off of the cuff if he had been asked the same question.

Ralph caught his first glimpse of the city towards the middle of the afternoon of the following day, but it was distant and almost featureless, and gave no impression of its true scale and complexity. It was a day further before they were able to start to pick out any great amount of detail, and a day more before that detail was such that it could start to overawe their senses with its forest of impossibly tall towers and aerial walkways. Even then the size was lost on them, though Ralph fancied that the tallest towers scratched the bellies of the clouds, creating eddies.

What Ralph and Nifnaff saw in the distance was only a part of the city. Like the flash of a bared thigh, there was far more to it than met the eye. It was almost as big below ground as it was above, but more than that, it had dimensions to it beyond the three most commonly associated with a physical space, dimensions where the physical laws that governed reality changed. More importantly and in some ways less easy to grasp than these strange places where the city extended beyond itself, was the way that it reached out and touched the lives and dreams of all Derrianites. For some like Northan and his wife, it was a doorstep upon which to lay all the ills of the world, for others it was a must see place, or a fabric into which generations of parents had woven many colourful bedtime stories. It was an example to a world inhabited by dozens of sentient species of how a diverse population could coexist peacefully, and an ever present reminder of what could happen if they did not.

Ralph and Nifnaff stopped at a quiet little hamlet along the way to fill their flasks and take a short break. Nifnaff had picked a spot for them under a large willow tree on the hamlet's well manicured green, and the pair rested there for a while. They had managed to find a day's work in the fields pulling and packing potatoes the day before, and the farmer had paid them with much needed provisions and a dry bed of straw for the night in one of his barns. Ralph was still sore from that unaccustomed work, and he groaned as he sat down and leaned his back against the tree.

The place had a romantic yesteryear feel to it with its perfect grass and planted borders, and its whitewashed picket fences and occasional trundling farm cart clattering along the cobbled lane. It was England in a bygone age with all the nasty bits taken out. Ralph felt that Englishness and was instantly homesick, even though home had never been so picturesque or so perfect as this place.

Nifnaff stuck out like a bassoon player in a string quartet sitting under the tree popping tiny new-potatoes into his mouth like they were sweets, and even Ralph did not exactly blend in in his cast off road worn elven clothing, but other than the odd greeting or doffing of a flat cap or boater in passing, their presence attracted very little interest.

Ralph might have forgotten that he was not on Earth were it not for the general lack of concern at having a huge hairy Mountain troll sat in the middle of their immaculate green. The pointed ears of a man who was playing a ball game nearby with his children spoiled the illusion somewhat as well. Ralph sat watching them, confused at first that the children did not have the same pronounced tip to their ears, then it occurred to him that their mother might not be an elf.

Ralph started to doze off as he watched their game, then woke with a start as the ball clacked loudly against the bat. This was accompanied by an encouraging cheer from the man who was grinning broadly and clapping. Ralph felt a stab of envy. This was their normal, their lives the way that they were meant to be. He wanted his life back as it was. He wanted it so much at that moment, that it caused a tight knot in his stomach that grew into a physical ache. It would have surprised him to know that his huge hairy companion was similarly affected.

The boundary of the hamlet was marked by a raised flower bed on each side of the cobblestone lane. Between the two flowerbeds was a metal cattlegrid, after which the lane turned to a mixture of chalk and small stones that had been tamped down to create a serviceable, if much less attractive surface over which to travel - serviceable most of the time that is. It had rained briefly during the night, then again as Ralph and Nifnaff left the hamlet behind them, turning the chalk and soil to a dirty scum that clung to their feet and caused them to slip, and it proved to be easier to walk on the grass alongside the lane than on it.

Ahead of them the skyline was now dominated by the city and its tall outer wall. Tumble Wilkins had told them that the lane would veer sharply to the right a mile or so after the hamlet, and that they should stick to it until they found the start of a track with a small painted stone marker next to it. Nifnaff who was still harbouring some doubts about Tumble, relaxed a little when they found that the track with its painted stone marker appeared to lead straight to the city wall.

There was a town to their right, the sky above which was darkened by smoke from its many chimneys as its residents prepared their evening meals, or settled down companionably - or not - in front of a warm fire. It was too far away though, and there was no reason for Ralph and Nifnaff to go there, especially when the city wall and the promised gate were now so close, and so they spent one more night together under the stars by a small hungry fire that constantly demanded their attention. The next morning they broke their night's fast with the last of their flat baked bread and hard almost tasteless cheese, then walked the last few miles to the wall.

They reached the wall just after midday and stood staring dumbly at the wall, or more particularly, at the door that was set back on a protruding ledge halfway up the side of the wall with no obvious means of getting to it!

"We could try and climb up to it," Ralph suggested.

It was a stupid suggestion, but Nifnaff humoured him by asking him how.

"We could try to find some rope," Ralph offered.

"Where?" Nifnaff asked him.

Ralph did not have an answer. "So how are we supposed to get up there then?"

Nifnaff shrugged his big hairy shoulders. "I do not know." He knew that he could jump maybe fifteen feet, and that he could throw Ralph at least that far, but even if he could manage to jump with him in his arms and then throw him at the last moment, it still would not be enough, and would likely result in one or both of them being injured.

Ralph put his hands on his hips and took a step forward. He stubbed his toe on something and swore loudly. Nifnaff looked down thoughtfully. He slid his foot forward a little until it met with something solid, but there was nothing there, or appeared to be nothing there. He bent down and tore up a heavy sod of grass which he shook vigorously just in front of his foot. Soil rained down and scattered across something unseen twelve inches from the ground. "Invisible steps," Nifnaff announced.

"Why?" Ralph asked as his hairy companion stepped up into the air. It seemed a bit pointless putting invisible steps where normal ones would have been much more sensible. "And why put a door half way up a wall?"

"Maybe it amuses them," Nifnaff offered.

"I'm in stitches," Ralph said dryly.

There were forty-nine invisible steps in total, each one adding twelve inches of apparent nothingness between themselves and the hard floor below! Ralph grabbed a handful of Nifnaff's fur and held onto him tightly. Nifnaff grunted his disapproval of Ralph's fragile nerves and shook him off, then grabbed him quickly again as he almost fell.

When they reached the top, Nifnaff shoved Ralph up against the wall to one side of the door. Satisfied that the human was safe, he pushed the door, then when it did not move, shoved it hard with his shoulder. Still it did not open, so he pushed even harder, then threw himself at it several times, getting more and more angry with each attempt. Ralph watched incredulously as the door and its hinges somehow resisted everything that the powerful troll could throw at it.

Nifnaff stood back, somewhat chagrined. "Now what?" he asked irritably.

"Knock?" Ralph offered.

Nifnaff gave Ralph a blank look that had it been a blank piece of paper, would have had I want to hurt you scrawled on it in invisible ink. He turned stiffly towards the door and banged a massive fist against it thrice very slowly.

A shuffling sound came from inside, followed by the screech of metal scratching against metal, the clank of locks, more screeches, another clank, and finally a long deep ominous creek that continued for a few seconds after the door had stopped moving. "Yes?" a short, somewhat portly man in a crisply pressed bottle green uniform and peaked hat enquired through a crack in the door. The pudgy face that jutted from below the peaked hat radiated something close to terminal levels of boredom, and his expression did not change a jot as he looked from Nifnaff's expansive chest to Ralph's face.

"We need to find a wizard," Ralph said as the guard opened the door a little further.

The guard nodded. "Then you've most likely come to the right place."

"Good," Ralph said, brightening a little. "Could you tell us how to find one."

The guard was thoughtful for a moment as he considered the question, then said, "yes."

Ralph and Nifnaff waited a whole thirty seconds for the guard to say something more. When it became obvious that nothing more was coming, Ralph said, "So how do we find one then?"

Again the guard thought the question over. "I think you might find that the best way is to ask me," he answered a little smugly, obviously pleased with his own cleverness.

Ralph frowned. "And will you?" he asked in a slightly irritated tone.

The guard raised his eyebrows disapprovingly and harrumphed. He knew how to deal with precise inquiries, which is as much as you can ask from a brain that is being powered by the equivalent of an AA battery, but this human seemed unhappy with any reply that he gave. It was vexing to say the least. "I usually will, but that very heavily depends on whether the *will* that you are talking about, is morally or legally acceptable," he told Ralph sternly. "So, what is it exactly that you want?"

"What do I want?" Ralph asked incredulously.

The guard shook his head and took a cautious step backwards. "I am quite sure that I do not know!"

"What?" Ralph snapped at him.

"Ah," the guard sighed dreamily. "That is one of the great ones; that and *why* of course."

Nifnaff watched the exchange between Ralph and the guard with growing amusement. He had detected the strong odour of oil and ozone as soon as the guard opened the door and quickly realised that he was not all that he seemed.

"If you don't stop mucking around," Ralph warned.

"Yes?" the guard asked innocently.

Ralph had not thought it through that far and sputtered out the first thing that popped into his head. "I'll get my friend here to sit on you."

Nifnaff opened his mouth to object, but did not get the opportunity.

"But I, but I, I am not messing you around!" the guard cried in alarm as he eyed Nifnaff. "I, I um, hummm, I might, I, I, I collect stamps. I, hummmm. My uniform itches a lot." He ran his finger around the inside of his collar. "I, I, I, referring to, to you, you, yooooou, hummm, hoooo, hooooooooooooo."

Ralph took a step backwards as a panel flipped open on the guard's hat. A small wisp of smoke coiled up into the air and was whipped away by the slight breeze.

"What!" Ralph said as he caught Nifnaff's look of disapproval. "I didn't do anything!"

"And neither did I, but I'm still going to have to fix the sodding thing!"

Ralph and Nifnaff both turned and stared at a pinch-faced little old man in a boiler suit who was stood clutching a screwdriver and glaring at them.

"We didn't touch him, it." Ralph took a quick peek into the open hatch, giving into curiosity as he said this. He coughed as a wisp of acrid smoke hit the back of his throat, and added, "whatever it is?"

"Did this to itself, did it?" the old man snapped back at him, then muttered, "damned tourists!" He went to the motionless guard, pulled its head forward roughly and peered through the open panel. "Ah!" he said, and started poking around inside with his screwdriver. There was a click and a whirr. "That should do it for now," he mumbled to himself as he closed the panel and put away his screwdriver.

The mechanical guard pulled itself back to attention and stood there smiling stupidly as though nothing had happened.

The old man grunted his satisfaction then turned around. "Now you two: what do you want?" He pushed passed Ralph and turned at the top of the steps so that he was facing him. "Well?" he asked again.

Ralph felt himself redden. "All we wanted was some information," he told him.

"And do you always vandalise other people's property when you don't get what you want?" the old man asked him.

Ralph was at the end of his tether. Since landing in Derrian he had narrowly avoided becoming the cabaret and buffet for a swarm of fairies, been ridiculed by elves, become lost, found, chased by a well intentioned Mountain troll, and almost become a toothpick for a dragon, not to mention the endless miles of walking and the nights spent sleeping on hard ground. Getting into the city should have been the easy bit, but it was proving to be anything but. "I told you, we didn't touch that damned thing," he said, raising his voice.

The old man clenched his fists and leaned towards Ralph, trying to appear as intimidating as his late years and willowy frame would allow. "You trying to suggest that my work's shoddy?" he asked angrily, "cus I built this one myself!"

"If the cap fits, feller," Ralph told him.

The old man jabbed a finger at Ralph's chest. "There was a time when I'd've made you regret your rudeness, boy," he rasped, reddening with indignation.

"I'm surprised you can remember anything that far back," Ralph said with a sneer. He looked up at Nifnaff's stern face and sighed. None of this was going any of the dozen ways that he had hoped it might. "Look," he said, turning back to face the old man. As he turned, the old man took a step backwards, into thin air. Ralph yelped and made a clumsy grab for him, but only made matters worse when his hand bumped against his boney shoulder.

Nifnaff was many things, but impetuous was not one of them. He resisted the urge to throw himself down the invisible steps after the old man, and instead followed him one careful step at a time. He reached the old man and knelt by his side on the grass. It did not need a physician to see that his neck and leg were broken and that he had stopped breathing. Checking for a pulse was merely a formality. "He is dead," he announced, answering the question on Ralph's worried face.

Ralph reeled like a man who has been struck unexpectedly. "Maybe one of the wizards can do something?" he suggested, trying to grab a glimmer of hope from the ashes. He turned and looked up at the guard who was descending the steps after them. "Is there a wizard nearby?" he asked, his irritation forgotten.

The guard nodded. "There are a lot of them nearby," he answered proudly, adding that this was their city after all.

Ralph tried to make the mechanical man fall to pieces with the power of his intense stare, but the thing remained annoyingly whole. He grimaced, took a deep breath, counted to five in his head and started again. "Could you..." He paused. "Will you..." he stopped again and thought about it then said, "go quickly and tell the first wizard that you see that we need help here. Tell him what has happened."

The mechanical guard nodded then knelt down next to the still form of the old man. "Mr Ethelthwaite, Sir, these two men would like your help." He/it frowned. "Now I know that might be a little bit difficult with you being dead and all, and I wouldn't normally bother you at a time like this, but if you could see your way to helping them while I go and fetch the city constables to arrest them for murdering you..."

Nifnaff stood up slowly and turned to face Ralph. "I am going to go now," he said in a restrained voice. "I suggest that you do the same."

Ralph looked nervously at the crumpled body of the old man and the guard who was knelt still, fussing over him. "We could explain," he started to say.

"Now I know that you was pushed down the steps," the guard was saying.

"I didn't!" Ralph objected. "I tried to grab him." He shook his head and again said, "I didn't." He sagged under Nifnaff's glare. "They won't believe me will they?" It was not really a question, and no answer was forthcoming. Ralph nodded miserably. "We should get going," he agreed.

Nifnaff took a small but purposeful step towards Ralph. "No," he said, his voice tight with restrained anger. "I do not think you understand me. Not together." He took another step towards Ralph. "You should go now, before the constables come and arrest you for murdering one of their wizards. I now have a very long walk ahead of me, and I think it would be better for both of us if we parted company."

Ralph was backing away and shaking his head. "But I didn't kill him!" he protested. "It was an accident."

Nifnaff closed his hands into fists and let out a growl of frustration that shook Ralph to his toes. That was enough for Ralph. "I'm sorry," he said, then turned and fled, leaving Nifnaff to his anger and a less than certain future.

Ralph wandered around aimlessly for several days. He did not know what to do next. The need to get home was often at the forefront of his thoughts, but he might as well have been pining after the moon for how distant the hope of getting home now seemed. The wizards; it always came back to the wizards. They alone of all Derrian's people had the means to send him home, but that bridge now appeared to be well and truly burned.

Ralph drifted like a boat without a rudder for a short while, picking up the odd bit of work along the way, digging ditches, mucking out pigs, anything for a meal and a dry bed of straw for a couple of nights. He resorted to begging when there was no work to be had, and when the begging left his stomach empty still, he stole. All of this time he lived in dread of bumping into anyone wearing uniform, fearing that he would be caught and taken back to Brace to face the wizards. It did not occur to him that people as powerful as the wizards were supposed to be, would have had very little difficulty finding him if they had wanted to.

Things continued to spiral downwards for Ralph. Somewhere along the way he started to lose himself, to lose his sense of worth, his self respect and principles as he was forced daily to accept his many inadequacies. He might have risen to the challenge, might have faced those inadequacies and dealt with them, but there was an irrational part of him that believed that if he suffered enough, the universe would eventually feel sorry for him and see the terrible mistake that it had made, and put things right again.

Ralph eventually staggered half starved and feverish into a small riverside town called Newford. Up until that point he had avoided any place with more than a few buildings, just incase, but he was desperate, and *just incase* had started to hold less fear for him than the very real possibility that he would die alone in a ditch somewhere of hunger and hypothermia.

Newford was small, but it was relatively prosperous due to its location, nestled as it was in the crook of a tight bend in the river. The river had been widened on the bend to accommodate a long wharf, and it was from there that the greater part of Newford's livelihood came, via the many barges that used it for transferring goods to other craft, or to wagons for transportation overland.

Ralph managed to beg a little food on his first day in Newford and found a dry place to sleep that night behind a shop. The next day he tried his hand at begging again and got himself arrested for causing a public nuisance. He waited in the cell, expecting at any moment to be told that he was wanted for killing a wizard, and consequently, the two hours that it took to process him turned into the longest two hours of his life.

One wall was covered in wanted posters, and he scanned these covertly, expecting to see some mention of himself and Nifnaff. There was nothing, and to his consternation, he was released later with the sternly given advice that he should find work and lodgings or move on.

Ralph had not considered getting a proper job. It smacked of permanence, and he was not yet willing to accept that he might never see his home again. He needed to live somewhere though, even temporarily, and Newford had more going for it than any place he had been to so far, so he cleaned himself up in a rainwater butt outside the jailhouse and went looking for work.

His enquiries took him to the wharf, where after talking to two boatmen who were returning to their barges a little worse for wear after an afternoon spent in the tavern, he found a ganger who was willing to give him a few hours work unloading a barge that had just tied up. It was back breaking work but it got him a meal and a cot for the night. The next day he tried to find something less strenuous, but though he did not consider himself such, he was a scruffy drifter with nothing to offer but his physical labour, and so he again found himself back at the wharf loading and unloading the barges as they tied up.

Newford's three taverns served as eating houses and brothels and lively community centres, as well as being the only places where Ralph could get a hot bath. It was not surprising really that he found himself spending more and more time in one or another of these establishments, feeling sorry for himself and - when funds allowed - getting drunk. And so it was that Ralph came to be sat in a tavern staring moodily at the door as it slammed shut behind Jarek, who had decided to risk bumping into a mob of angry Lowland trolls outside, rather than spend another minute listening to Ralph prattling on about pyjamas and blue skies and bolts of lightning.

Ralph staggered to his feet and pointed himself towards the door. Between him and it were two occupied stools, a spittoon, and an embarrassing drunken brawl that was just waiting for a chance to happen. Halfway to his goal he stumbled into one of the stools, lost his balance and landed in the lap of the occupant of the other, then lurched to his feet and tripped over the spittoon, the contents of which splattered over the shoes and trousers of two of the tavern's regular hard men. Ralph stood there listless and swaying slightly, and waited for inevitability to catch up with him.

Ralph woke up with a start and stared at a familiar wall with its crumbling plaster and flaking whitewash. It was covered with bits of nonsense that had been scrawled or scratched into it by the cell's many former occupants. Some of it was statements of rebellion, like, 'buGGer of U

Constable' or attempts at vagueness that did not quite work, such as, 'Guess hoo?' followed by 'and it weren't Mauler Edwards neither, if that's what U was thinkin'. Ralph searched through bleary eyes for his own modest little effort tucked away neatly in a dark corner where it was less likely to catch the attention of one of the guards. It read 'Don't let the buggers break you'. It was a pointless statement really, but he had not wanted to be left out.

Ralph rolled over with a groan and pulled the thin blanket up over his head. He slid quickly back into a troubled half sleep, bobbing up and down through its various depths like a float on a baited line that is being toyed with from below. This was due in varying parts to the scratchy blanket, the beginnings of a hangover, the hard straw filled pallet with it's many blood sucking denizens, and a recurring bad dream where his actions or his lack of reaction - take your pick - had culminated in the death of another human being.

How many times Ralph had replayed that scene in his sleep and awake, trying to rearrange those terrible events in a way that left him blameless, but each time the wizard was always dead, and Nifnaff was always there passing silent judgment on his guilt, his disappointment cutting Ralph far deeper than his anger had.

Ethelthwaite had clung to the appearance of death with the greatest difficulty while the troll fussed over him. Ralph had hovered there at the edge of his reduced perception, concerned, but mostly afraid and frustrated. Guilt he knew would come later. There was a saying in Derrian that guilt and fairies take their time eating into you.

Ethelthwaite lived in a city where tales of magical misdoings were bandied around like old wives' tales, where rumours flowed like spilled beer at a bawdy house during happy hour, and where a human from Earth popping out of thin air would have scarcely caused an eyebrow to lift. It was different beyond Brace though. Magic was like spicy food away from the city: people wanted it, then complained bitterly about it afterwards.

Far more than a fair share of these complaints were levelled at the wizards directly, yet it was the witches with their midwives and healers in almost every community, who had by far the greatest impact on the ordinary lives of Derrian's people.

Like a coin with two tails, it often seemed to Ethelthwaite that it was the lot of a wizard to disappoint someone somewhere whichever way he turned, and he had long ago stopped worrying about it on a personal level, but he was Brace's spymaster - his official title being, Minister for external affairs - and it was his job to protect not only the reputation of Bracian wizardry, but by extension of this, the reputation of Brace itself.

Ethelthwaite hated and loved his work. He would have given it all up in a heartbeat given half a chance, and then skinned an angry bear with his teeth to get it all back again. The fact was that he cared deeply about Derrian, its people, and even those meddling witches most of the time.

He stopped pacing and took a couple of deep breaths to calm himself, then went and sat back down behind his desk to wait. There were several thick reports lying on his desk. There were always thick reports on his desk. Some were good, some/most were bad. The good ones were the closed ones. Ethelthwaite's system was simple: closed meant done, finished, no longer requiring his attention; open reports meant acid indigestion and a lot less sleep.

Most of the reports on Ethelthwaite's desk were open. Many of them concerned the activities of an organisation - mostly women - who had set themselves against the wizards over recent years. Publicly they were a suffragette type movement who were campaigning for the right to be able to become wizards, their argument being that the brotherhood of wizards was acting in a chauvinistic and elitist way by not permitting women to join their order. It was a nonsense of course. A woman could no more become a wizard than a man could become a witch. It was this gender distinction that preserved their two separate orders, and it was their adherence to this rule among many others that helped to maintain the exclusivity of both.

Ethelthwaite suspected that what was really at the heart of it, was good old fashioned jealousy. These suffragettes only saw the city and the status that it gave the wizards; they did not see the mire of statutes and legislation that girdled them, restricting their activities beyond Brace's borders. The witches were not so encumbered. They had won the trust and the hearts of their host communities, and enjoyed a level of autonomy that the wizards never would. Ethelthwaite had no complaints about this. The wizards and the witches were two sides of the same coin, despite their little wrangles, and Ethelthwaite had used their skills and their integration within their communities to his advantage on more than one occasion.

The wizards were a checking mechanism of sorts, providing a bulwark constructed from chaos to protect Derrian's people from a more destructive type of chaos. Their prominence and exclusivity were key components of this. Derrian had only stories from the time when it had stood on the brink of an abyss, ready to tear itself apart. Magic had helped to nudge it there, but more importantly, it was magic that had pulled it back from that crumbling edge. It was the wizards who had done that - albeit clumsily - and it was the wizards who protected Derrian against a repeat of those times.

The sisterhood of witches understood this, for all that their way of doing things was very different to the wizards, yet there were suffragettes and their sympathisers even among their ranks. Ethelthwaite would not have minded if the suffragettes had restricted their activities to soapbox speeches and the occasional banner waving march through Brace's streets, but there was a more disruptive, more destructive element that had chosen a far more proactive approach. A battle of the sexes! Ethelthwaite would have laughed were it not for the very real harm that it was causing. Of course it was preposterous to think that they might succeed with their aims, but they were a growing irritation that he knew he would have to deal with sooner rather than later. It would have been a simple matter to expose them and simpler still to deal with them quietly, were it not for their unsanctioned connection with the witches.

There was a longstanding understanding that prevented wizards and witches interfering in each other's business directly. That put the onus on the witches themselves to deal with the problem, except that the witches could not easily do so without acting against the suffragettes within the communities where they themselves lived, and to do so would be to betray the trust that they had spent so long nurturing.

Ethelthwaite saw the glint of a golden nugget in a mess that was partly of the witches own making. He might justifiably have exposed them, condemned them for their apparent complicity. He could have made them wash their dirty laundry in public for once, but Ethelthwaite knew that there would be a few dirty socks from his own wizards in their wash basket. Handled properly, the suffragettes would be made to go away though, and the wizards who had so stoically endured their spite and their attempts to undermine them, would appear in a more sympathetic light. The witches on the other hand, had played their hand badly by not dealing with their wayward sisters sooner, and when the dust finally settled, people would be wondering if they had spent so much time looking for a wolf at their door, that they had completely missed the fox that was snuggled up next to their hearth. Ethelthwaite smiled. The idea of their Mother Superior squirming a little held a certain appeal.

A few months had passed without any word from the witches. This was consistent with how long it usually took them to make any kind of collective decision, and Ethelthwaite was not greatly concerned by this. He used the time to call in a few old favours and to make certain preparations, and all the time he continued to receive reports from his many agents scattered throughout Derrian, adding to the pile of open folders on his desk.

Most of these agents had been in Ethelthwaite's service for years. In some cases generations of the same family had served him, yet he had not met more than a handful of them in person. He knew many of his agents well despite that. Ethelthwaite prided himself on knowing them, and always asked after their health and that of their families whenever he corresponded with them. It was a rather quaint and colloquial form of spying really, that allowed him to not only know what was happening beyond the city wall, but also through their observations and opinions, why.

Ethelthwaite had amassed a considerable amount of information about the conspirators this way. He already knew who many of them were, and it would not take long to discover the names of the rest when they started rounding them up. It was a simple matter of knowing where and when best to twist the knife.

Tumble Wilkins was one of Ethelthwaite's best field operatives. Ethelthwaite had recruited him at the tender age of seven from the gutter where he had been surviving as a petty thief and little league trickster. He had looked beyond the boy's many failings and seen the twinkling-eyed rascal with quick hands and a quicker wit, who had not yet been taught to know better. Ethelthwaite had taken the boy from the streets and placed him with a couple who ran a safe house just outside the city. They were good solid dependable people who he had known would give the boy the discipline and care that he needed, as well as the training that he would require if the he was ever going to be of any use to him in the future.

There were risks of course. There were always risks when investing that amount of time, effort and emotion into a person, but he had felt at the time that it was a risk worth taking. It was a decision that Ethelthwaite had rarely found any cause to regret. For Tumble's part, Ethelthwaite was as much of an uncle to him as an employer, and he enjoyed a level of familiarity with the old wizard that few others within his sphere would dare to attempt.

When a coded note arrived from Tumble requesting a private meeting, Ethelthwaite had immediately looked for the sub-message that he knew would be there within it. It was this latter simpler message that was of more interest to him: 'I'll have a lady friend with me.'

Tumble brought a rather nervous young witch to an arranged rendezvous the following night. The fact that the witches had sent this whip of a girl rather than one of his normal backdoor contacts, left him in no doubt that she was considered by them to be not only trustworthy, but also deniable and disposable should things go badly. He wondered briefly if the girl knew just how limited her future might now be? Ethelthwaite pushed the thought aside; he had been playing this game far too long to get sentimental about such things.

"I have a message, Master wizard," the girl said a little uncertainly as she stood there. She gave Tumble Wilkins a sideways glance.

"You can speak openly," Ethelthwaite told her, indicating that she should take a seat. The noise from the barroom down the hall provided an undulating backwash of noise that would make eavesdropping difficult. The bar itself was owned by one of his people, and there were a dozen more among the patrons who would ensure their privacy.

"Don't mind if I do," Tumble said, taking a vacant seat himself.

Ethelthwaite frowned at him then turned his attention back to the girl. He looked her over with something more than a professional eye, privately chiding himself for allowing her pretty face to distract him. "You have some dissension in your ranks." he said, surprising her a little with his directness. The young witch recovered her composure quickly. "That's our problem," she told him.

Ethelthwaite sighed. He brought his hands together in a steeple and tapped his index fingers together thoughtfully as he held her eyes. "If that were true, you wouldn't be standing here now, so I must insist that we stop this nonsense, otherwise..." Ethelthwaite let the threat hang there for a moment then moved on. "And so to your specific purpose for being here?"

The witch nodded. "The problem is not of our making, and many of those involved are..."

"Not witches," Ethelthwaite said, finishing the sentence for her. "We know this. And so you want us to do what your own rules will not allow you to do yourselves."

Ethelthwaite returned to his rooms later at the old university building and retired for what little remained of the night. He half woke in the early hours of the morning and steered himself like a ship with a rubber rudder through the shreds of a fading dream in which he was just a normal man, unencumbered by position and responsibility, able to go where he wanted, to do what he wanted to do, when he wanted. It was a wishful bit of nonsense, he knew; a recurring bittersweet dream that left him longing for that other life that he might have had.

Ethelthwaite got up and started to dress. While he was dressing, he tried to recall the last time that he had left the city. He was dismayed at the answer. The problem was that there was always so much to do. He thought about the world beyond his city's gates. He knew it intimately through reports and correspondence and his countless maps, yet almost not at all in any direct sense. He shook his head and tutted loudly as he made his way to the door that led from his bedroom to his private office, and the open report on his desk about a man from Earth who was travelling to Brace with a Mountain troll. It was a curious choice of companion for both, but not as curious as a human from Earth just popping out of thin air. It was not impossible that his appearance was in some way connected to the other mischief that was going on, but he doubted it. It was difficult enough to transport a living creature between two fixed points in time and space; transporting a human between two shifting dimensions was another matter entirely.

Ethelthwaite knew of maybe five or six people who could have performed that sort of magic, and one of them was staring back at him from the mirror that was hanging on the far wall. It was high magic; difficult to perform and hard to conceal. That left a random occurrence as the most likely explanation, but - and this was the problem for Ethelthwaite - he did not believe in random or chance occurrences. Things did not just happen, they happened *because*: the postman had teethmarks on his leg *because* the dog bit him, the kitten had flees *because* it tried to use a hedgehog as a scratching post, the man from Earth appeared out of thin air *because?* Ethelthwaite did not know why, and he was intrigued by it, especially when the Earthborn human was travelling to Brace. He needed to know if he posed any kind of a threat before allowing him into the city. It was a simple matter to arrange an encounter away from the city gate where he could, if necessary, make the problem go away without too much fuss.

In hindsight Ethelthwaite felt that he might have overplayed his role as a crotchety old mechanic a little, but his stunt fall down the invisible steps and subsequent death was a masterful piece of improvisation. Ethelthwaite found nothing to suggest that the human posed a threat, but he also found nothing to suggest that he was from Earth either. He would have written it off as a hoax, but there was a trace of something; a kind of fading afterglow that he did not recognise, and until he knew what it was, he was not prepared to let the human into the city. When Ralph stood at the top of the steps ranting at him, it was one percent decision and ninety-nine percent impulse that decided the matter. After that it was a relatively simple thing to shield himself as he fell down the invisible steps, and simpler still to lower his pulse and breathing to a point that was indistinguishable from death.

It was only while he was lying there being fussed over, that Ethelthwaite gave any thought to what he had done or why he had done it. He was known for acting swiftly and decisively, and some took this for impulsiveness, but rarely had he taken any action that had not been thought through properly, however quickly. That he was now truly acting impulsively, even recklessly, was as much of a surprise to him as it would later be to the others when they discovered what he had done.

The theatrics aside, Ethelthwaite was not being completely irresponsible. His network of agents and spies were such that they needed no direction from him at this late stage in the game. Everything that could be done had been done, and it was now simply a waiting game. He knew that he could keep informed almost as well beyond the city as he could from behind his desk, and should circumstances require it, he was only ever a portal away from where he was needed. Even so, there was a moment where he considered just sitting up and shouting, 'surprise!' That moment passed in the gulf between two drawn out heartbeats, and so he kept very still and gave some thought about what he would do next.

Ethelthwaite was eventually carried back into the city by two constables and taken back to the old university. The physician who attended him in his private rooms was only mildly surprised when he opened his eyes and sat up. "Enjoy your nap?" she asked him as he stood up and started to hunt for his slippers.

Ethelthwaite smiled a little awkwardly. "Yes thank you," he answered, then asked, "would you mind signing a temporary death certificate? Oh, and send for my secretary if you will."

Ethelthwaite's body was laid in an open casket until the midnight of the following day in the old university's tiny chapel. This was to give him the opportunity to change his mind about being dead. It was not unheard of for a wizard to do just that - even one who was really dead. During this time six sergeants took turns watching over his dormant body.

It was the same six sergeants who once the casket had been closed, pulled the cart with it on at the head of a somber torch-lit procession to the underground tombs. A wizard dying was an uncommon event, and people stopped and watched quietly out of respect or curiosity as they trundled passed. Quite a few joined the procession, driven by the same two motives, and it was a large crowd that finally gathered at the great blackened iron gates of the catacombs to see Ethelthwaite off.

The guards stopped and waited. Beyond the gates, beyond the rows of crumbling moss covered gravestones that were left from a time when the wizards had buried their dead in holes, at the end of a pathway of diamond encrusted slabs of the blackest jet, was the entrance to a world that only dead wizards and their caretakers could enter.

There were only two young wizards with the procession. This was owing to the fact that Ethelthwaite was not really dead, but they managed to look suitably dour as they stood one to either side of the sergeants, each bearing a torch, the dancing light from which sparkled off of the path for a short distance ahead. The sergeants rested easy while they waited, their hands wrapped loosely around the age darkened oak crossbars.

Several minutes passed with the gates firmly shut and no activity beyond them, but this was normal. The caretakers were well known for being unpunctual to the point of rudeness. Many people, including those now watching, wondered why the wizards put up with what seemed to be so obviously intended to cause them offence, but the proceedings as they were - the undertakers tardiness included - had been conducted in this manner since before even the longest lived of the unnaturally long lived wizards could remember, and it was now expected rather than simply accepted.

A heavy clank broke the expectant silence finally and brought the waiting sergeants back to full attention. They watched as the gates started to swing slowly inwards on their heavily greased pins, then leaned into the crossbars and pushed, setting the cart rolling along the path, its ironbound wheels making tiny popping noises as they crushed tiny pieces of grit beneath them.

An attendant who was stood waiting deep within the shadow of the tunnel entrance motioned for the sergeants to enter, leaving the torch bearing wizards outside. They were halted just inside and instructed to transfer the casket to a waiting gurney, then dismissed. The attendant - a suitably dour fellow - grabbed the handrail and leaned into it, muttering a complaint about the unnecessary weight of the casket and its lavish fittings as he pushed it into the hidden depths of the catacombs.

It is not until you have been dead for a while that you realise just how painful being alive actually is. Every itch and irritation, every caress, every brush of fingertips against a lover's skin or resistance against the fall of a foot on hard ground, every beat of the heart and drawing of a breath is a little agony that we have learned to live with from before birth. A magically induced prolonged near death state is not so very different from actually being dead - the likely permanence of the latter aside - and returning from either is something of a mixed blessing.

Ethelthwaite gasped loudly in the closeness of the casket as his various organs resumed their full pre-death functionality. He tried to sit up and banged his head against the lid, adding another point of pain to his other discomforts. It was a knee-jerk reaction and he felt rather foolish for having done it, and he forced himself to relax. He had to wait, had to be patient.

As it happened, it was only a matter of minutes before the lid was removed from the casket. Ethelthwaite sat up and stretched the moment it was. "Keep your flensing knives sheathed," he snapped irritably as two bibbed attendants stepped forward. "I've a mind to keep my flesh on these old bones a little while longer, so if you'd be good enough to fetch your master undertaker for me. I believe that he is already expecting me?" He raised his left hand and it started to glow, throwing a dull red light over the scene that was intended not be too severe on their unaccustomed eyes.

The master undertaker had been there all along and stepped from the shadows. He always attended the rendering process. Wizards were a tricky business that required a certain degree of care, otherwise dried bits of them would start turning up on key-rings and bracelets like lucky rabbits' feet all over the place. "I am here, Master Wizard?" The undertaker said. He was a severe chisel-featured little man with pale, almost translucent skin and large bulging eyes.

"Did my secretary contact you?" Ethelthwaite asked.

The undertaker stepped closer. "These are the catacombs, not a common thoroughfare," he complained bitterly.

Ethelthwaite smiled grimly. "I'll take that as a yes then," he said as he climbed out of the casket and adjusted the stiff burial robe that he was wearing in an effort to make it a little less uncomfortable. "This place keeps many secrets; yours included," he told the master undertaker. "That is in no small part due to us choosing to keep them for you." He gave the undertaker a significant look then said, "I need to remain dead for the foreseeable future."

"That can be arranged," the undertaker answered coldly.

Ethelthwaite frowned at him. He had seen and memorised maps of the catacombs and could likely have found his way without a guide, but these tunnels covered a vast area that was home to more of the living than the dead, and the living here did not welcome having breathing up-worlders among them. "Do you think to tease and frighten me as though I were a jumpy little schoolboy?"

The undertaker stared back at the wizard, trying to match wills with him. "It has been arranged as you requested," he answered with a sniff after a few moments. "Your things are there on the table. The guide will wait for you outside while you, ah, change."

In the between hour as the birds were just starting to clear their throats for the dawn chorus, an odd looking creature crept furtively out of a hole in the ground and slinked into the shade of a nearby tree to avoid being seen. The creature was economical in both stature and dress, whip thin and almost hairless, with small restless eyes that seemed intent on missing nothing. Dressed in a dun coloured skirt and vest and carrying nothing but a simple drawstring satchel over its shoulder, it would have attracted little attention, but for its obvious intention not to draw attention to itself. The creature - a Lowland troll - took a long look back at the city, searching its detail like a man standing at the front door reassuring himself that everything is as it should be before he leaves the house.

The eyes that Ethelthwaite was staring out of were as hard as flint below their heavy brow ridges, and showed none of the doubt that had suddenly flared up behind them. It had been far too many years since he had last ventured beyond Brace's high walls. He knew this, but the realisation that he had allowed himself to become a little agoraphobic annoyed him, and it was that annoyance as much as anything else that strengthened his resolve to carry on.

Ethelthwaite loved Brace deeply. He knew it by brick, cobble and citizen, its many flaws and its wondrous creations, its ideals, objectives and dreams, the whole of which he deemed of greater value than anything individual within it. A building could be rebuilt, and there were far too many people there anyway. Even guttering dreams could be rekindled, but it was more even than that: Brace was the great dream, the grand vision, an evolving aspiration, reaching towards something. These things were precious to Ethelthwaite. If he was now giving in to a personal desire for a little freedom and adventure, it was because all the cards had been dealt and were falling where they needed to. He simply wanted to see where some of them landed for once, rather than hearing about it secondhand from his people.

Ethelthwaite thought about some of the more recent reports that had found their way onto his desk. Some of it was quite theatrical, even comical from an outsider's perspective. A lot of it was simply attention grabbing, like a sly infant throwing a toy out of the pram to elicit a response. Viewed as a whole, people might have rightly suspected that a different hand than that of the wizards was stirring the pot up, but people had a habit of seeing only what they wanted to see, and the wizards were always a favourite target for Derrian's rumour mill. Ethelthwaite remembered his dad saying to him once that it does not do to be built like a barn door when the farmhands start slinging the muck around.

Ethelthwaite remembered the months of absolute horror that he had put his mother and father through as he struggled to deal with the double whammy of puberty and his own very particular kind of magical awakening. How many of his childish tantrums had been accompanied by levitating pottery and flying cutlery he could not now fully recall, but there had been very few windows in the house that were not panelled over or being held whole with hastily applied tar and brown paper until a new pane of glass could be fitted. Even his attempts to make amends went wrong more often than not. The thirty-foot sunflower that had exited noisily through the roof when he had tried to produce a flower for his mother had stood for some time as a monument to this. Finally at their wit's end, his father had packed Ethelthwaite's bag and marched him halfway across the continent to a place where he hoped someone might know what to do with his boy.

Ethelthwaite closed his eyes and saw his father again: the big man who he had worshipped, the memory of his abrupt goodbye as he turned and walked away, his shuddering shoulders betraying the tears that he had tried to hide from his frightened son. Each detail was perfectly preserved in his mind like flies caught in amber. Ethelthwaite - the boy - did not run after his father. He did not cry or call out to him. As frightened as he was, even then he had understood that the world was not coming to an end, just changing in ways that he had yet to discover.

Ethelthwaite put the memory away. It was one of many such that he wheeled out and examined as a particular moment or mood required it. It usually helped to centre him, to restore his sense of balance and purpose, but this time his mood still turned like a weathervane caught between two storm fronts.

The sky overhead seemed to reflect the turmoil in his mind. Clouds frothed and barrelled into one and other like rutting stags. The air below them was oppressive and dead as though gathering all of its energy for something monumental. The conscious part of the living world within the shadow of those boiling clouds, hunkered down and waited, or fidgeted nervously; and then the rain started to fall in heavy globules that caused leaves to sag and bounce on their branches as muddy rivulets raced across the dry ground below them, forming into deep dark puddles as and where the terrain dictated.

Ethelthwaite was somewhere between resignation and excitement. He liked storms, he liked to watch with a wizard's sight, the interplay of forces from the broad windows in his private rooms in the old university, but as the first fat drops of water exploded on his bald troll head, and the first deep rumbles forewarned of the violence that was yet to come, he decided that he did not like it quite as much as he thought he did...

... Murdlight broke through the clouds and warmed Daphen's soaking clothes, causing them to steam slightly. He smiled with pleasure, closing his long toes around the warm mud in which he was standing. Water was something to be cherished - even muddy water. Rain came almost as frequently to the Barrens as it did to other places, but the ground in the Barrens was high and thirsty, and the water table was very low, so that water seldom settled for very long on the surface.

Daphen tried to think of a time when he had felt quite so content with his lot. He was hit by the realisation that he could not remember a time before this one at all. "Now why would that be?" he wondered aloud. He sat down in the puddle with a satisfying splosh and curled a grimy fingernail beneath the belly of a worm that had come to the surface to escape its waterlogged hole, only to find itself in a wetter and far worse predicament. He flicked the unfortunate creature into his mouth and...

... Ethelthwaite had the strangest taste in his mouth. It was sweet and metallic and earthy, and it brought back childhood memories from before his awakening when he had still been considered a normal boy, of making mud pies with the other children and daring each other to eat them.

He looked down and harrumphed loudly as he realised that he was sitting in a puddle. He was curious about it and more than a little put out, but not greatly surprised. Short term memory loss was one of a number of possible side effects of assuming another creature's character, as well as its appearance. Put in its simplest terms, Ethelthwaite was temporarily forgetting himself and becoming fully immersed in his Lowland troll persona, but everything that it was, was still Ethelthwaite, and he trusted himself not to do anything too stupid or dangerous during any brief absences that he might have. Besides - he thought - retrieving those missing bits later, and seeing what he got up to when he was not around, might be amusing. If the memory gaps became too much of an issue, he knew that he could simply shed that personality and try to wing it as a Lowland troll.

Ethelthwaite knew that it might be years before he roused himself to leave the city again, and he wanted this busman's holiday to be as immersive as possible. It was not enough to simply look like one of the natives; he wanted to experience it from their perspective, to shed the rosey-tinted glasses and live it as an ordinary Derrianite might. His choice of vessel for this was - he realised - driven in equal measure by inherited guilt, and by curiosity. Lowland trolls were amongst the least liked, least understood, and most commonly misunderstood of all of Derrian's peoples, and this was in no small part due to the meddling of his own wizards centuries earlier. He wanted to better understand the consequences of that from how others behaved towards him as a Lowland troll.

The Barrens was a long banana shaped strip of barely habitable land nestled between the Randhorn steppes and the provincially governed elven lands to the southeast. The people who lived closest to its borders - especially those on the elven side - had a number of colourful names for the place, and the people who lived there, very little of which was not to some degree deserved.

The Lowland trolls were a product of an environment that gave nothing to those who chose to call it home. It was a harsh and - as the name implied - barren place, where subsistence living was the rule, the alternative to which was often not living. The male Lowlands lived in small nomadic packs with their young, travelling along the borders, buying, selling or stealing as need required, while the adult females led a more solitary existence for most of the year.

The few settlements along the borders that tolerated Lowlanders, used them as a kind of mobile news service, and though the news and gossip they carried was not always accurate, it was at least plentiful and entertaining. It was partly for that reason that Ethelthwaite was making his way towards the Barrens.

Ethelthwaite spared a thought for his secretary, William. Maybe he should have listened to him. William had not been happy about him leaving the city like this, just because he was going through - as he had put it - some sort of late life crisis. "Late life crisis indeed!" Ethelthwaite had fumed. "I'm a hundred and sixty-seven, not three hundred!" "You're a hundred and ninety-four next Wedding's day," William said, correcting him.

"Which is still nothing for a wizard, as you well know," Ethelthwaite snapped back at him, irritated at having been corrected.

That conversation had hardened his resolve. Of course it was out of character and of course it was impulsive, but years of responsibility had only made him subdue a mercurial nature, not lose it completely. This was important to him in a way that went beyond easy rationalisation; it was just something that he felt that he needed to do.

He climbed to his feet and shook himself like a dog, sending a shower of tiny brown globules flying in every direction. He frowned slightly at the way his sodden clothes clung to him. This was - he realised - not going to be quite the romantic devil may care little jaunt that he had envisaged.

Ethelthwaite covered the better part of three hundred miles over the next few weeks, sometimes by foot and occasionally on the back of someone's cart or wagon. During this period he suffered no more blackouts, and he did not give it any more thought. The few rides that he did manage to get were from people belonging to his 'old boy's network' of agents.

The use of the word 'agent' tends to suggest something very covert in nature, but these people were on the most part just ordinary people, living very ordinary lives, who saw Ethelthwaite as more of a pen-pal than a spymaster. The reception that he received when he turned up unannounced on some of their doorsteps was - after their initial surprise at finding a Lowland troll standing there - heartwarming.

The route that Ethelthwaite was travelling was not without its risks. In a form that was barely tolerated so close to The Barrens, he might easily have fallen foul to a party of elves and been forced to use his powers to extricate himself. Elves! So haughty and ridiculous on occasion, clinging to their old grudges like precious family heirlooms. Of all Derrian's people, they were the ones that Ethelthwaite had the least time for.

Nifnaff was lost again! The trouble was that he was born and raised to a life in the mountains. Forests were a sprawling mess where every direction looked the same and smelled like rotting vegetables to his unaccustomed nostrils. Every tree and shrub seemed to be in his way, making it almost impossible to walk in a straight line, every path ran in circles like a confused dog chasing its own tail! In clean mountain air he could have told the difference between North and South blindfolded from the smell of the rocks and the rivers, and yes, even the distant forests. The air was purer and much less congested, less polluted away from the sickly sweet decay that dominated the lowlands.

Nifnaff blamed Ralph for his situation, at least in part. If Ralph had not caused the wizard to fall down those steps; but then he could not avoid his own share of the blame in that. If he had been just a little more open with Ralph to start with, the human might have acted less rashly. And even there Nifnaff knew he was walking on thin ice. Ultimately it was his own rashness all those years ago that had set his feet on his current path. And there was the wizard. What was that damned fool doing dressed in a workman's clothes any way, and standing at the edge of an invisible step of all places! It made no sense to him at all. Something had happened at the city that was other than what it appeared to be, but he could not quite put his big meaty finger on what it was.

Nifnaff wondered briefly if Ralph had been as unlucky as he had so far. It would have taken a team of horses to drag the admission from him, but he did not like to think of the human coming to any harm. There had been times when he would have gladly throttled him, but there were other times during their journey together when he had not felt an inclination to hurt Ralph, times when he had actually enjoyed his company.

Nifnaff was socially challenged; he was also slightly xenophobic and had a very low tolerance for silliness in other people. Smalltalk made very little sense to his direct way of thinking. He hated how people jabbered on without ever seeming to get to a point, as though the only thing that mattered in a conversation was the sound of their own voices. He was also without ever trying to be, very intimidating to creatures who were not of his own race or stature, and it was a rare person who could get passed that. This made making friends outside of the Mountain troll society from which he was banished, a bit of a problem. Ralph had after his initial bout of terror, become quite inured to all but Nifnaff's foulest moods, and had seemed almost oblivious to anything short of being growled at. It was something of a revelation to Nifnaff, but even after everything that had happened, if someone caught him off guard with a request to indicate on one hand the number of friends that he had in the whole wide world, a single finger might have twitched, slightly.

Nifnaff had been banished from the mountains of his birth for the crime of sibling assault. The only thing that had made his banishment bearable was the knowledge that it was not forever, and that he would one day go back home. It was a condition of his ten year exile that every step he took should take him further away from his home. Nifnaff had been truer to the spirit of this instruction than anyone might have reasonably expected him to be. Now that those ten years were over, he wished that he had been less severe upon himself.

Nifnaff would not allow himself to consider the possibility that his family might be strangers to him when he finally got home, or that he might not be welcomed home as warmly as he wished to be. He had paid for his stupidity heavily and owed nothing more. His exile at an end, if his impatience could have taken a form, that form would have had the swiftest wings ever to cut through Derrian air. As for the lowlands! Everything about life at this altitude was uncomfortable, even after ten years. The air was too thick and wet, and the people were - in his evaluation - too wet and thick. He longed for the harsh bite of mountain air filling his lungs and the crisp metallic smells of his communal cavern.

Nifnaff remembered again the fateful day that had changed not only his life, but the lives of the people who were most important to him. He remembered the pride that he had felt when his older brother Minfar had done well in the proving, and he remembered his consuming bitterness when he found out that Minfar had joined with a female that he had hoped to become mated with when he himself came of age.

It had been childish of him to think that a sexually mature female would wait for him to reach maturity. He had not seen that her affection towards him had been that of a close childhood friend, and that she had been forming a different kind of relationship with his brother. It had been childish, but Nifnaff had been little more than a child at the time, contending with the hormonal baggage that went with that stage of his life.

Nifnaff had watched them secretly, guiltily. He had felt Minfar's excitement as though it was his own, enjoying it and being torn apart by it in equal measure, but when the she troll bit Minfar's shoulder and groaned his brother's name and not his, the spell broke like a flood through a collapsing dam, sweeping away any last shreds of thought and reason in Nifnaff's jealous young mind.

Nifnaff had thrown himself from the ledge where he had been hiding and landed heavily on his brother's back. Minfar rolled sideways, caught completely off guard, and fetched up against a fallen boulder, dazed and winded by the hard blow to his back. He tried to stand, but Nifnaff having had the easier part of their collision, was on him again quickly. Minfar raised his arm to try and fend off his younger brother's continued assault, but disbelief sapped the strength that might otherwise have been behind it, and his arm was forced backwards across the top of the rock against which he was sprawled, tearing the flesh at his shoulder and snapping his arm in two places. After that there was nothing. Minfar's mate let the bloody rock that she had hit Nifnaff with drop from her hand, then roughly pulling his slumped body away, she knelt at Minfar's side.

Mountain troll law where violence was concerned was as hard and unbending as the rock of their mountain home, and as clear as springtime melt water from the peaks. It had to be for creatures who could tear the leg from a horse as easily as a human could pull the leg from a cooked chicken.

There were places and occasions where it was permissible with mutual consent to try and mutilate and murder each other, such as in a proving or in the quarrellers' pit, but these were the exceptions without which the strict enforcement of the law in this matter would not have been considered fair. When Nifnaff had been made an outcast for attacking his brother, the only bitterness that he had felt was aimed at himself.

That was ten years ago, and Nifnaff was ten years older and - in theory - wiser for the experience, but it had left a gaping hole in his life that had become filled with unfulfilled dreams and shattered hopes. He might have had a mate by now, might have had children and the fullness of the feeling that comes from belonging to something. He might yet have these things, but oh the time that had been wasted!

Nifnaff grew angry at himself. Nothing good ever came out of self pity. What was done was done. He needed to think about the present, and at present he was walking around in circles and getting nowhere! Every damned tree looked the same to his unattuned eye, and the canopy was so thick that he could not get a proper bearing.

Nifnaff trundled on through a world of stately Red-barked columns, uncaring of their awe inspiring beauty, or the way that the shifting leaves dappled the forest floor in dancing light. He did not feel humbled by the forest's great age or get a sense of his place within the grand scheme of things. He did not get a sense of life's intricacies; the interdependence of so many things, the endless recycling of materials that allowed so many species to move forward rather than stagnate in endless sameness. He did not consider any of these things as he walked through a forest that was old before his own people had even learned to walk upright. The place stank of rotting vegetables and confused his senses, and he would have burned the lot down to see the back of it if everything was not so damned damp!

Part of the problem was that he had been following a stream for several days under the assumption that it would eventually lead him out of the forest. He had not considered the possibility that the stream might not be straight or - as was the case - that it might run in a nearly perfect circle. If he had known that this part of the forest was called Ring Brook Weald, he might have worked it out and saved himself a great deal of time and effort.

When it eventually dawned upon Nifnaff that following the stream was getting him nowhere that he had not already been, he left it and headed away at an angle in what he hoped was something like a straight line. Unfortunately he was on the inner bank of the stream, and two days later he was stood yet again upon the inner bank at the opposite side of the circular waterway, staring down in disgust at its cheerfully bubbling surface.

Nifnaff sat down on the bank with a dull thump that caused a few stones to come loose and roll into the water with several loud plops that sent ripples skittering across the surface in overlapping circles. He pulled a small bush out of the ground and passed several of the branches sideways between his lips, stripping away the leaves and eating them. It was not a bush that he recognised, but there were few plants on this part of the continent that a Mountain troll could not digest.

Here and there tiny fish moved lazily below the surface, or held themselves stationary in the slight current before shearing away like little guided torpedoes, only to stop again a few inches away. Nifnaff envied them their apparent freedom, their immediate considerations that took no account of tomorrow or yesterday. Reflected light danced over the surface of their world like a shiny undulating force field, drawing Nifnaff's senses, soothing away his many worries until - remarkably - he found that nothing seemed to matter. He could not remember a time when he had felt quite so relaxed, so at ease with the world and his lot within it.

Nifnaff lowered his head slowly onto his great chest as an unprecedented bout of weariness took a hold of his mind and body. His left arm slipped from his knee with a jolt and he toppled forward into the water, his expansive nether region sticking up into the air like a small volcanic island as his forehead and knees settled into the silt and gravel.

The cold shock of the water against his body was as welcome as a chill breeze coming down from the caps of his mountain home, and he was there, or at least he would have been if someone would stop stabbing him in the buttocks long enough for him to complete the illusion!

Nifnaff rolled over angrily and opened his eyes onto a world that was undulating like a bag full of baby snakes. He found himself staring up at the face of a small wobbling creature that was perching on top of his chest, jabbing at him viciously with a stick. Nifnaff watched its mouth working furiously as it continued to prod him, but he could not make out the muffled words over the gurgling of the stream. He reached one big furry hand up and grabbed the creature by the throat, only realising as he sat up and dangled it in mid air, that he had been watching it from below the water. Nifnaff still had the gnome by the throat as he asked, "was I drowning just then?"

The chubby scarlet-faced little creature nodded furiously, which given that it was suspended by the neck, involved its head staying quite still while its body jiggled slightly. "Let go of me you great flea ridden carpet!" it croaked angrily as it clawed at his branch-thick fingers.

Nifnaff did as the gnome asked. He smiled with satisfaction at the pleasing little plop that it made as it hit the water.

The gnome dragged itself from the stream and turned to face him from the bank. "That's a fine thank you for saving your life!" it said as it removed its boots and started pouring the water out of them.

Nifnaff stood up and joined the gnome on the bank. "Thank you," he said as he sat down with a heavy thump next to it.

The gnome plucked a few leaves from the discarded bush and rubbed them between its fingers. It sniffed them and shook its head. "You should be more careful what you eat," it said reprovingly as it leaned forward and washed its hand in the stream.

Living up a mountain where plants are as tough as the creatures that live on them requires a very tolerant digestive system. Nifnaff had not thought that there was a need for him to be cautious. It was a mistake that he did not intend to make a second time. He thanked the gnome again and offered his name.

"I mean, what sort of fool thinks that they can go about shoving..." The gnome paused its berating long enough to insert its own name. "Gellah," it said, then carried on.

Nifnaff tried changing the subject. "If you are neither male or female, how should I address you?" he asked, drawing upon his sketchy knowledge of gnome anatomy.

"So, all in all, you were really very lucky that I was here, otherwise..."

"I know," Nifnaff said, and thanked the gnome again for the umpteenth time.

"Not that you deserved my help after what..." Gellah shot Nifnaff a look that was pure acid. "I am not neither, I am both male and female if you don't mind."

Nifnaff shrugged. "There is no reason why I should mind," he said mildly.

Gellah huffed. "Not that I would expect any creature daft enough to eat a poisonous bush to have much sense," it snapped.

"Sorry."

"But what thanks do I get?" Gellah continued, getting back to its original train of thought. "Eh?" Nifnaff did not answer, so Gellah nudged him. "I said, what thanks do I get?"

"The same that I have been giving you for some minutes now," Nifnaff told the gnome, and again thanked the creature.

"Not that any words can repay the saving of a life," Gellah told him. "It's a selfless thing I guess. Fortunately a compassionate act carries its own rewards, but a little unsolicited thanks is still nice."

"I did say thank you," Nifnaff pointed out, adding, "several times."

"But no, I guess thats..."

Nifnaff grabbed the gnome by the back of its collar and tossed it into the water. He waited long enough to be sure that it would not drown, then stood up and walked away, the sound of its loud rebuke ringing in his ears.

Nifnaff continued to walk in circles, variations of circles, triangles and even the occasional square. He almost started to believe that he was being punished by the wizards for his part in that wizard's death, but what had he done but take pity on a stranger who would surely have died without his help? "Well that will not happen again," he muttered angrily as he stomped along.

A heavy net dropped suddenly from the trees above Nifnaff's head, catching him by surprise. Nifnaff stood there for a moment, unbending under a weight of a rope that would have floored a bull as he contemplated this new and unexpected turn of events. Part of him was excited at the prospect of something other than endless walking, but by and large it was anger that drove him to start tearing at the thick ropes with his hands and teeth until his head, right arm and shoulder were poking through. He stopped when four darts thumped into his chest and upper arm and stared down at them in dismay. He tried plucking at one, but the poison they were carrying was already taking effect, and he could not coordinate his movements well enough to close his numbing fingers over the tiny projectile.

The world seemed to jump up at Nifnaff with a jolt, and it was a few moments before he realised that his knees had given way beneath him. Even then he found some fight still, and he managed to tear the hole in the net a little wider, but in doing so, he lost his balance completely and toppled sideways. Finally, incapable of moving his limbs more than a few inches, Nifnaff was reduced to slinging futile threats at the legs of his unseen attackers.

A tall whip thin man sauntered into Nifnaff's line of view after having watched unobserved from the trees for several minutes. He came to within ten feet of Nifnaff and stopped. "Now what do we have here?" he asked with feigned surprise. "Too big for a rug, I'd say." He stroked his chin thoughtfully. "You might make a good mattress cover, or possibly fur lined boots for my people here. You'd make a fair few pairs I'll bet."

Nifnaff glared at the man. "If I get out of this, I will rip your backbone out and strangle you with it," he slurred thickly.

The thin man darted forward and kicked Nifnaff hard in the jaw, then danced back out of the way again. He might as well have kicked a canon ball for all the damage it caused the huge troll. "But you won't," he replied confidently.

Nifnaff took stock of the human. There was nothing exceptional about him physically. He was tall but not excessively so, stringy to the point of appearing fragile and ill, and had a general sort of look that would not excite much in the way of envy or desire from others of his kind. Nifnaff only looked him over the once, then looked into his eyes and knew that he was looking into the soul of a madman. This was - he realised - a man who might kill out of boredom and be bored whilst doing it.

He fought back his anger, deciding that it would be better to hold it in check for a more advantageous moment. "In time," he promised silently, then asked, "now what, human?"

"My name is Ronl, troll," the skinny man told him, "but you can call me, Master, if you like." He turned away then turned back again. "That's until I have you put to death. Then you can just scream."

Nifnaff let out a growl that was so low that those closest imagined that they had felt it through the soles of their feet. Ronl shrugged. "Any way it goes, troll, I'm going to have my sport from you before you die," he told Nifnaff. He looked up at the trees and shouted, "we have ourselves a new pet, lads."

Nifnaff watched impotently as Ronl's people clambered down from their hiding places in the trees. They were a rag tag bunch of misfits on the most part, and Ronl seemed to be by far the shiniest button in the packet and was very obviously their leader. Nifnaff still had enough wits about him to be curious when a Lowland troll and an elf gingerly approached him with a heavy pole and worked together threading it through the netting in which he was ensnared.

He turned his wilting attention back to Ronl again as the man pulled a long blowpipe from his belt and took his time fitting a dart into its end. Ronl put it to his mouth and puffed out his cheeks until they were white almost, and blew. "We've been following you for days you know," he said conversationally as he waited for the darts to take full effect. "It was quite funny at first. That bush you were eating when you fell into the water is what we use to make the paste that we dip our darts in." He frowned and fitted another one into the pipe. "Two darts would kill most men." He shrugged. "Still, no great loss if I overdo it, eh?" He raised the pipe and blew it again.

Nifnaff caught the blur of the dart's swift flight and felt it slam hard into his cheek. It did not surprise him in the least that the man had deliberately aimed it at his face, even though his body would have made a much easier target, but there was something about this Ronl that he was missing, something crucial to him understanding the situation. "Why... you... doing... this?" he slurred as he finally started to lose consciousness.

"I have my reasons, troll," Ronl hissed at him. "I have my reasons."

It took three teams of sixteen very nervous men the better part of a day to carry Nifnaff's snoring bulk back to their camp. Nifnaff stirred just once during that time. It was nothing much really. He smacked his lips, mumbled something incoherent and started snoring again. The men carrying him dropped their poles and put several feet between themselves and their burden. It took two more darts and a lot of coaxing to get them to pick him up again.

They were bone weary nervous wrecks when they at last staggered back into their camp, and more than one of that put-upon party dared to voice their disgruntlement within earshot of their leader. Ronl was too full of his own success in capturing the Mountain troll to care much. He even allowed them to rest a little before having them haul Nifnaff up against a tree with blocks and tackle.

Tying him to the tree took a lot of good thick rope that might have been better used elsewhere, and a working knowledge of knots. As they stood staring at their handiwork afterwards, most of them were wondering why they had gone to so much trouble to catch such a dangerous creature. Many of them knew of their leader's obsession with Mountain trolls, but this was taking that obsession too far.

"Should've tortured and killed it where we caught it," one of Ronl's men said as he finished putting a whip at the end of a rope to stop it fraying.

"Aye, would've been the sane thing to do," somebody else agreed.

It was utter madness, but Ronl had wanted it, and Ronl usually got what he wanted. Nobody knew quite why that was. He was not the strongest or even the brightest of them, and nobody liked him very much. Even his relationship with the king's daughter had somehow managed to backfire on them, and they had been forced to move their camp deeper into the forest to avoid getting into a scrap with his soldiers as a result.

Nifnaff opened his eyes onto a shifting canvass of animated blurs. One of those blurs came closer and kicked him hard in the shin. Nifnaff was in no doubt about who that blur was. He sucked his breath in as he struggled to hold his temper in check and tried to bring Ronl's cruelly grinning face into focus. "Why are you doing this to me?" he asked again. Whatever the reason, he doubted that it had anything to do with Ralph or the wizards.

Ronl stepped closer. "Because you mock humanity by walking on two feet," he answered dryly as though supplying a fact that should have been obvious to him.

Nifnaff studied Ronl's face; the telltale twitch at the corner of his right eye betraying some inner torment. "How can my existence mock you?" Nifnaff asked him. "What hurt have I caused you that compares to what you are now doing to me? Does my presence give you a sore neck from having to look up at me? If so, stand on a stool, or better still, let me ago and you will never need to look up at me again."

Ronl spat at Nifnaff, then jumped back in alarm as Nifnaff jerked forward suddenly. The ropes creaked as their fibres were stretched almost to breaking point, but remarkably they held, and he was impotent to do more than growl his frustration into his captor's shocked face.
"Fight all you like, troll," Ronl said in a shaky voice. "It won't do you any good, but it'll keep me entertained for a while."

Ronl composed himself as best he could before walking back across the camp. He went back to his hut and threw himself onto his cot. "You want to know why I'm doing it to you?" he sobbed into the fur hide that was draped over it. Ronl shut his eyes tight against the soft fur and replayed a terrible event from his childhood that was pivotal to understanding the twisted creature that he had become. "You killed them," he whispered softly. "And by the wizards, you're going to beg me to kill you before I've finished with you," he promised.

Years earlier, a much younger Ronl had woken abruptly to the sound of his mother screaming, and the heavy thump of something large crashing into the wall that separated his bedroom from the living area. Curiosity overrode his fear, and he climbed from his bed and tiptoed to the bedroom door. He opened it far enough to see without being seen, and watched his mother as she clung desperately to the arm of a huge crouching Mountain troll, begging it not to kill her husband/his father.

Ronl did not understand what was happening at first. He would have stayed transfixed upon that scene until its end, but for the sight of his father crawling broken and bloody across the floor towards the door behind which he was hiding. Throwing all thoughts of personal safety aside, Ronl ran into the room. He stopped and screamed as the troll swatted his father with a club, snapping his head sideways with a sickening dull crack.

Ronl remembered all of these things as clearly as if they had only happened yesterday, the blood and the gore that had spattered across his face and bed shirt, his mother momentarily so shocked that she could not breathe and almost suffocated, the loud exhale and juddering sob that followed. There were other things that he did not remember/would not let himself remember, because if he did remember them, then the true monster would have become too familiar for him to bear.

The Mountain troll had put as much force into that blow as the limited space in the room would permit, showing more consideration in that moment than the man at his feet deserved. He caught sight of the child only at the last moment and tried to turn the blow aside, but it was too late. The deed done, he moved his leg slightly, putting it between the boy and his father's still twitching body.

Ronl screamed again and ran to his sobbing mother. The troll looked down at them both sadly, his anger at last spent. "What the boy has seen," he told the woman sadly, "nobody should ever see. I would have spared him that, had I known he was there, but my child was tied up and used as bait to catch her mother. She was made to watch as they killed her and cut trophies from her dead body, then they clubbed my daughter senseless and left her for dead. Be thankful at least, that I did not seek to take my revenge in a like fashion." This was said with a meaningful look.

Nifnaff had not been there of course. He had been little more than a cub at the time that these terrible things took place. His only crime was being a Mountain troll and conveniently being in the wrong place at the right time. Had he known what drove Ronl's hatred of his kind, it would not have made him less inclined to carry out his threat to extract his spine and feed it to him.

Ethelthwaite stopped next to a solitary wind-sculpted twist of almost barkless wood that was only technically a tree. He stared in dismay at the shale bank that he was about to attempt to climb. This was where The Barrens began in earnest, and Ethelthwaite could not imagine a more fitting threshold to such a miserable stretch of land.

He briefly considered carrying on in the hope of finding an easier way up, but he had already wasted two days on that vain hope, and the map that he had memorised before leaving suggested that he would only be wasting more time, unless he intended to venture deeper into elven territory. Ethelthwaite sighed and shook his head. He knew that it might yet come to that, but that would only be as a last resort. There was nothing for it, so he muttered a few choice words, hitched his skirt higher and started to climb.

Ethelthwaite was nothing if not pigheaded, but even wearing the form of a creature that was renowned for its toughness, it was a fool's task. Every foot that he climbed cost him dearly in skin and dignity as he scrabbled up the shifting shale. Twice he slid several feet on an avalanche of his own making. Both times he threw himself flat and lay there with his legs and arms outstretched, wondering if what he was about was worth any of this. He knew that it was. The cold, the wet, the cuts and the bruises; it was worth these things ten times over to stop himself decaying inside as he had been doing back in the city.

Ethelthwaite started to make some progress finally, and it was not long before he felt the incline lessen to the point where a braver or more foolish man might have stood up and tried walking. Ethelthwaite was no coward, but neither was he a fool, and so he continued slowly on all fours. "Didn't think you were gonna make it."

Ethelthwaite jumped with surprise and started to slide backwards again. He threw himself forward so that he was lying prostrate in an effort to gain some kind of purchase on the shale as it shifted dangerously beneath him. Fortunately it moved only a foot or so and stopped.

"Didn't mean to startle yer. Need a hand there?"

Ethelthwaite lifted his hand slowly without looking up, and felt it taken in a strong grip. He waited a moment, took a deep breath and with his unseen helper's assistance, made the top in a flurry of hissing shale. "Thanks," he said panting heavily as he rolled onto his back and stared up into the face of a genuine Barrens Lowland troll...

... Daphen caught his breath a little then sat up.

The real troll said, "name's Susna," as he offered his hand again in greeting. "So what possessed you to go shinnying up a nasty-arsed skinner like this one?"

"Don't know," Daphen said uncertainly as he realised that he could not remember anything either before or after the storm. "Reckon I must've banged my noggin on the way up," he mused. "Still, it'll come back when it's got a mind to."...

... Ethelthwaite's nose was insisting that he was very close to something that had been dead for a while. "What a gods' awful stink!" he exclaimed loudly, gagging slightly as his nostrils closed in protest against the unprepared for stench of an unwashed Lowland troll. He caught himself too late. "I mean, it could be worse I s'pose," he added quickly.

"Do you think so," Susna asked, sounding almost disappointed. "Can't really see how."

Ethelthwaite nodded. "Me neither."

"So, where're you off to then?" Susna asked, changing the subject.

Ethelthwaite shrugged. "Not really sure," he lied.

"Must be the bump," Susna decided.

"What bump?" Ethelthwaite asked him.

Susna gave him a look that translated into, 'my point exactly'.

Ethelthwaite decided that it would be better not to go any further down that path, and instead asked where Susna was going. Susna told him that he had been to Little Pelham on an errand and was now rejoining his pack. Ethelthwaite knew of Little Pelham from maps and from a haberdasher there who sent him the occasional letter. It was further along the border, some fifty miles southeast of his current position.

The town was as its name suggested, a smaller annex of a place called Pelham. Although it was loosely speaking still elven territory, the decentralised nature of elven government meant that a few of the more out of the way towns like Little Pelham enjoyed a certain degree of autonomy. Unlike most of its neighbours, it was heavily dependent on trade, and far more tolerant of strangers. It could still be a dangerous place, especially if you were a skirt wearing Lowland troll with acute halitosis and an aversion to soap, but if you kept your head down and got on with your business, people tended to mind their own.

Susna was concerned about Daphen/Ethelthwaite. The man was lost and confused. He made the suggestion that if Daphen did not know where he was going, they might travel together until he figured it out. Ethelthwaite readily accepted the offer. In fact, he had every intention of remaining confused all the way to Susna's camp if necessary. He had never seen a Lowland camp and he was curious.

To know about something is a world away from knowing it. Ethelthwaite knew about The Barrens, but he did not know it. The only way to really understand a place like that is to experience it first hand. To live there required certain qualities that would not be seen as admirable elsewhere. Lowland trolls had all those qualities and a few more besides. They were a frustrating contradiction who might steal the bedding from under a sleeping baby one minute and risk their lives to save it the next. It was contradictions of this sort that had helped them to survive in The Barrens, but their unpredictable inclinations did nothing to endear them to their neighbours, the elves. The elves had a saying: you need seven hands when you meet a Lowland troll: two holding your pockets, two pinning its hands, two around its throat and one spare just in case it's one of the trickier ones!

Susna made several sour faced references to the approaching breeding season while they walked. The female Lowlanders were tough solitary creatures who shunned the company of the males and other females alike, until the breeding season that is, then the females would come together in aggressively competitive packs to hunt males.

Shortly before the breeding season gets underway, the male trolls hold a week long festival where they catch up with old friends and family and formally bring their male offspring into adult society. It is also a time for them to say goodbye to daughters who have reached the age where it is no longer safe for them to remain in the camps with the males. Susna's errand had something to do this upcoming event, though he would not be drawn on what exactly.

Ethelthwaite had seen a few female Lowland trolls in Brace. They were infrequent weary-eyed visitors who never seemed quite comfortable in the city's crowded streets. Similar in size and appearance to the males, the only significant difference, aside from the obvious, was a vicious looking dewclaw above their wrists and ankles. These they used to latch onto their reluctant copulative partners, and to administer a stimulant into their bloodstreams to make them more, responsive.

Ethelthwaite observed on his first day travelling with the troll, that he was one of those rare souls for whom cheerfulness was a natural state of being. That Susna was growing less and less so as the second day wore on at first perplexed him, until the troll confided to him that his village was not where he had left it.

The Lowland trolls were a transient people who moved from place to place as resources and circumstances demanded. They travelled light, taking with them only what they could carry on stretchers between them or on their backs. On foot and with no carts or pack animals to leave heavy tracks behind, they could break camp quickly and be gone with almost no trace. This was the predicament that Susna now faced. His errand had taken a little longer than expected, and the camp had for whatever reason, been moved in the meantime.

Fortunately the village had not been moved very far, and an unexpected shout from a watcher the following day put the greater part of the troll's concerns to rest. Ethelthwaite looked to where the shout had come from and saw a distant figure rise up in a shower of dust from beneath a sheet of canvas. He had taken the young troll for a rock and his surprise was almost as great as his travelling companion's relief.

The camp itself was a couple of miles further on still. The dun colour of the canvas on the tents hid it very effectively at a distance, so that they were almost there before Ethelthwaite realised it. He looked around as they entered the camp, taking in its sparseness, its tents made from worn canvas laid over bent poles and held down with rocks, the complete lack of clutter because nothing could be wasted, signs of excessive wear everywhere, and he wondered that anyone would choose a life that was so bleak and devoid of anything that was not absolutely necessary.

There were many places in Derrian where the Lowland trolls might have lived far more comfortably, less economically; places where they could have built with permanence in mind. The gods knew, but the elves would have paid them to go, and helped them to pack their camps up if necessary!

News of their arrival had gone on ahead of them, and there were dozens of trolls waiting to greet Susna. Susna's son was among them, and the lad barrelled into his father the moment he clapped eyes on him. Susna swept him up with rough affection and bear-hugged him until he squealed his submission.

"This is my lad, Marci," Susna said as he put him down. He ruffled his hair playfully.

The boy cuffed his hand away and made a lunge for his bag. "What you got me?"

Susna pushed him away and fished around in the haversack. "Here," he said grinning, and tossed a parcel to the boy.

Marci clutched it to his chest and gave his father a sly look. "It's shoes, int it?" he asked, as he caught the unmistakable smell of leather. "Thanks dad!" he cried, then was off at a jog to find his friends and show them.

Ethelthwaite had become quite choked up as he watched the interaction between the boy and his father. Their simple and unrefined closeness touched something in him that he had not even realised was still there, and he found himself momentarily hating Susna for having managed to touch that rawness in him so easily...

... Daphen was confused. The last thing that he remembered was being at the top of a shale bank. His scabbed up hands and knees attested to the accuracy of that memory at least, though there was little enough before that, and nothing at all between then and now. Who was he? He knew nothing beyond his own name, and even there he could not be certain. He was relieved at least to see that he was in a Lowlander camp. Daphen looked at his companion who seemed perfectly at ease, and chose not to say anything about his latest lapse of memory.

Teenagers were busily hanging strings of small jerked lizards between the tents. They had been dyed to make them decorative, but would later be taken down and eaten. Daphen watched the teenagers and searched his memory for something that would explain why they were doing this, but he drew a blank. They were obviously getting ready for some kind of party or celebration, but for who? Was it in his honour? He did not think it very likely. He looked down at his torn and filthy clothes and his heart sank.

Did he have a change of clothes? Daphen could not remember where his home was, but he did not think that this was his camp. He dug into his small but unusually deep shoulder bag and started to rummage around in it, but the bag was Ethelthwaite's, and it did not recognise the wizard and the troll persona as being one and the same. Consequently his questing fingers came out empty but for a bit of lint that snagged onto a broken fingernail.

Susna noticed the sudden change in Daphen's mood and asked him what was wrong.

Daphen shook his head miserably. "I haven't got any clothes. I don't even know if I own any! I can't remember anything much before I bumped into you!"

Susna smiled sympathetically and patted his shoulder. "I should be able to do something about the clothes at least," he said, shoving Daphen gently towards his tent.

Daphen sat quietly on a rug and watched Susna digging through a small stack of clothes.

"I know I had a spare smock knocking around somewhere," Susna mumbled to himself in an exasperated tone. He stopped what he was doing and looked over his shoulder at Daphen. "There's lizard jerky in a bag over there. Help yer sen." He looked back at the pile of clothes and frowned. "I'm going to go 'nd see if Marci knows where that smock is. I'll not be long."

Daphen watched him go…

… Ethelthwaite watched the troll leave and frowned. "This's really got to stop!" he snapped angrily as he realised that there was yet another gap in his memory. He put the half chewed piece of jerky down and shuffled over to the door flap on his knees. Susna's haversack was near the door flap, and he moved it aside. As he did, the bag flopped over and a brown paper parcel dropped out onto the floor. Ethelthwaite picked it up and tried to shove it back into the bag, but the paper ripped, then ripped a little more when he pulled it back out again. Ethelthwaite cursed under his breath as he imagined how it would look to his host when he returned…

… Daphen sucked his breath in as he caught the glint of sequins through the tear. Without thinking he pulled the rest of the paper off and let the garment fall open in his hands. He must have dozed off and been asleep when Susna had come back in with it. He looked at it admiringly. The material had been painstakingly stitched with enough coloured steel sequins and polished bone beads to turn a knife attack aside. He held the smock up to his shoulders. It was too much. "I can't take this," he said with a resigned sigh.

Susna caught what Daphen had said as he pulled the door flap aside. He froze in horror halfway in. "Yer damned right you can't take it," he shouted angrily. "That's fer the Quiny!"

Susna made a grab for the smock. Daphen was confused still. He did not know what was happening or why, and he pulled away. Both trolls stopped and stared down in horror as the cloth tore between them. Several beads pitter-pattered off of an empty clay pot on the floor, punctuating the silence as each contemplated their own roles in what had just happened, and the likely implications...

... Ethelthwaite was face down in a bush with his hands bound tightly behind his back. It was dark and cold and there was a very definite smell of stale urine. He moved slightly, groaned and added a number of cuts and bruises to the list of indignities that his body had been subjected to in his mental absence. He cursed his other assumed personality under his breath and resolved to remove it at the first opportunity.

The thing that was Daphen had realised that it would be discarded once its host had finished with it. This conclusion had not been reached by independent thought, as Daphen's thoughts were in every respect still Ethelthwaite's own, just the part of Ethelthwaite who had started to think that he really was a Lowland troll called Daphen. Ethelthwaite could feel him there, a frustrated simmering presence at the edge of his thoughts, loitering uncertainly like a cat that has just had its camouflage taken away.

Ethelthwaite knew that Daphen would try to regain control again; it was in its/his nature not to give up without a fight. No longer able to gain access to the thing that gave Daphen the ability to think, there was only instinct, and there is no greater instinct than the instinct to survive. Daphen acted on that one instinct without thought, and attacked. Ethelthwaite recoiled from the attack, momentarily stunned by its unexpected intensity, then dug down into the wellspring of his memories for the strength to resist it and push back.

Daphen was new and had no core memories of his own. His personality was a thin veneer that lacked the depth of character, the intricate flaws and callouses that can only be accumulated with a lifetime of experiences. In the end, he simply lacked the necessary substance to overwhelm Ethelthwaite, and with nowhere left to go, he faded away, leaving Ethelthwaite with a few more bad habits, and an unpleasant guilty feeling that he did not care to examine too closely.

Ralph opened his eyes and stared dully at the flaking whitewashed ceiling above his head. It was a familiar sight - or at least it was getting to be familiar. How he had come to be there this time was still a bit of a blur to him, but the why was pretty easy: he had gotten drunk again. He knew the routine well enough. Eventually someone would come along with a mop and bucket and tell him to clean the cell, then give him the standard lecture about behaving like a responsible adult and such. He closed his eyes again and pulled the thin scratchy grey blanket back over his head. With luck, if they were not too busy, they would leave him to sleep his hangover off before that happened.

"Come on, Mr Chambers, let's be havin' you up 'nd out. I've got some respectable villains as're waiting to get in here once you've cleaned yer puke up."

There was a jangle of heavy keys and a loud grating noise that set Ralph's teeth on edge.

Ralph shuddered and groaned. He waited for the throbbing to recede a little then turned his head slowly and looked at the guard. "You'd've thought with all those respectable villains that you've got, you'd not have any time for the likes of me," Ralph ventured.

The constable grinned at Ralph from the open doorway. "Now Mr Chambers, you know we're never too busy for the likes of you. Mind though, this must be startin' to feel a little bit like home from home."

"At least nobody bumps their heads on the ceiling where I live," Ralph answered acidly, making reference to the constable's height. The effort it took to be indignant caused his head to throb again and he winced.

"Now Ralph, I know as you claim not to be from this world, but you've been around here long enough to know that dwarves only appear short next to long folk, and I've already told you this more than once, that I couldn't bang my head on my ceiling, owing to the fact that I'm the right height for my house," the constable said, correcting him mildly.

Constable Buller was one of those annoying people who could remain cheerful no matter how hard a person tried to be disagreeable with him. Ralph would not go so far as to say that he liked the dwarf, but there were other constables who he liked less. For Constable Buller's part, Ralph was just one of the many that he had to deal with who insisted on wasting their lives and their wages in the local pubs. Sober, Ralph was a tolerable sort of fellow who could hold a reasonably intelligent conversation when he was not prattling on about being from another world.

"So now; come on then, Mr Chambers," the constable said when Ralph had finished mopping the floor, "or am I to tell the pretty young lass who's come to collect yer, to bugger off?"

Ralph coughed out an involuntary laugh, then asked, "what lass?" when he realised that the constable was not pulling his leg.

While Ralph was being led through to the reception desk he overheard someone being asked if they were quite sure that he - Ralph assumed this to mean himself - was really the one that they wanted. There was a note of doubt in the questioner's voice that Ralph knew he should be offended by, but he was more interested in the person who was being spoken to.

The woman - he was fairly sure that it was a woman - was wearing a blue fur trimmed cloak with a deep hood that effectively hid her features. The cloak was expensive and stylish rather than practical, and covered her from her head to her dainty ankles.

Ralph stooped slightly in an effort to see her face. "Do I know you?" he asked.

"I do not believe so," the woman answered, extending a delicate lace gloved hand for him to take, "but I know of you." Ralph took her hand, thought to kiss it, thought better of it, and gave it a little shake instead before letting go of it. He leaned a little closer to catch her softly spoken words, then closer still to catch the smell of her scented skin. The woman stepped back as he did and moved over to the door, where she waited.

It was several seconds before Ralph realised that she was waiting for him to open the door for her. When the penny dropped he hurried over. "After you, er, Miss," he said a little uncertainly, opening the door and stepping to one side so that she could leave.

"Don't it warm yer heart to know there's still some real gents about, Mr Buller?" Lucius asked, suppressing a giggle.

"It does indeed, Mr Periwinkle, it does indeed," constable Buller agreed.

Ralph closed the door quickly on their laughter and hurried after the woman.

"Are you sure we haven't met?" Ralph asked as he caught up with her. He tried to peer under the hood again, but was again frustrated by its depth.

The woman stopped. "Oh, I am so sorry!" she answered in a slightly embarrassed honey-sweet voice. "No. As I said, I do not believe so." She rested a delicately boned hand on Ralph's arm. "I seek your services," she said, leaning in as though confiding a secret to him.

Ralph smiled nervously and his pulse began to race. "Services?" he asked hopefully.

The woman let go of Ralph's arm and took hold of both sides of her hood. "You are Ralph Chambers, are you not?" she asked, pulling it back.

Ralph's jaw dropped faster than a one legged footballer taking a penalty. The woman was beautiful! "No," he thought as he reconsidered her looks, "not beautiful", she was immaculate, which was not quite the same thing. "Yes, I am," Ralph agreed, a little surprised at someone other than the town's police using his full name.

"The Ralph Chambers whose fame has spread far and wide?" she asked.

"Well, I wouldn't say fame exactly," Ralph answered, growing a little uncomfortable.

"The one who slew the mighty wizard, Ethelthwaite?"

Ralph's blood went cold. He shrank into himself and waited for bolts of lightning to come stabbing down out of a sky that was suitably moody. Long moments passed. A dog vomited in the doorway of a shop and yelped as the shopkeeper caught it a 'good en' with a bunch of well aimed radishes, a spider in a tree got more than it bargained for when it tried to pounce on a fairy that had been stripping the glue from its web, but though these things were of great consequence to the parties involved, none of it presaged the arrival of a horde of revenge hungry wizards. "Yes," he said cautiously, "but it was…"

"Truly heroic." The woman grabbed both of his hands in her own and shook them. "And it is you that I seek," she insisted, not giving him a chance to say that it had been an accident, "and it is you who will save my father's kingdom."

"Kingdom?" Ralph repeated, then, "I'll save your father's kingdom?"

The woman squealed with delight. "I knew you would," she said, intentionally misunderstanding him. She looped her arm through his and pulled herself in close to his side. "I am the Princess Miriam," she told him, adding, "and as grateful as I will be, it is nothing to what my father will have in store for you."

Ralph managed to say, "oh."

Miriam pursed her lips thoughtfully and asked, "where are your arms?"

"On my shoulders," Ralph answered uncertainly.

Miriam tittered and gave his wrist a playful swat with her glove. "Heroic and witty," she exclaimed. "You know of course that I refer to your weapons and armour."

Alarm bells that had clanged dully in a head that was still suffering the after effects of too much alcohol started to ring more clearly. "I haven't got any," he told her, then said,

"You're not kidding, are you?" He waved her answer aside. "So, just who do you think I'm about to save your kingdom from then?" He was catching up quickly now and beginning to realise that wherever she was going with this, it was probably not going to be somewhere that he wanted to go.

Miriam pretended not to notice his question. "We will have to take care of that this instant. Whatever the misfortune that has brought you to this, I would see you restored in your standards to something more befitting your station. Walk me to your armourer and I shall correct the matter this instant," she told him. She touched a finger to his bare arm and stroked it lightly. "So firm," she whispered as though to herself. "I do so love the sight of a suited man. It makes me..." Miriam stopped there, leaving Ralph's imagination to fill in the blanks.

"We've got an ironmonger," Ralph offered with renewing enthusiasm.

Ralph swaggered into the ironmongery five minutes later in Miriam's perfumed wake and called out, "hey there, good fellow," as he spotted the owner. "Attend to us this instant."

"You can attend to my ar..." the ironmonger started to say, then stopped as he noticed the young lady who had come in with Ralph. His expression softened slightly, but when he turned back to look at Ralph, he might as well have been eyeing an annoying stain on the counter. 'What do you want Chambers? Ain't got no work for you, nor any charity neither." He wiped his dusty hands on his apron. "Now what can I do for you young miss?" he asked, switching the smile back on again.

Miriam arched an eyebrow at the man. "I require suit and arms for this, the finest of men," she said icily, her expression daring the shopkeeper to challenge her stated opinion of Ralph's worth.

The shopkeeper took in her fine clothing and her aloof manner and did some quick mental arithmetic. You could almost hear the ca-ching of an opening cash register in his voice as he smiled at Ralph. "If sir would follow me," he said, switching tack seamlessly. He stepped from behind the counter and led them both into an adjoining room. "Now let me see." He started rummaging through an assortment of dusty crates and boxes. "We don't get much call for armour these days," he said with a grunt as he tilted a barrel onto its edge and rolled it out of the way. "Ain't been a proper dust up around here in years. It's hammers and nails fer these folk, and I'm glad of it," he told Miriam without turning. "I got me hands on some old army surplus and a few bits of dress armour from the niece of General Wellwreck when he passed on a while back though. Meant to get it melted down for horseshoes and nails and such, but I never got round to it." He pulled out a rusty chainmail shirt and held it up. "It might not look much, but I reckon it'd dull a fairy's teeth quickly enough."

Miriam ignored it and waved at the box that he had dug it out of. "Elf made if I am not mistaken?" she said, indicating another mail shirt, the sleeve of which was hanging out of the box limply.

The shopkeeper nodded. "That'd hardly be a recommendation, Miss," he told her.

Miriam waved her hand dismissively. "But it has such lovely big rings," she said, talking over him, "and it would look wonderful with that big helmet there. Yes, that one there with the big purple feather on it, and oh and oh, and I think those thingy-majigs over there, and..."

Ralph stepped from the store forty minutes later looking like something out of an amateur production of a Gilbert and Sullivan opera, dragging a huge two-handed ceremonial sword behind him that gouged the floor. Miriam led him by the elbow, all the time cooing and petting his ego, and eyeing him in a way that had all the trappings of admiration, but none of the sincerity.

Ralph was about to say that the chainmail was chafing him a little when he heard someone laughing loudly. He turned awkwardly to stare at a red-faced dwarf who was sat on a bench holding his sides and choking on the carrot that he had been eating. "What're you looking at?" he snapped hotly.

The dwarf's wide eyes were streaming, and he was banging his chest with his fist in an effort to eject a piece of carrot that had gone down the wrong way, otherwise he might have told Ralph.

Miriam turned her head away and stifled a laugh. She stopped Ralph and fished a few coins from her purse and pressed them into his hand. "I have some business to take care of," she told him, "but I will meet you later in the tavern that we passed on the way here. I am staying at the hotel across the road."

Ralph was not about to do anything that would put his own skin at risk, but he was not about to tell Miriam that. As long as she thought that he was going to be her knight in shining armour, there existed the possibility of an adventure of a more amorous nature that would not involve putting his life at risk, so he nodded and clanked away smiling like a cat that has just found the back door into pigeon heaven.

Miriam collected Ralph from the jail just before dusk. He was too drunk to walk, and had to be helped/dragged out by two constables, who Miriam pressed further by asking them to put him onto the back of a mule that she had hired for the purpose. Several attempts were made to get him into the saddle, but Ralph was an unresponsive dead weight. Finally - to the great amusement of the small crowd that had started to gather - the saddle was removed, and he was dragged over the poor animal's back like a sack and tied into place.

Miriam climbed onto her own horse and took the mule's lead rope from a constable who had been holding it for her. She nodded at him curtly and gave him a few coins, then after securing the rope to the pommel of her saddle, startled her horse into motion with a few quick jabs of her heels. The mule resisted just long enough to inflict a rope burn on Miriam's thigh where the lead rope dragged across it, then grudgingly fell into step.

Ralph came to with a start as he was toppled unceremoniously from the back of the mule an hour or so later. He sat up quickly - a little too quickly - and let out a loud groan. "Where the hell am I?" he asked thickly.

Miriam stepped into view as a boy led the mule away. "How is your head?" she asked in as neutral a tone as she could manage.

Ralph stifled another groan. "Falling from that has taken my mind off of it," he said, nodding at the retreating mule."

Miriam smiled inwardly, her expression all concern. "I'm sorry," she said simpering sweetly, "I tried to catch you, but you are such a big man. You did drink rather a lot though, from what I was told. Do all warriors drink so much? I guess they must, to dull their terrible memories. Is that so?"

Ralph forced a smile on to his face. "Drink hard, fight harder," he said with unconvincing bravado.

Another woman who was sat warming her hands by a fire a few feet away, sniggered. Ralph shot her a cold look, and in doing so, noticed that there was a third person present, stood just beyond the fire watching him. "That thing that I'm supposed to be doing for you," he said as he felt the first flutters of apprehension, "exactly what is it?"

Miriam was smiling at him sweetly still. "Oh, it's nothing much," she reassured; "a bit of a problem with an airy-plane, but you know what a pest they can be." She knelt down next to him and stroked his bearded cheek with her fingertips. "It almost seems insulting to ask a man such as you to do this for me."

Ralph breathed in her perfume. "An aeroplane?" he asked, desperate to be convinced by her. "Didn't think you had those here."

"A small one," Miriam said reassuringly. "And the reward, well..."

"And the reward?" Ralph asked just a little too quickly.

Miriam lowered her head slightly. There was a shy smile creasing her full lips as she said, "my hand if you would have it, and the kingdom that will one day go with it."

Ralph scratched his chin. It itched annoyingly. "And you say I've just got to sort out a small aeroplane?"

"Yes," Miriam agreed.

Ralph smiled nervously and made a clumsy lunge for her.

Miriam was up and out of reach in a flash, her petite hand out of sight, resting on the petite bone handle of a stiletto knife that was concealed within her cloak. "Oh, sir knight!" she said in a shocked voice. "As much as I might wish it otherwise, I will not, I can not be yours yet," she insisted. 'How would it look?"

Ralph frowned. "Who are they?" he asked thickly, still very much under the influence of the large amount of alcohol that he had consumed while waiting for Miriam.

"Marguerite is my personal lady," Miriam told him. "The other is a warlock who I have hired to transport us to my home."

"A wizard?" Ralph asked in sudden alarm.

"A warlock," the man corrected as he stepped into the firelight. He hunkered down next to the fire and extended his hands towards it. "I am my own man."

A fortnight earlier Miriam had stood boldly in front of her father - the king - and announced that she was going to marry Ronl. The announcement had been made solely to needle her father, and it was doubtful whether she had any real intention of seeing the threat through. The old king was at first amused, then incredulous at her stupidity and arrogance in believing that he would ever allow his kingdom to fall into the hands of a brigand like Ronl! When after a week confined in her suite, Miriam stubbornly declared that her mind had not wavered on the matter, the king flew into a violent rage with her. "You spoilt brat!" he had shouted at her, shocking his scribe out of his stupor. "You will not marry Ronl as long as I still suck Ithmarian air," he vowed.

Miriam had stormed from the throne room in a very un-princess-like manner after that and ran up to the battlements. There were parts of Ithmar's battlements where a voice could carry a long way. Miriam was not one to keep her tantrums to herself and took full advantage of this. "Ooh, I hate you," she screamed at the top of her lungs, stamping her feet. "I wish an airy-plane would burn your precious little kingdom to the ground around your ears,"

Two things happened quite quickly after that. Firstly, a sentry upon hearing the princess cursing two things that he loved dearly and was sworn to protect, became quite outraged at her words and tutted, quietly, under his breath - she was a princess after all! Secondly, an incredibly bored dragon who had been drifting among the clouds overhead looking for mischief, heard her.

A dragon is a rather odd creature, even by Quathliom's very broad standards. It lives its life floating upside down suspended from a grossly bloated belly, with its neck and tail hanging down limply, their great length and weight preventing the creature from lifting either more than a few feet. Being necessarily quite lazy, a dragon will pretty much go wherever the wind takes it. When pushed to exert itself, it swings its pendulous appendages a few feet at variance with each other to create a shimmying kind of movement that it controls with four - proportionally speaking - small, bat-like wings that it uses like rudders.

A cross between a hot air balloon and an airship, a dragon's stomach works like a chemical plant, creating among other things, helium and hot air. These it feeds separately into two inflatable cavities, the combination of which it uses to maintain and regulate its buoyancy. One byproduct of this process is a superheated mucus discharge - a kind of napalm snot if you like - that it vents through a boney nostril-like aperture below its mouth, or in short bursts to defend itself or stun larger prey, which it then sweeps up in its wide flat mouth and breaks down with enzymes into a digestible sludge over a period of several weeks. Mostly though, a dragon will feed on the wing - so to speak - confusing its intended prey by changing the colour of its scales rapidly in an effort to blend in with its background. This often sparse source of energy it supplements by using other specially adapted scales like solar panels, and by creating carbohydrates through photosynthesis in a similar way to the way that a tree does.

Dragons mate on the wing - awkwardly - and give birth to their young several feet from the ground. The young remain grounded for several days while they slowly inflate their lift sacks for the first time, and this is when a dragon is at its most vulnerable. The same infants then return to their birthing site as juveniles once every three years to stretch their sacks further as they mature into adults, after which they become too big to ground themselves.

But for this vulnerability, Derrian's people might have been at the mercy of the dragons, as was very nearly the case several centuries earlier. It had taken a cruel and bloody campaign, and some serious mediation afterwards by the wizards to bring about an uneasy stalemate between the land and the sky dwellers. But for the occasional sheep mysteriously catching fire, that stalemate had proved effective.

An invitation from a member of a ruling house was however an invitation, whether it came on a gold trimmed card or via the mouth of a rash young princess who might have been expected to show a little more maturity and self-control; at least that was how Baelbeth chose to see it. He dropped from the sky quickly, his rapid venting searing the lichen from the crenelated tower above the wall walkway as he did. The air rippled angrily above Miriam and the soldier, and it was an unprocessed instinct that sent them both scurrying for the safety of the steps just in the nick of time.

King Roberin upon hearing what had happened, immediately sent his soldiers to the walls with crossbows, but the walls had not been built to protect its defenders from an aerial attack, and the bowmen were dangerously exposed. Baelbeth swept the wall again and again with a long exhalation of superheated gas that drove its defenders back towards the steps, or sent them jumping from the wall walkway to an uncertain fate in the moat below, screaming loudly and trailing smoke.

Baelbeth was pretty average as adult dragons went. That does not mean much if you are a bowman firing bolts upwards at a creature that measures a little under six hundred feet from its head to the top of its elongated lift sack. Consider also that a dragon's brain and all of its vital organs are located just below its lift sack, above a thick protective plate of fused ribs and vertebrae, a few feet of muscle and a layer of scales, and you will realise just how futile their efforts were.

Few people get close enough to a dragon to study its anatomy, so it is no surprise that the soldiers loosed most of their bolts at Baelbeth's head where they shattered against his scales or bounced off harmlessly. One or two found soft crevices between his scales and stuck, but they were like tiny little splinters to Baelbeth, and only served to irritate him. Baelbeth turned this irritation on a small cavalry unit that rode out of the castle in a valiant attempt to draw him away from the wall. They barely made the end of the drawbridge, and it was a pitiful few who reached the safety of the castle unscathed.

Roberin listened in dismay and growing anger as his newly appointed sergeant - the old one having been taken to the infirmary - made his report. Fortunately most of the reservists were at home on their smallholdings, mucking out their pigs or bent over a plough complaining about rocks in the soil, otherwise the butcher's bill might have been much higher than it was. As it was, of the forty regulars that Roberin kept at the castle, nineteen were either dead, or so close to it as to make very little difference, and a further five were too badly injured to be of any further use. Of those who were still able to stand a watch or fight, several had painful burns that needed treatment. This left Roberin with a handful of frightened soldiers, a rapidly promoted sergeant, an ageing half crippled training yard master and an assortment of domestics to defend the castle against the single biggest threat that his tiny kingdom had ever faced!

Roberin's mind turned to the infirmary as he listened. As good as his physician was, he would have given his right arm for a magical healer. He was a warrior king who had stood shoulder to shoulder with his men twice in a shield wall, and had earned enough scars and aches to prove his credentials to any man, yet the thought of that place was enough to send him into a cold sweat. He could almost hear their screams and moans, could almost smell the blood and the sickly sweet stench of more pungent bodily expulsions if he closed his eyes and dwelled on it. Roberin gripped the arms of his throne tightly. The age-blackened wood was hard and ungiving beneath his white knuckles. It anchored him, reminded him of his duty and helped to focus his thoughts as it had so many times in the past.

Any hope that Miriam might have harboured that her father was unaware of what she had done up on the battlements were crushed when a curt summons was delivered to her by a serving boy. Miriam swept into the assembly hall after what she considered was an appropriate delay, her face a fine blend of innocence and insolence. She stepped forward and kissed the king's cheek, but it was like kissing a stone for all the warmth he returned. "Are you annoyed at me, father?" she asked, knowing full well that he was livid.

Roberin stood up and stepped menacingly towards his daughter, his fists clenched into tight balls of rage. "Annoyed!" he roared down at her, stepping to the edge of the dais upon which his throne stood. "If you were not my daughter, I would have a pike-man spit you and hang your flailing body from a flagpole in the hope that that creature might take you and choke on your sour carcass." He shook his head and sighed. "I've been advised however," he said with an irritated glance at five old men who were sat off to one side of the dais trying to look as un-there as possible, "that in this more enlightened age, even I must follow my own laws. They have suggested that I should send you away until I am feeling more..." He looked at them again and ground his teeth together as he said, "rational."

Miriam had lowered her head, for once not daring to answer him back. "Sire?" she said meekly with a little bob.

"Scribe," the king growled, turning to face a wizened little man who was sat at a desk to one side scribbling away, unaware that he was being personally addressed. "SCRIBE!" he repeated with more volume.

The scribe looked up slowly, "Sire?" he asked.

"You're a deaf old fool," the king told him.

The scribe nodded. "Should I write that down, Sire?" he asked.

Roberin liked his scribe and tolerated a lot from him. He liked, respected and - importantly - trusted all of the people who held positions in his court, otherwise they would not have held their positions. They were a thick skinned and bolshy bunch who had opinions that they were generally not afraid to express. He liked that about them too. It is likely that they liked him for much the same reasons, though he had never felt the inclination to ask them if that was the case.

Roberin grinned despite himself, but the grin was gone when he turned back to face his daughter. "Write this down you old twit: Miriam is to leave my land until the dragon has gone, or until a way can be found to get rid of it. If she should then choose to return, I will decide on a suitable punishment."

The scribe could not help but smile to himself as he wrote. This was a detail that was not lost on Miriam.

Miriam had never been one to let little things like a dragon and banishment keep her from what she wanted. She was already hatching a plan as she was being led from the hall. Miriam would find some useless imbecile to pose as a dragon slayer, then come home with him. With luck the dragon would have destroyed her father's little army by then, allowing her to seize power from him with Ronl's help. Miriam would then allow Ronl to marry her as payment for his services. Afterwards, a poisoned drink to toast their union or a sharp stiletto from beneath the pillow on their wedding night, then the throne would be hers to command along with his men. Afterwards she would be seen as the heroine who saved her people from the vicious outlaw who had tried to take her throne. Ronl's ragtag band would enlist in her own army in return for full pardons for their crimes against her kingdom. It seemed like the perfect plan to a pampered young princess who had no idea how things worked in the real world.

"Temtan!" Nifnaff mumbled as the name of the she troll came unbidden to his thoughts. Temtan was the sound of a hammer striking granite; 'Tem' as the hammer strikes, 'tan' the smaller second strike after the slight rebound. 'Tem-tan, tem-tan, tem-tan, tem-tan', as his adolescent pulse raced at the very sight of her. They had been playmates for a while, despite her being a few seasons older than he was, and she had learned a great deal about the male of the specie during some of that play, but their age difference and her swifter journey into puberty had ended all of that, and a juvenile Nifnaff had thought that his heart would break.

His mind swam on, finally arriving at the pivotal moment when he had attacked his brother. He relived it again. How inevitable it seemed to him now, and how utterly avoidable. He had been barely more than a child at the time, immature and driven by urges that even now he did not fully understand. This time he did not attack his brother. This time he grabbed his shoulder and pulled him around, desperate to explain, to beg his forgiveness, but it was Ronl's face that stared back at him.

"He's wakin' up, Ronl," someone said.

"I know that you bloody fool," Ronl snapped back at the man, adding, "I've got eyes."

Nifnaff dipped back into that memory moment and drew all of his juvenile anger from it. His temples throbbed with the ache of holding on to it, then he let all that hate and jealousy go in a single blinding and murderous movement. His arm flew forward against the ropes, tearing strands, pulling fibres apart. Fortunately for Ronl the thick ropes held still, but Nifnaff had the satisfaction of seeing the man go white with shock.

Eight men ran forward with their swords drawn, but Ronl raised his hand. "No!" he shouted in a trembling voice. "Drug him again. I don't want him dead; not just yet."

It was early evening when Nifnaff regained consciousness again. There was a single guard watching him - the second having gone to attend to a call of nature. The guard heard him stir and called to the other guard who was just returning to go and tell Ronl. Nifnaff used that unobserved moment to flex his arm against his already weakened restraints.

Ronl came quickly. He had five men with him, their blowpipes held ready lest Nifnaff make another attempt on his life.

Nifnaff ignored the men. He watched Ronl's eyes. There was fear in them still, even though his stance and expression suggested otherwise. "I guess that we are both prisoners. The difference is that I have no choice in the matter."

Ronl laughed, but it was weak and unconvincing. "I'm not the one who's tied up," he pointed out.

Nifnaff smiled despite his discomfort. "There are many kinds of imprisonment," he answered. "You are mad, and you can no more escape that than I can my bonds."

"And if I am mad?" Ronl asked. "What good'll that do you? You'll still end up as a rug on my floor when I've done with you."

Nifnaff shrugged as much as the ropes that were restraining him permitted. "And you will still be mad."

Ronl turned his back on Nifnaff. He gestured for one of his men to come over. "I want that thing beating, then drugging again," he snapped, then added, "and throw some water over him and get the dung cleared away; he's starting to smell like a cesspit."

The man looked nervous. "Can we drug him first, then beat him?"

"A little," Ronl said, relenting slightly.

Roberin ordered his people into the lower halls and cellars to wait it out. The dragon finding no ready targets for his sport soon got bored and left, but any hopes that Roberin harboured that the dragon was gone for good were swiftly dashed as the first fleeing families from the surrounding villages and farms started to wash up at his gates.

Roberin sent what riders he could spare out to warn others about the dragon, and to round up his reservists. Just over a third of his part time soldiers answered his call to arms, and a good many of these were reluctant and needed some coercing when they learned what had happened to those who had already tried to fight the beast off.

Roberin was more disappointed than angry. It was a point of honour with him that he should try not to expect more from his people than he was willing to give himself; it was a point of pride that he was prepared to spill the last drop of his own blood to protect them and his kingdom should it be required. They had given as much and more in the past to defend Ithmar, the result of which had been a lasting peace with their neighbours, but peace softens the spine. His father had told him that. Roberin had not agreed with him at the time, or at least not agreed with his solution, which was to go looking for trouble. Now he was not so sure.

The castle was built to hold out against a siege. Roberin had never needed to put it to the test before, but he had lived there all of his life, and his intimacy with the castle left him in no doubt that it would hold against several such dragons, should they come. The castle was built on top of two converging underground streams that fed a lake further down in the valley. It boasted among other things, two communal toilet blocks, several small sanitation stations, two bath houses, a pub, an ice cellar, three large storehouses, kitchens, a smithy come armoury, stables, and an infirmary. The only thing that it lacked was enough space to accommodate all the people who were now seeking refuge there!

Roberin had never imagined that he had so many people in his little kingdom! Every morning saw more and more of them banging at his gates, staring nervously over their shoulders while they waited to be let in. He let them in - of course he let them in. They were his people, and he would have seen them crammed into every last inch of his castle rather than leave even one out there to face the dragon.

Baelbeth was off having a rare old time, burning farms and killing anything that was daft enough to be on foot under his particular patch of the sky, then a few horsemen showed up. Armed only with crossbows and unencumbered by heavy armour, they led him a merry old dance, charging at him, firing their bows and wheeling away at the last moment.

Again and again they attacked, coming at him in twos and threes then riding away as others took their places. It was a rather courageous if somewhat futile gesture on their part that Baelbeth indulged for the sport it provided. When after a couple of days the riders showed no sign of giving up, he tired of the activity and went back to burning the surrounding farms and villages, except that most of them were now deserted. Baelbeth was furious when he realised that the riders had been sent to distract him. Frustrated and angry, he headed back to the castle.

Castle Ithmar held against the worst of the dragon's rage, but Baelbeth was persistent and imaginative. One of his favourite tricks was dropping flaming sheep on to the castle's many roofs. It is amazing how much damage a well placed burning sheep can cause when dropped from a great enough height, but though they caused a lot of damage to the rooftops and a few wooden outbuildings, it also provided the castle's beleaguered defenders with a ready supply of cooked meat.

Roberin was listening to a report about a fight between two men that had apparently started over food. The men involved were stood before him. One had the makings of a black eye and the other sported a thick lip and a broken nose. Neither of the men could meet their king's eyes as he started to berate them. "We've grilled mutton dropping out of the heavens, and you're fighting over scraps like starving dogs!"

he growled at them. He was about to say more when a soldier hurried in and crunched to attention. "What?" Roberin snapped irritably.

The soldier was young and barely filled his uniform, but he was used to dealing with his king's occasional peevishness and took nothing of it. "Your daughter, Sire," he said with a slight inclination of his head, "Princess Miriam has..."

Miriam picked that moment to come waltzing into the hall with a reluctant and road wary Ralph in tow.

Roberin gave the two shamed brawlers a withering look and waved them away. The look only intensified as it swept across Ralph and settled on his daughter. No words were needed to express his opinion of either one of them. "Why have you come back?" he asked her.

Miriam dropped a slight curtsy and smiled nervously at her father. "I have brought someone to deal with your little problem."

"Little problem!" Roberin was on his feet, his face red with rage.

Miriam glared back at her father for a moment then dropped her gaze to the floor. "This man," she said, bridling her temper, "dared the wrath of the wizards by killing one of their own right under their noses, and he lived to tell the tale! A little old airy-plane should be nothing compared to that."

Roberin raised a skeptical eyebrow at Ralph. "Are you salvation, folly, or the salt in my wounds?" he asked with typical bluntness.

Ralph looked from father to daughter and back again. "I, I," he stammered.

That was all the answer that Roberin had expected. He knew his daughter for the conniver that she was and found himself almost pitying the fool in front of him. "That's what I thought," he said dryly, then looked at Miriam. "I should have you hung from the battlements by your pretty ringlets and let that damned creature get gut-rot feeding on your sour flesh," he spat at her, then shouted, "get out of my sight."

Miriam was about to object, then thought better of it. Being told to get out of his sight was not quite the same thing as being told to leave the castle, which meant that she was at least where she wanted to be for now, albeit not quite as she had planned it. She raised her chin slightly and gave a haughty little sniff at the room in general, then turned slowly on her heel and walked casually from the hall.

Ralph watched her go. He stood in the middle of the throne room fidgeting nervously, not sure whether he should stay put or follow her.

Roberin stared at him long and hard and asked in an almost conversational tone, "are you a brave fool or a foolish trickster?"

Ralph reddened intensely. "I'm not trying to trick anyone," he answered in an offended tone, then admitted with some chagrin that he was feeling pretty foolish though.

Roberin allowed a brief flicker of a smile to cross his troubled face. "Go," he said, waving his hand in dismissal. "You don't need to be here."

Ralph turned to leave then stopped. He turned back to face the old king again, frustration showing clearly on his face.

Roberin turned a quizzical eye on Ralph that further puckered a small fold of skin under his left eye, where the cheek guard of his helmet had been driven into his face by a big brute of a fellow in a shield wall many years earlier. "Yes?" he asked impatiently.

Ralph felt the strength of the man. It was more than just his physical presence, which even dimmed by his advanced years could not be ignored. It was there in the directness of his stare. It reinforced and gave weight to his words. This king was not like the monarchy that he saw on television greeting visiting dignitaries and performing state ceremonies. There was no pomp or ostentatious display of personal wealth, no simpering entourage hanging onto his coattail. This was a king who lived in the same world as his subjects, able to reach into their lives directly if he chose to. Such a man might be a tyrant, a father or a pompous old fool to his people; might be loved, despised or feared by them, or be indifferent to their needs. The words of such a man had the weight of a judgment behind them. "I don't want to go," he said, scarcely believing what he was saying.

Roberin eyed him coldly. He was more annoyed by his daughter, but this fool was starting to test his patience.

"You can't just send me away without at least giving me a chance," Ralph mumbled as his already weak resolve, crumbled further still under that unforgiving gaze.

"I've given you the chance to stay alive, and to walk away from something that doesn't concern you, which I daresay is probably more than you deserve." Roberin waved his hand in dismissal again. "You've nothing to prove here."

"Maybe I have," Ralph said, surprising himself further.

"Be careful of your words," Roberin warned him. "Some people think that they are just sounds that get hung together for effect. I am not one of those people."

Ralph knew that he should walk away. The lowest stable-hand in Roberin's castle was more of a soldier than he was. He shrugged and smiled uncomfortably, not knowing what else to do. "My sister used to say that my mouth would get me in trouble," he answered lamely.

Roberin chortled. "I would imagine that she was right?"

"More often than she deserved to be," Ralph agreed.

Roberin stood up and stepped down from his dais. He gave Ralph a thoughtful look then took hold of his hands and turned them so that they were palm up. Ralph pulled away instinctively, but Roberin's bony hands were like vices. "You're not a fighter," he observed, releasing them. He seemed to reach a decision, which he then duly announced. "You can do nothing here that'll make things worse, and I would be a fool to turn away any man who can point a spear with things as they are." He looked at a young boy who was sat on a stool against a wall trying not to fall asleep. "Find him a bunk, then take him to the yard master, and for the gods sakes tell him to find him something more sensible. How you intended to fight a dragon with a sword like that is beyond me!" he told Ralph.

Ralph actually staggered. "Dragon!" he sputtered in surprise. "She asked me to get rid of a small airy-plane, not a dragon!" Roberin said, "Ah!" as the final piece thumped home. "They're the same thing. Everyone knows that."

"I didn't," Ralph told him.

"Then you're stupid as well as foolish," Roberin snapped a little more harshly than he had intended. He sighed. "You can still leave if you wish."

Ralph looked at Roberin uncertainly, but did not speak. He knew that anything that he said now would be a decision, and he did not have enough courage or conviction to make a decision either way at that moment. Roberin could see the fear and doubt in Ralph. He took his silence as a stubborn refusal to give in to it and he approved. He grunted a dismissal and turned his attention back to more pressing matters.

Ralph followed the boy from the hall. He needed time to think, to consider his options. A lesser person than King Roberin might have conscripted him against his will or had him turfed out on his ear. He might even have suspected some duplicity on his part and had him thrown into a dungeon, or worse. That he had done none of these things was not lost on Ralph, and he decided to sleep on it and make a decision in the morning.

The yardmaster was a squat brick of a man with no discernible neck and a profusion of scars. He took the measure of Ralph with a single glance and pronounced his judgment in the form of a grunt. "Kit him out you say?" he asked the boy.

The young boy could not help but grin as he nodded. "Bunk and kit is what the old man said."

The yardmaster grunted again and said, 'this way then."

Ralph followed the man across the partially covered yard to a studded oak door and waited while he fumbled with the heavy bolt.

"Here," the yardmaster said, pushing the door open and motioning for Ralph to go in. He followed Ralph in and took a lamp from the wall next to the door. This he duly lit by igniting the end of his thumb and holding it to the oil soaked wick. The yardmaster could not help but notice Ralph staring at his hand as he did so. He raised his thumb and conjured up the flame again, then laughed at Ralph's obvious surprise. "What sort of man marvels at the most basic elemental magic?" he asked.

"The sort that gets hit by lightning on a world without any magic and wakes up on this one," Ralph told him.

"Ah," the yardmaster said, "that sort." He took the lamp and lit two more from it as he went further in, illuminating all but the furthest edges of the chamber. "Most humans have some magic, even a bit. I think it has something to do with how we first got here. There are other races with magic, but nothing like as powerful as our witches and wizards have," he said with some pride. "And you have none at all?" he asked, then shrugged. "Some come to it late, or not at all."

The yardmaster walked over to a wooden throne. It was a simple chair that had purportedly been cut from a fallen limb from one of the first great oaks to sink its roots into Derrian soil. The yardmaster did not know if that was true or not, but the throne was ancient and almost black, and its arms had become worn with many years of use. He sat down heavily on the throne and leaned back. "This throne has had more royal arses polishing it than I care to consider," he told Ralph. "The old king had it replaced when Roberin was just a lad, but Roberin don't like getting rid of stuff like this. He's sentimental about the past, so it ended up in this storeroom gatherin' dust 'nd mould with the other crap."

The throne was stood between four squat pillars on its own. Around it trestle tables and shelves were stacked up with old weapons and armour that were waiting to be repaired or recycled.

"This stuff should be in a museum," Ralph said, adding, "some of it must be worth a fortune."

"To who?" the yardmaster asked. He seemed to consider the possibility, then frowned. "Get rid of that rubbish you're wearing over there," he told Ralph.

Ralph left the storeroom less encumbered and less ridiculous than he had been going in. The cumbersome metal armour was gone and had been replaced with a padded bowl shaped helmet, vambraces and greaves, and a quilted over-shirt that smelled of horse. Instead of the two handed ceremonial great-sword, he had been given a short stabbing sword, a knife, and a long-handled pickaxe that was hung on his back alongside a steel buckler. The buckler was blackened steel and had a bronze boss that had been crafted in the shape of a goat's head. The boss put Ralph in mind of the scar on his chest, and he had asked if he could have the small shield. The yardmaster did not care one way or the other and said as much.

The yardmaster had a vague recollection of the buckler having been a battle trophy from one of Roberin's grandfather's run-ins with a tribe called the Illefed. The Illefed were for the most part goat herders, hence the design on the small shield. They had moved onto an area of land that was mostly scrub and rocks, believing that no one would care about a piece of Ithmarian territory that was barely habitable. They had been wrong in that assumption, as had King Billfarlen in assuming that they would leave without a fight when he ordered them off of his land.

The Illefed had stood their ground, matching the Ithmarian soldiers almost shield for shield, but their leader surprised the Ithmarian's by making his people remove their weapons before coming forward to meet the Ithmarian shield wall. The sergeant leading Billfarlen's soldiers knew what it was to stand in a shield wall pinned against an enemy who was trying to hamstring you or stick a blade into your groin. Albeit that he was somewhat bemused by their actions, he ordered his own men to do likewise. And so it was that the two shield walls came together on a misty morning in a loud and brutal shoving match that lasted for nearly three hours, during which time not a single life was lost.

Ralph asked the yardmaster who won. "I reckon we all did," he told Ralph. "Billfarlen heard what they did and decided to let them stay put under the condition that they become Ithmarian citizens, and our bloodlines are the richer for it."

"Yes," Ralph said, "but who won the battle?"

The yardmaster grunted. He grabbed two blunted training swords from a barrel and tossed one to Ralph. Ralph caught the weapon - just - and raised it uncertainly.

"Defend yourself," the yardmaster said coldly, "or I'll give you a cut that'll sit pretty on yer face fer a lifetime." He flicked his blade forward and tapped the edge of Ralph's sword. "You were bold enough when you came riding in with the princess I heard, so let's see what yer've got."

Ralph gripped the handle of the training sword tightly and lifted it into what he hoped was an on-guard position. He struggled to hold it there as he tried to decide what to do next. The yardmaster was not so indecisive. He stepped forward, catching Ralph off guard, and drove his elbow upwards into his cheek. Ralph dropped the sword and staggered backwards. He could taste blood welling warm and salty in his mouth as he tongued the torn flesh in his cheek. He had not expected the old man to do that, which he guessed was probably the point!

There are two kinds of violence. Boxing is one type. It involves two people choosing to get into a roped off square with the intention of trying to punch each other's lungs out. The other kind of violence, the one where at least one of those who is involved wishes that they were not, Ralph did not like. It scared him, made him feel sick; it demoralised a person, left them feeling ineffective and inadequate, but more than that, it destroyed a person's faith in the goodness of others.

There were times in Ralph's life when he had walked away from a fight knowing that it was the right thing to do, yet despising himself for not having stood his ground, and there were times when he had stubbornly stood his ground when a wiser man would have walked away. Taken on balance, it was the times when he had not stood his ground that had caused him the most regret.

Ralph picked the training sword up and took a clumsy swing at the yardmaster. As angry as he was, he still held his blade short of the point where it might actually strike him. The yardmaster had expected as much, and swiped the sword from his hand as the blade passed. He stepped in close and hooked his ankle behind Ralph's and pushed hard, sending him sprawling on the floor.

The yardmaster was on Ralph almost before he hit the ground and brought the tip of his sword to rest firmly on his chest. "Tell me, who has one this fight," he said, pushing down slightly.

"You have," Ralph answered grudgingly when the yardmaster applied a little more pressure.

"No," the yardmaster snapped at him. "Everybody loses something in a fight. The trick is to lose less and to live long enough to learn that lesson."

"My dad once told me that any fool can pick a fight, but it's a wiser man who knows when to pick a fight, and a wiser man still who also knows when not to," a boy said, surprising both men as he stepped from a doorway. He had been watching the exchange between the two men and felt that maybe it was a good moment to step in.

"Sire," the yardmaster said, greeting the young prince. He lifted the sword from Ralph's chest and smiled at the lad.

"Illefed wasn't the name of the tribe. My dad said it was a misspelling," the boy told Ralph. "The rider who came back and reported that they were squatting on our land was asked who they were, and he said that he didn't know, but that they looked as though they were ill fed. My dad says that they were just a bunch of scraggy arsed land thieves, with more balls than brains." He looked at the sky thoughtfully. "The dragon's off causing mischief elsewhere today," he observed, changing the subject.

The yardmaster grimaced. "Don't imagine that that foul bag of wind has got bored with us," he said.

The young prince nodded his agreement and turned to Ralph. "You're not a fighter." He raised his hand to stall any reply that Ralph might make. "That's not a bad thing, unless your standing with a sword in your hand pretending to be one."

Ralph was burning up with embarrassment when he walked away from the yard. He expected to hear laughter pursuing him. The silence was somehow worse. He would have left the castle there and then, but he did not relish the idea of being under open sky if the dragon was still about.

Unable to leave, he opted for the next best thing and went looking for somewhere where he could get drunk. Ralph eventually found what served as a tavern in the castle, but was disappointed to discover that all of the barrels and bottles had been put under lock and key on the king's orders. "It's cus' ov what's happenin'," the tavern keeper explained. "The king reckons people need to keep their wits about 'em." He smiled apologetically and went back to wiping the empty counter.

Ralph was depressed, humiliated and sober, none of which he could do much about the way that things were. He was smarting still at the young prince's unvarnished assessment of his worth, but as hard as he tried, he could not bring himself to dislike him, or the old training yard master for having so forcefully demonstrated the point. Even King Roberin for all his bluntness had not been unfair with his evaluation. Ralph had not said that he would help to defend the castle against the dragon. He had not said that he would not either. He had thought that he might, but that was - he now realised - a world away from actually doing it.

With nothing better to occupy him, Ralph succumbed to his natural curiosity and went exploring. He was in a castle after all; a real castle with real soldiers and creaking doors, and an actual drawbridge that went over a moat that had water in it that was not full of shopping trollies and floating carrier-bags! His humour improved a little, then ebbed when his wandering brought him via a different route, back to the training yard.

Ralph turned to go, but he had not been noticed, and instead sat down on a step and watched as the yardmaster took advantage of a dragon free sky to exercise a group of youngsters who had grown lazy and fractious cooped up as they were.

"Shields and sticks, and smartly to it," the yardmaster bellowed, clipping a boy who was moving too slow for his liking around the ear as he sauntered passed. "Pair off and form up in two lines facing each other." There was a collective moan as they realised the significance of this instruction. "Close up and lock yer shields, and quit yer bellyaching," he growled at them.

What followed was a slow and brutal contest of strength, endurance, and a struggle to get traction in the dirt. This was punctuated with groans and curses as their wooden shields ground and clacked together. Here and there Ralph caught furtive little movements as short wooden poles were thrust blindly through gaps between the shields or swung over the top. As often as not the wood found nothing but air or glanced off of a shield edge, but every now and then a squeal rose above the general hullabaloo, reminding Ralph that these fiercely determined little scrappers were children still.

For long minutes both lines held their ground, then a girl in the middle staggered when a boy managed to kick her hard in the shin. The children who were stood to either side of the girl moved to close the gap before any advantage could be gained, but the girl took her place again quickly with tears of anger streaming down a face that would have been pretty, were it not for the murderous look that was now on it.

The wall collapsed anyway, but the girl's spirit and determination made a lasting impression on Ralph. Her efforts had not been missed by the yardmaster either, and the ugly little man showed his approval with a wink that brought a bright blush to her cheeks, one of which was sporting the makings of what would be a glorious bruise.

Ralph waited until the yardmaster had finished with the group, then putting his pride aside, went to speak to him, to ask if he would give him some basic training. The man was an unsettling mix of hard and ugly, much of which was the result of souvenirs that he had picked up in various fracases, only some of which had been in the defence of his king and country. Ralph's earlier encounter with him did not leave him hopeful, but the yardmaster surprised him by agreeing.

When Ralph was not at the training yard adding to his collection of cuts and bruises, he was on watch up on the walls, hoping and hoping not to see the dragon. He still knew next to nothing about dragons, for all that the other guards spoke of little else, and his quest to rectify that took him to a small room with a flaking sign above the door that made the exaggerated claim that the dark dank space beyond it was a library.

The library as it was, consisted of an old table, a chair, three shelves, a rusted mop bucket and four fusty stacks of books that had not found their way onto the empty shelves. In one of the stacks was a children's book with its back cover missing and several pages so badly damaged by mildew that they were unreadable. The book was entitled: An encyclopaedic journey for the young adventurer. Within its damaged pages Ralph found a few short chapters on dragons that described them in the most dramatic terms. This was accompanied by a simple drawing of a creature that resembled a hot air balloon with its strings trailing from having lost its basket.

Ralph's one and only close encounter with a dragon had been quick and mostly viewed from inside its mouth. The only thing that he had discovered from that unhappy experience was that a dragon's breath smelt a lot like what he would have expected a coal miner's socks to smell like after a twelve hour shift.

Ralph closed the book and ventured up to the castle wall. His shift on the wall was not due to start for an hour, but the evening was drawing in and he wanted to see if he could catch a glimpse of the creature in the distance before it was too dark to see anything. Despite several reported sightings, he had yet to see the beast, and would have begun to doubt its existence, were it not for the nervousness of the guards on the wall and the extensive fire damage to the castle's many rooftops that was visible from the wall.

Ralph did not know it, but the spiral stairway that he used to get up to the battlements was the very same one that Miriam and the guard had fled down. The stone steps were worn from a great many years of use, and one or two of them had been carefully chiseled down and refaced with new stone. Ralph thought about how many soldiers had trudged down those very same steps, yawning after a long and uneventful watch.

Ralph dragged his finger along the sooty scorched brickwork and rubbed it against his thumb. He rested his hands on the cold stone between two stumpy merlons and looked out. The land that he could see from his vantage point was a breathtaking expanse of blotchy windswept foliage, and exposed rocks that fell away into a wide grassy plain. It was wild and beautiful and humbling and uplifting, and a hundred other words that did not do the place enough justice, and he understood as he stood there, why generations of Ithmarians had fought to make this land their home, and why they would not abandon it even now.

Ralph straightened and shoved his hands under his armpits to warm them. It was cold at this elevation, and made cuttingly so by the ever present wind that tousled his hair. He thought about Miriam standing on this wall, petulantly issuing her invitation to the dragon. Maybe if he called out to it, maybe it would come to him? He opened his mouth to shout, then closed it again. He felt suddenly very exposed and fragile, and this feeling drove him down from the wall before the end of his watch, leaving a nearby sentry looking nervously skyward and wondering if some prescience on Ralph's part had caused his hasty departure.

Ralph spent the remainder of that night and the next day on the edge of a precipice. The dragon hung over him like a great cloud. Even the mention of the creature was enough to cause his chest to tighten and his hands to tremble so badly that he had to clench them behind his back so that others would not notice. He wanted to believe that he would stand and fight alongside Ithmar's soldiers if the dragon returned, but the truth of the matter was that he did not know what he would do. Standing up on the wall playing at being a soldier did not alter that truth or diminish it any. He was afraid. He was afraid that others would see that he was afraid and think him a coward. He was afraid that ultimately that would prove to be the case. Stay or leave. Those were his choices, and neither would make a difference to these people. The dragon was a spite filled force beyond his or any of their reckoning, and he was just one man among many, the least of whom was more accustomed to pointing a weapon than he was. Stay or leave; live or possibly die. Looked at in those terms, there was only one sensible course of action.

Ralph loaded his old armour and a few other bits onto a small handcart then slipped quietly into the night. This raised only the mildest interest from a bored guard on the gate, who having received no orders to the contrary, inspected the contents of the cart and allowed Ralph to pass.

Roberin nearly choked on a syrup cake when a soldier burst in on his breakfast unannounced the following morning.

"Begging yer pardon, Sire," the soldier said quickly. He noted with some concern, the funny colour that the king had turned and asked, "would you be wanting me to pat you firmly on the back, Sire?"

Roberin shook his head angrily. "This had better be important," he warned, wheezing slightly.

The soldier nodded. "Sorry, Sire, but yes it is. It's that foreign feller," he said. "He's outside the castle. He's..." He paused uncertainly.

"Get on with it man!" Roberin bellowed, using the room's acoustic qualities to good effect.

The guard started slightly and swallowed hard. "He's lit a bonfire and he's stood there jigging about and waving his arms, and hollering all sorts of obscenities about the airy-plane's parentage and the likes, and..."

There were dozens of people up on the wall when Roberin got there, and he had to order it cleared. When there was enough room, he crossed to the wall and looked out. What he saw left him open mouthed and mute. True enough, Ralph was stood there in the silly suit of armour that he had been wearing that first day, jiggling around and shouting all manner of abuse at the sky. In front of him was a bonfire that had been covered with damp leaves, and was belching a plume of thick white smoke into the air.

Roberin half guessed what he was up to and was about to order some of his men to go and drag the fool back in to the castle, but Ralph was some distance away, and Roberin had to weigh the risk of putting his few soldiers at risk -

soldiers that he could ill afford to lose attempting to rescue a madman. There was also a part of him that was curious to see how this silliness would play itself out, and so he waited and watched.

Ralph was not in fact jiggling around in front of the bonfire. He was actually huddled in a shallow hole that he had dug during the night, peering out from underneath a big unwieldy long-shield. He was tugging on a length of rope that was attached at the other end to something that only vaguely resembled a human form, at a distance, squinting. The chainmail and other paraphernalia that Miriam had coerced him into wearing, was dressed over a wooden frame that he had nailed together, and tied to the two-handed great-sword which he had hammered into the ground as a stake.

Baelbeth did not hear Ralph's words in quite the same way that a human would have heard them. He felt them across countless millions of fine hairs that covered the surface of his head and floatation sack. Long before he saw the bonfire and the jiggling metal marionette, he new where Ralph was hiding.

Of course there was some sort of deception intended, but great size and great power breeds greater arrogance, and so it did not enter his mind to be overly concerned about what one frightened little human might do.

Ralph squinted as he tried to see more clearly through the smoke, but his eyes were starting to smart and the heat was making the air tremble. The dragon was coming though, its outrageously long neck descending down as though a rope had been dangled from the very heavens by a visiting god. At the end of that impossibly long neck, was a head that resembled a gargantuan doggy poop scoop. Ralph did not see any of this from his place of concealment, but some sixth sense had the hairs on his neck standing up like guards at a royal parade.

An adult hunting dragon's camouflage although far from perfect, is still pretty remarkable. It is difficult enough for a small creature like a chameleon to blend in effectively with its surroundings even when it is keeping very still; to do so when you are the size of a dragon, moving against a moving background, requires a much more complicated process. Most of the scales on a dragon's body are photo-receptive, and each one is paired to a scale on the opposite side of its body. The paired scales transmit and receive average colour information, which each then reproduces by adjusting its pigment. The delay in transmitting, receiving and reproducing a colour, along with the size of each individual scale and the massiveness of a dragon, impacts upon the effectiveness of a dragon's camouflage, and a person would need to be drunk, blind, or blind drunk not to see a dragon coming, but it does however allow it to get closer to its prey before being seen than would otherwise be the case.

Ralph saw the sky start to ripple and blur in a sickening way that could not possibly have been the result of the heat and smoke from the fire alone. He lowered his head quickly so that he could just see over the top of the shield and pulled on the rope even harder. The armour waved its hollow arms like a crazed marionette then proceeded to fall to pieces, but it was too late to matter; Baelbeth had started to vent, and the superheated discharge had engulfed the armour completely.

Ralph cowered in the shallow pit. The shield covering him was big enough and strong enough to absorb the blow of a sword, or even an arrow fired from a distance, but it had never been intended to withstand a mucus discharge that was not too dissimilar to napalm. Ralph could feel the heat radiating through the shield and around its edges, singeing the hairs on the exposed areas of his skin, and warming his clothing to the point where he was sure that they would soon burst into flames. His alarm grew in proportion with the temperature, then it stopped suddenly - the heat that is - leaving behind a deathly silence that was broken every few seconds by the crackling and popping of his charred shield as it started to cool.

Ralph jumped up and threw aside what was left of the smoking shield. It hurt to breathe, and he gasped loudly. He realised that the sleeve of his undershirt had caught fire, and quickly fumbled open the buckle on the shoulder of the gambeson that he was wearing over the top of it. Ralph pulled both garments off and threw them aside. He stared down at the weeping red burn on his arm, then collecting enough of his wits to remember the dragon, turned and stared transfixed into one of its eyes as it slowly turned its wide head towards him.

Every instinct in Ralph's being screamed at him to run, but he resisted it, knowing that he could not possibly hope to outrun the dragon's burning breath, now that he was so close. He stood there for the briefest moment, completely overawed by the dragon's size, then crouched quickly and reclaimed his pickaxe. Ralph took one last longing look over his shoulder, shouted loudly and ran straight at the dragon. It was a matter of several steps taken at a run, a short scrabble up the side of its flattened head, and a moment later he was clinging to its neck for dear life, and wondering what madness had possessed him.

Baelbeth was more put out than surprised. He filled his sack enough to gain a few feet then tilted his head forward in an effort to tip the human off. Ralph did not fall off though. The scales that he was clinging to were thicker at the top, each one overlapping the scales above it. This arrangement of its scales was a consequence of the creature being to all intents and purposes, suspended upside down from its hugely extended stomach, and had the added benefit of giving it more protection against an attack from below. Unfortunately for Baelbeth, it also gave Ralph something to cling to.

A dragon of Baelbeth's size could not raise its head more than a dozen feet with such a long neck, and though the paddle shaped end of his tail could cradle his head in repose whilst in the air, it was not dexterous enough to use as a swat. Perplexed now by this stubborn little man-bug, he inflated his lift sack more. As he rose into the air, he started flapping his small wings vigorously, causing his head and tail to swing back and forth, back and forth like two huge pendulums.

Ralph clung there for dear life with his eyes closed tight shut. He nearly lost his footing twice, but somehow managed not to fall off. Fortunately for Ralph, Baelbeth was only able to keep it up for a minute or so before growing tired, and the movement gradually subsided, leaving both man and dragon dizzy.

Ralph opened his eyes when the motion had almost stopped, and looked down at the diminishing ground. The time when he might have considered letting go had passed. He looked up at the dragon's vast lift sack high above his head and his heart sank. He knew that he could not hold on forever. Damned if he did nothing and caught between a rock and a hard place, Ralph opted for the hard place over the rock that was getting further and further away, and started climbing.

Ralph stopped several times during that long climb, exhausted, but each time he dug a little deeper and found something more. His arms and legs shook with the effort, yet his hurting fingers found their holds and he pushed on, right hand, left foot, push and pull, left hand, right foot, push and pull; and so it went, every foot gained, a tiny victory over his growing despair, every foot the dragon gained in height adding to the ever present fear that he would lose his grip and fall to his death.

How easy it would have been to give in to that fatigue and simply let go; no guilt for having been beaten by odds that had been stacked against him from the outset, just a few gnawing regrets and a long fall cradled by the rushing wind, then oblivion. He did not/could not bring himself to let go though. Giving up was not an unavoidable consequence, it was a decision, and Ralph was either too pig stubborn or too much of a coward - depending on your point of view - to make that decision.

Baelbeth was rising quicker now. Deep inside his body the organs that produced his lift gases were working furiously, taking him higher and higher into the thinning atmosphere. He reasoned that if he could not shake the human off, he could carry it to where the air was too weak for it to breathe.

It was there where his kind lived in their thousands. Massive gasbags drifting on the wind, many of them so big that to descend towards the ground would mean certain death. They were like great lazy sky cows, drifting sedately in the wind, siphoning what nutrients they could from the thin air and soaking up their sun's radiation. The oldest of them were introverted to a point where they were barely aware of themselves, let-alone each other, living their lives in a thoughtless sensory bliss.

Baelbeth hated it there; he hated the sedentary nature of his kind and the thought that he too might one day be as unconscious and uncaring as a clump of spindrift. On the ground there was living as apposed to just life, struggle and change as apposed to endless stagnation, and there was fun to be had. Baelbeth liked to have fun. Fortunately for the objects of his fun, it was not a commonly held view amongst dragons - even those that were still capable of having a view.

Ralph did not know it, but he was very close to the top of the dragon's neck. Weak and almost delirious with fatigue and the effects of the lowering level of oxygen in the air, he barely noticed when the living terrain that he was climbing curved towards the horizontal. Cradled between two thick straps of muscle, he rested for several minutes, but a niggling sense that he was still not safe stopped him giving in to his exhaustion completely. Ralph groaned and pushed himself up onto his hands and knees again and crawled over to where the creature's fused shoulder blades and huge bulbous lift sack were joined together. The scales were much larger there, and he sagged against one of them. He was surprised to find that it gave a little like a firm cushion under his weight.

Ralph stared out at an horizon that was starting to take on a definite curve. He found himself wondering what was beyond it, and regretting that he would probably never get the chance to find out. He giggled at his own silliness as he realised that he was hankering after something that he would not have given two figs about an hour earlier. What had he been thinking of, what had possessed him to be so reckless, and what had he hoped to achieve by forcing an encounter with the dragon? Had he secretly hoped that by facing the dragon and ending it, that he would end the surreal nightmare that he was in and wake up back on Earth? He knew that was stupid, but even so, a part of him still entertained the possibility.

The air was unbearably thin, and the cold cut like knives across Ralph's skin now that he was no longer exerting himself. He wanted to sleep, needed to give in to the dizziness and the intense fatigue that was gripping him, but the sound of his teeth chattering loudly in his head were an annoying distraction. Instinct drew him tighter against the slight warmth that emanated from the base of the dragon's lift sack at his back, but that warmth did little to fend off the bitter cold.

It was then that Ralph saw them, or at least became aware of them; huge blurry hints of thereness betraying the presence of dozens of camouflaged dragons. The shifting colours on their scales did nothing to help Ralph's dizziness as he stared at them. He teetered, almost blanked out, then snapped back to his senses like a man who has just been woken up abruptly.

Fearing that he would pass out at any moment and slide off, he fumbled his hand into the lanyard on his pickaxe handle and pulled his wrist so that the loop tightened about it. Ralph grabbed the handle with numb fingers and tugged the weapon from his back. He sat there listless for a moment, then mustering his strength, swung the pick clumsily in a backhand fashion. The scale that it struck was flexible and somewhat thinner than the scales on the dragon's neck, and the pickaxe tip bit deeply and held fast.

Ralph slumped sideways, his weight dragging at the weapon, twisting it. He gripped the shaft with both hands and tried to pull himself upright again, but there was blood running down the handle, and his fingers slipped a little. He kept his hands there and endured the hot-aches as warm blood ran over his cold-numbed fingers. He watched appalled and fascinated as the dark liquid spilled from the wound in small gushes that kept time with whichever of the dragon's five hearts was pumping it.

The hole that the pickaxe made was little more than a pinprick to a creature the size of Baelbeth, and the blood that was running from it was already starting to slow noticeably. Ralph grew alarmed at the thought of losing that source of warmth, then disappointed, and finally angry. For the briefest moment he had allowed himself to hope that his sacrifice would not be entirely for nothing, but that hope had begun to fade as the blood slowed. Ralph cried out and yanked at the pickaxe hard, twisting and turning it, and again the blood started to flow. He knew then what he had to do, knew in those last terrible moments that he would give his final breath and his last ounce of strength to the task, even if all he achieved by it was to give the dragon a small scar to remember him by.

Ralph pulled himself up onto his knees and drew his short-sword from its sheath. He started stabbing at the fleshy scale a little way from where the pick was embedded. It stuck in a few inches only, but he worked the handle up and down furiously with each stab, shoving the blade deeper and deeper.

The scales covering the dragon's vast lift sack were necessarily elastic, allowing them to expand and contract with it. At that moment the dragon's lift sack was fully inflated, and the flesh and scales covering it were stretched almost to their limit, putting them under more stress than usual.

Ralph's sword cut through the last inch and slid in to the hilt. He held onto the handle and stared at it dumbly as escaping hot gas whistled around the blade, mixing with the blood and spraying his hand and arm with a fine red mist. It was a full thirty seconds before the significance of what had just happened registered on his oxygen starved brain. When it did, he came to his senses with a start, and gripping the handle tighter, started sawing at the scale.

Ralph did not stop despite feeling sick to the stomach at what he was doing. It was crude butchery, as offensive to his nature as any single act could be, but the dragon was a bully and a killer, and he knew in his heart that it enjoyed what it was doing too much to ever stop. He cried out in anger and frustration, but the sound was lost within the greater noise of the gushing gas. He tried to stand up, tried to get more leverage, then slipped in the blood and fell awkwardly, dragging the sword down and out as he did so. It was the loop on the still embedded pickaxe that saved him, preventing him from sliding further as he finally lost consciousness. He was not aware, but as the sword came free, the gas gushing from the wound tore the stretched flesh further, until there was a ragged trembling tear.

Baelbeth realised that he was not rising as quickly as he wanted, and tried to compensate by increasing the pressure in his lift sack. That ultimately proved to be his undoing. As the pressure grew, so did the stress on a wound that was already significant, until at last it gave completely with an almighty whoosh, leaving a flapping hole that was big enough for a double decker bus to drive through.

Baelbeth fought desperately to stay aloft, but his wings were not strong enough to do more than slow down his rapid descent. He hit the ground hard, his head, neck and tail twisting beneath him, flattening, spreading and tearing as his hollow vertebrae were forced apart; yet somehow he still lived, still fought franticly to try to get free of the ground with what little gas remained in his sagging lift sack. He rose a few feet, then fell again as riders from the castle bent low across their horses in a breakneck race to get to him before he could escape.

Ralph was insensible throughout. He regained consciousness only slightly as he was dragged away by two soldiers who had spotted him lying dangerously close to the fallen beast. They were excited, their faces and hands animated as they switched back and forth between praise and commentary, but it was mostly meaningless sounds as he slipped in and out of what was happening around him.

The courtyard was crowded when Ralph was brought in on a cart with an injured soldier. Everyone was asking the same incredulous question: was the dragon really dead? It seemed hardly possible that they should now be free to walk under an open sky without flinching every time a cloud passed over their heads!

Everybody wanted to see their saviour, to touch him in the hope that some of his staggering good luck would rub off onto them. Ralph was delirious again by this point and had only the fuzziest notion of where he was. He did not see Roberin hovering over him, questioning the soldiers who had brought him in. He was not aware of being carried gently from the cart to the infirmary, or of having his fractured arm and cracked rib strapped up, and his numerous scolds and lacerations treated and dressed. One thing alone occupied his thoughts in his more lucid moments: the dragon was dead.

Miriam had watched in stunned disbelief from the windows of her private quarters as Ralph was brought back into the castle. "Well, I am most certainly not going to marry him!" she hissed at one of her maids, then turned and stormed out of the room. She screeched a few more observations on the matter as she quickly changed into her riding clothes and hurried down to the stable.

"Get my horse ready now, you half-wit!"
The groom dropped his shovel with a clatter and grabbed a tangle of tackle from the wall. He hurried away to do his mistress's bidding and returned ten minutes later with her horse in tow. The mare knew the princess's moods all too well and eyed her warily as the groom led it out into the yard. He

rechecked the girth strap and adjusted the stirrups as she got on, then handed the reins up with a mumbled, "Milady."

"Out of my way you maggot!" Miriam snapped at the youth as she snatched the reins from him. She pulled the horse around sharply and jabbed her heels into its sides more forcefully than was necessary.

The groom stepped aside quickly, narrowly avoiding being trodden on. He made a gesture at her retreating back that was probably one of the few things from Earth that had not changed over the years.

"We'll be havin' none of that lad," the stable master scolded, surprising him. "She be a princess, rot her gangly bones, and if you value them two digits you've just saluted her with, you'll be doin' it from the privacy of yer pocket in future."

The groom grinned broadly. His right hand sought the privacy of his pocket and stayed there for a few moments before he retrieved his shovel and went back to mucking out.

Miriam flew through the castle grounds like a small whirlwind, scattering pigeons and people alike. The poor mare's hooves skidded across the cobblestones, striking up sparks and flecks of stone as she pushed it on recklessly. Twice the mare nearly lost its footing, only to recover at the last moment after scrabbling to get traction. Miriam had no care beyond that which fuelled her anger though, and only reined in long enough to sling an insult at the gate guards before riding out of the castle. One of the guards shoved his hand into his pocket and kept it there for a few moments.

The mare was not trained for battle like the bigger destriers, and though Miriam had never been the kindest to her, she had never treated her quite so carelessly before. Seeing the open road beyond the drawbridge before her, the mare gave in to her fright and broke into a breakneck gallop. Miriam clung grimly with her legs and let the mare have her way. She was an excellent rider even if she was not fit to own a horse, or any other feeling creature for that matter.

Miriam threw wild curses at everything and everyone that had ever gotten in the way of her ambitions as she rode away. Not surprisingly it was Ralph and Roberin's names that rolled most frequently from her acid tongue. She even cursed her poor mare to the marrow of its bones for having the audacity to become tired. Fortunately for the mare, Miriam was able to change her horse at a way station and continue on with a creature that was at least as wilful and ill natured as its rider.

It was early evening when Miriam reached the wide stream where she and Ronl had first met a couple of summers back. She had no great sentimental attachment to the place because of that, and she would have ridden on without stopping, but for her horse deciding to take a drink at the water's edge. Miriam dug her heels in and gave it a couple of keen swipes on the rump with her riding crop to get it moving. The horse was a highly strung creature, and rather than trot on timidly as Miriam's own mare would have, it reared and bolted, spilling her messily from the saddle. Fortunately for Miriam the water broke her fall, otherwise she might have broken her neck. Miriam sat there sodden and bedraggled, screeching insensibly and slapping at the water with her dainty little white-knuckled fists.

Miriam stood up and stomped across to the other side of the stream. Three small trees stood together a few feet from the waters edge on the far side, huddled together and hunched by the wind so that they looked like a trio of conspiring old-aged pensioners. The trees were all but leafless now, their fall a soft carpet of pungent smelling mulch under Miriam's feet as she passed beneath them.

Miriam and Ronl had spent time together under those trees. Ronl had later said that it would always be a special place for them, though in truth, neither felt that anything particularly special had happened there. At best it had been a not unpleasant means to an end.

Ronl was the bad boy that every wayward and unworldly-wise little princess dreams of goading her daddy with, and Miriam was the royal brat that every thug with an ambition would kill to get his hands on. As is so often the case with such relationships, there was a big difference between expectation and realisation, leaving both Miriam and Ronl feeling that they had gotten the worst of a deal that had given neither of them more or less than they had deserved, i.e. each other.

Miriam staggered into Ronl's camp a few hours later looking more like a banshee than a human, and was nearly shot for that likeness by two of the camp's guards who she had startled into guilty wakefulness. It was only the hoity-toity way that she cursed their mothers, fathers, nephews and nieces, that led to one of the guards recognising her and exclaiming loudly, "strewth, if it ain't the guvners bit!"
"Take me to Ronl immediately, you half-witted morons!" Miriam snapped in reply.
Both guards secretly toyed with the idea of shooting her anyway and claiming that it was a mistake.

Ronl heard the commotion outside and jumped from his bed. He grabbed his dagger and sword and shook them from their sheaths. His first thought was that the Mountain troll had somehow broken free of its ropes, and he stood there in the dark, as afraid and vulnerable as he had been the night that he had watched a Mountain troll kill his father. A knock on the door made him jump. "What's happening?" he called out nervously.

"Yer woman's here."

Ronl let his breath out slowly and took a moment to steady his nerves, "I'm coming," he snapped angrily.

Ronl almost laughed when he saw Miriam standing by a fire warming herself and looking like something that had been dragged backwards and forwards through a hedge several times, but her disheveled appearance and the lateness of the hour were not in keeping, and he grew concerned. "What's up my darling?" he asked carefully. He caught Miriam in his arms as she ran to him, and held her close, but though he cooed and mollycoddled her, his eyes flitted nervously around the shadows at the edge of the camp. "Tell me my love, now, what is wrong?" he asked again a little more insistently. His left hand moved slowly to the back of her slender white neck still clutching the dagger.

Miriam pushed away slightly so that she could look at Ronl. She was about to speak when she noticed the Mountain troll tied against a tree. This was the first Mountain troll that she had ever seen, and she took a moment to thrill at its size and obvious power. She dragged her attention back to Ronl almost regretfully. "Oh Ronl!" she cried pitifully, falling back into his arms again. "It has all gone so dreadfully wrong.

That Ralph actually killed the damned airy-plane!" she sobbed.

Ronl stroked her hair almost mechanically as he absorbed her news. "There, there," he soothed.

Miriam stepped back again and looked up into Ronl's eyes. "Do you love me darling?" she asked. "I mean, really love me."

Ronl smiled reassuringly and pulled her close again. "Of course I do," he lied.

Miriam snuggled in closer. "A lot of my daddy's army are toast now. The reservists will be seeing the farmers back to their hovels in a day or so, and there will be a lot of coming and going for a while. You could sneak in easily now, and take the castle if you wanted. You could make daddy your prisoner and kill that Ralph for me, and we could rule Ithmar together as man and wife. It would be so easy-peasy," she persuaded sweetly.

No one had noticed Nifnaff stiffen at the mention of Ralph's name. Nifnaff only knew one Ralph. It was not a common name, and the odds against it being the same one were great, but another Ralph with a knack of getting himself into trouble with a dragon, and messing up someone's plans so badly that they wanted to kill him? "As if I did not have enough problems!" he grumbled under his breath.

Nifnaff looked over at the guards. They were too engrossed with what was going on between Ronl and the woman to pay him any attention. He had weakened and stretched the ropes that were holding him when he had tried to lunge at Ronl a few days earlier, and he been working on them steadily since, but though he believed that he could free his arms with an effort, he doubted that he could get free before his captors could turn their blowpipes on him. It was that doubt that had stopped him from trying to get free before, but Ronl was giving the woman's suggestion that he attack the castle serious consideration, and if he decided to do as she asked, he would not waste a single man or woman on guarding him. Nifnaff doubted very much that Ronl would simply let him go.

Nifnaff tensed against his restraints and took a deep breath. "You," he shouted.

Several people, including Ronl and Miriam, stopped what they were doing and turned to look at him.

"Are you with him?" he asked Miriam. "Only, I was wondering if you fancied something a little more..." Nifnaff paused a moment for effect, then said, "manly?" He forced an outrageously toothy smile onto his face as he added, "actually, something a little more than manly, if you get my meaning?"

Miriam looked shocked, though she was not as shocked as she looked. "Are you going to let that creature speak to me like that?" she asked sharply.

Ronl was almost purple with rage. "By the gods, no!" he cried loudly. He drew his sword again, and brandishing it, stomped towards the tied up Mountain troll. "I'll cut you to shreds for that!" he rasped.

Nifnaff met his fury with a slightly bored expression. "It will be better than listening to any more of your mad prattling," he answered dryly.

Ronl paused for barely a second to reassure himself that the troll was securely tied still. Satisfied that he was not in any personal danger, he gave in to his madness and swung the sword at Nifnaff.

Nifnaff was ready for him. He gave a mighty roar and thrust his arm forward against the weakened ropes. They held for the space of a heartbeat then snapped. Nifnaff's arm shot forward and came around like a swinging sledgehammer. He caught Ronl's sword close to the hilt, stopping it mid swing and yanked downwards, tearing it from his hand and pulling him forward slightly. Ronl yelped in surprise and tried to back away, but Nifnaff caught his hand and pulled hard, spinning him around so that he staggered backwards into Nifnaff.

Nifnaff wrapped his arm around Ronl's chest and held him close like a shield as he kicked off the last of the rope. Several blowpipes were already aimed at him, and a few of Ronl's men had their swords or axes in their hands, but everything had happened so quickly and they were unsure what to do. Nifnaff squeezed Ronl's chest ever so slightly, causing him to cry out. "I only want this man and his mistress," Nifnaff told them.

There was a few seconds silence, then someone said, "that seems reasonable."

"Fine by me," another voice added. "Never liked the mad bastard anywise."

"Yeh, good riddance if yer askin' me."

"Didn't ask yer," someone else said. "He's been good to me and my Sarah."

'He's been good to your Sarah alright!"

That caused a few giggles.

Someone else added, "reckon a few'n us've been good to his Sarah."

There were a few ayes and a couple of embarrassed coughs.

Two men who were as yet undecided about the extent of their loyalty took an uncertain step forward.

"He will only be the first to die if you try and stop me," Nifnaff warned them. "No one will win if we go down that path," he reasoned carefully. "You have to ask yourselves now before it is too late, do you owe a dead man so much that you would die with him?"

Ronl's second in command was stood closest to Nifnaff, and most eyes were now on him. He was no coward, but neither was he a fool. It was a simple enough choice that the troll was offering them. He gave the troll a long hard look, weighing up their options, then shrugged finally and nodded. "Take him and his bitch then. He's brought us more trouble than gain of late anyway." He waved the others back with his sword. "This fight has no purse for us lads. The rug's right; Ronl is dead whichever way we play this'n out. I reckon it's time we cut our losses and toss our camp on our backs and be off. King Roberin will turn his mind to us once he's licked his wounds, thanks to Ronl and his pet princess, so I say let the troll have 'em both and have done with the matter."

Roberin visited Ralph in the infirmary during the evening. Ralph was delirious and babbling on about the sky being full of dragons. Roberin stayed with him for a short while, listening and contemplating the oddity that was Ralph, but it was a mystery that went beyond his understanding of the way that the world was meant to work. Ordinary little men did not go around single-handedly defeating dragons. It was against all the rules. He giggled and shook his head, then got up and left.

Roberin had intended to drop in on Ralph again the following morning, but there was so much that needed his attention that he could not find the time. Squatters, petty thieving, not so petty thieving, bad plumbing, roof repairs, a little matter of recruiting/conscripting enough regulars from the reservists to replace those that he had lost, and then there were the funerals; and so the list went on.

Later that evening Roberin returned to find Ralph both conscious and coherent. "Nice to see you awake," he said, stifling a yawn as he sat down on a stool next to the cot that Ralph was in. "My sawbones says that aside from a few scars, you'll mend well enough."

"You look tired," Ralph observed.

Roberin shrugged it aside. "My daughter left the castle shortly after you were brought back," he confided.

"She's bound to come home sooner or later," Ralph said, trying to reassure Roberin.

Roberin laughed bitterly. "Of that I have little doubt! A bad penny is always to be found somewhere in a full pocket. I regret the day I sowed her seed. Had I known then the trouble that she'd cause, I'd've gladly foregone that pleasure. She'll come back alright," he agreed, "and she'll doubtless be planning some mischief for me with that cutthroat gold-digger of hers. I should've dealt with him and his band long ago."

"Why has she got it in for you?" Ralph asked. He had so far found nothing about the king to dislike. He was blunt, but Ralph was not so sure that he would call that a fault.

Roberin smiled grimly. "You know very little of royalty. Miriam is hungry for power, but I have stubbornly kept her from it by not dying," he explained, then added apologetically, "I think she would also like to see the man who thwarted her latest little scheme, stop breathing too."

"Who's that?" Ralph asked stupidly then said, 'Oh, right, me." He smiled nervously. "You've got a great big castle that'll keep them out though?"

"Castles stop armies. Few walls have ever stopped a determined thief or a cut-throat." Roberin assured him.

Ralph's relief at having survived an almost certain death turned to anger. "So I went through all that for nothing? Even after all that, your castle and people are still not safe," he said bitterly.

Roberin shook his head. "No," he agreed. "But then," he said with a meaningful look, "I think that you had your own reasons for that daft little stunt out there, eh?' Ralph was about to protest, but Roberin shushed him and stood up. "Did you hear that?" he asked as his hand came to rest on the bone handled hilt of the dirk at his waist.

"Hear what?" Ralph asked nervously.

"That!" Roberin snapped irritably, shushing him again.

Ralph heard it this time; shouting somewhere out in the passage. There was the sound of running feet, then a loud crash as something hit the wall outside with force.

Roberin hurried over to the door and almost skewered the guard who came spilling through it. "What the blazes!" he roared at the man.

The guard was red faced and puffing like a bellows. He had just run up three flights of stairs in chainmail, and it was several painfully long moments before he could speak. "Your, ah, daughter, huh, ah," he wheezed. He saw the sudden wariness in his king's eyes. "No, no!" he said, waving his hand. "She and, ah, and, ah, Ronl, and ah, huh, ah, captured by..."

"Nifnaff?" Ralph said uncertainly as a wall of muscle and fur filled the doorway. "Is that you?" He tried to sit up, but he was still too weak. "I didn't think I'd ever see you again."

Nifnaff stooped in the doorway and peered in. "I heard dragon, Ralph and murder uttered in the same breath," he told Ralph.

Ralph waited for Nifnaff to say more, but Nifnaff obviously felt that nothing more needed to be said.

Ronl and Miriam knelt on the floor in front of Roberin's throne. Both were in shackles. Miriam had gone from being offended at her treatment, to apologetic, and was presently in sulky denial. Ronl on the other hand met Roberin's iron edged glare steadily, neither shrinking from it nor rising to its challenge. He listened in smouldering silence as Roberin tore shreds out of his character.

When the king had finished, he raised his chin a little, and in the mildest of tones asked, "but what exactly am I being accused of?"

"What are you being accused of!" Roberin roared at him. He gripped the arms of his throne tightly, not trusting himself to speak until he could master his fury.

"I have not committed any crime within your borders," Ronl continued confidently. "As for my relationship with your daughter; it was she who sought my company and pursued what was for me a useful dalliance. I was not aware that ambition was a crime, even here."

Ralph slipped out quietly, unnoticed, and returned to his room. His sympathy was with the old king, but family feuds were messy things and he wanted no part of this one.

Ralph and Nifnaff stayed on at the castle as King Roberin's guests until Ralph was fit enough to travel. They might have stayed longer, but Nifnaff was keen to be on his way again. Ralph toyed briefly with the idea of staying in Ithmar, but though he never thought that he would hear himself say it, he had just about had his fill of being the object of hero worship.

Ralph the hero! He was sure that a hero was supposed to be brave, that a hero would never make excuses to a drunken soldier who fancied his chances with him on the training square, or cash in on his fame with a young woman who was flattered enough by his interest in her, to be easy game. Ralph had never had a good name before - not like this. Now that he had one, he was afraid that if he stayed any longer, he would do something that would irrevocably tarnish it. Ultimately it was this reason more than any other that decided him to leave.

Ralph went back up to the battlements the night before they were to leave. The lichen on the stone was black in places still and smelled strongly of damp soot. There were plenty of reminders of what the dragon had put these people through: collapsed roofs, blackened timbers that had yet to be replaced, a line of fresh graves alongside the road. Some things - he new - could never be mended.

He rested his hand on a merlon and stared out into the star punched blackness. The moat below him was in darkness, but for the occasional reflection where a swimming rat disturbed its surface. He wondered what rubbish had been dumped into the moat over the years, wondered what forgotten secrets were stuck fast in the silt at its bottom? If Ralph had been on Earth, he would have put a small bet on there being a couple of shopping trolleys rusting beneath its algae coated surface.

Ralph smiled to himself as he recalled the private meal that he and Nifnaff had shared with Roberin earlier that evening. Nifnaff had made his excuses after the meal, leaving him and the old king chatting by a log fire over a jug of mulled ale. The conversation had flittered around like sparrows, sometimes serious, sometimes light-hearted. Ralph had soaked it all in as though every word and syllable that the king spoke was wrapped in a bit of worldly wisdom.

The evening had passed far too quickly, ending when Roberin slipped into a contented snooze. Ralph stared at the half full jug that the king was holding loosely on his lap. He took it carefully and put it on the table. Not so many weeks ago he would have drained it first. Ralph could barely bring himself to think about how low he had sunk, and how much further he might have sunk if Miriam had not collected him from the jail that morning. He had that at least to thank her for!

Ralph wormed a fleck of stone away from the wall were it had been blown by frost and extreme heat. He tossed it into the darkness, then jumping up slightly, leaned out and tilted his head so that he could listen for a plop. It landed in the grass on the narrow berm below him without a sound.

Nifnaff leaned over his shoulder and looked down with eyes that were much better suited to the dark. "You could not hit a mountain if you were standing on it," he observed.

Ralph had not heard him arrive and jumped a little. "Been having fun?" he asked, turning slightly.

"Not as you would say, fun," Nifnaff answered vaguely.

Ralph watched Nifnaff for a moment. It saddened him, the thought that they might go their separate ways again in the morning. They had not spoken about what each would do after they left the castle, but travelling together had been a disaster that he doubted that Nifnaff would want to repeat. "I might stay here," he lied, trying to give Nifnaff the opportunity to leave alone and thus avoid an awkward moment. "They think I'm a hero, you know."

Nifnaff laughed. "I would give it a month before they ran you out."

Ralph liked Nifnaff's laugh, even when it was at his expense. It was honest and as loud as a colliery brass band. "Maybe," he admitted, "but I'll give it a day before I get myself into trouble again out there," he said wistfully.

"I am leaving tonight," Nifnaff announced unexpectedly. "We could travel together for a while if you want," he suggested, adding, "we might yet find a wizard who does not want to see your head on a stick."

"And what if we didn't?" Ralph asked him.

Nifnaff shrugged. "Then we might find one who does want to see your head on a stick, who will send me home for having delivered it to him."

They stared out into the darkness in silence for a while, each locked in their own thoughts. Nifnaff was wondering why he had offered to let Ralph travel with him again. It was clear that their journeys were different, for all that their paths had crossed twice now. He needed to get home as did Ralph, but unlike Ralph, his own journey could be measured in miles. "Have you thought that you might not be able to get back to your world?" he asked.

Ralph nodded grimly. Of course he had. He had not thought about it much since coming to Ithmar, but when he did, it caused a knot in his stomach as it did again now. He wanted to kick Nifnaff for making him go to that dark place again. A moment earlier he had been thinking that things were really not that bad in Derrian once you started to get used to it, now it seemed almost as alien again as it had on that first day.

"We should go now if you are travelling with me," Nifnaff said, breaking into Ralph's thoughts. "I would prefer to leave without any fuss."

Ralph considered it for a moment, then nodded. "I'll get my stuff and meet you at the gate," he told Nifnaff. He wondered briefly what prompted his large companion's urgency as he went back down the steps, but he doubted that Nifnaff would have told him if he had asked. He would have liked to say goodbye to Roberin before leaving, but he realised that everything important had already been said earlier.

Roberin looked up from his breakfast. "How do you write this one up, eh old friend?" he asked his scribe gently, then said, "pass the jam please."

The scribe leaned over and passed the pot to the king. They often sat down to breakfast together and discussed the business of the coming day. It was a familiarity that Roberin shared with very few people, but the scribe had been with him for more years than he cared to dwell upon.

"That a young fool came to Ithmar and that a better man left?" the scribe offered.

Roberin thought about it for moment and nodded. "Aye," he agreed. "A bit flowery mind you, and I guess you'd better say something about him killing that dragon."

Ronl was found just before the change of the watch. The wall of his cell had been taken down brick by brick and stacked neatly to one side. His body had been placed on top of the stack of bricks and covered over with a piece of canvas that had become bloody. Resting on top of the canvas, pinned down under the edge of a brick was a note. The note was short and to the point, apologising for the inconvenience and explaining that a promise had needed to be kept.

Amazingly the jailer had heard nothing. He claimed later during an interview with the king, that the reason that he had smelled so heavily of alcohol was due to him having been so shocked by the grisly find that he had immediately gone and taken a stiff drink to calm his nerves before reporting it.

The man had been so scared as he stood there in front of his king, that when Roberin suggested that Ronl might have been so consumed by guilt that he had torn his own spine out and strangled himself with it, he almost wet himself with relief. The scribe grinned and raised a disbelieving eyebrow. "And the stacked up bricks and note?" he asked, his pen poised over the page.

"Who knows what goes through the mind of a man like that," the guard said, shaking his head sadly.

"Just so," Roberin answered. He slapped the arm of his throne and smiled. "That's an end to the matter then; suicide it is." He added in the privacy of his thoughts, "which means I won't need to send my men out to bring Ralph's hairy friend back to face trial."

"Suicide Sire," the jailer agreed eagerly, his relief palpable.

"And get that wall rebuilt."

"Yes Sire."

"And when I say, get it rebuilt, I mean do it yourself."

"Yes Sire."

"Oh, and hang the body on the hangman's bough as a warning to others. It's been far too long since that tree bore any fruit."

"Yes Sire."

"And..."

"Yes Sire?" the jailer asked when his king paused.

"If you get drunk on duty again, You'll be needing more than a stiff drink when I've done with you."

The jailer nodded. "Yes Sire."

Nifnaff was not the most talkative of people. He was even less so after three weeks of listening to Ralph bleating on about his aching arm and ribs, and his cramps and saddle sores, and sleeping on the ground and.... With the clarity that comes with hindsight, Nifnaff reached the conclusion that travelling with Ralph again might not have been one of his better ideas. He could find many good qualities in the man that more than compensated for him being human, but Ralph was very much like he imagined whisky to be from having witnessed its effects on lowlanders; pleasant enough in small amounts, but too much of it can pickle your brain.

Ralph looked down at Nifnaff gloomily from his saddle. There was something bothering Nifnaff still, a ghost that had briefly left him alone during their stay at the castle. Ralph doubted that his hairy companion would ever confide in him about it. He toyed briefly with the idea of parting company with Nifnaff, considered that maybe Nifnaff would be happier travelling alone, but even thinking about doing it made him feel guilty. He knew that he was a burden to the Mountain troll, but then Nifnaff was the most physically completed creature that he could imagine; how could anyone not be a burden to him! Yet despite that, inexplicably, Nifnaff seemed to need him around. Ralph owed Nifnaff too much to simply ride away.

The road that they were travelling along was the first that they had seen since leaving Castle Ithmar. It was long and straight and well compacted from regular use, and the going was much easier than they had become accustomed to.

Nifnaff took full advantage of the easier going and set a pace that took any pleasure away from it for Ralph, even on horseback!

Ralph stared ahead dully. He had long since stopped being concerned about the possibility of an ambush from the forest that was hugging both sides of the road. Indeed, he almost welcomed the possibility, if only to relieve the boredom. He looked up at Murd - this world's sun - and figured that there was probably an hour or so of useful daylight left to them. He was tired and sore, and both he and his horse were desperate for a rest, but he knew from past experience that Nifnaff would not even consider stopping until it grew too dark for the horse to find its way. When Nifnaff stopped abruptly and told him that they were going to make camp, he had to ask him to repeat himself to make sure that he had not heard him incorrectly.

Nifnaff had jumped down Ralph's throat earlier because he had dared to suggest that they stop and take a rest. Now Nifnaff was standing there showing more brass than a pawn shop on a Monday morning, suggesting that they do no less than he had, because suddenly it was convenient for him! Ralph glared at him. He briefly considered insisting that they push on a little longer just to make a point, but his horse was worn out and did not deserve that from him, so he held his tongue and reined the mare over alongside a section of fallen tree so that he could dismount more easily.

The tree had fallen in a storm years earlier. It was mostly dust and shavings beneath the bark, and it gave beneath Ralph's foot the moment he put his weight down on it, and he fell backwards with his right foot still in the stirrup and landed on his back hard, narrowly missing cracking his head open on the exposed root of another tree nearby.

Nifnaff reached for the reins to steady the horse, then grabbed a handful of Ralph's shirt and pulled him to his feet. "You must be the clumsiest creature alive!" he exclaimed. "You have been nothing but trouble since the day we met." He turned and walked away, not trusting himself to say anything more.

Ralph stared after him open mouthed. He was momentarily taken aback, but his surprise quickly turned to anger. "Wait a bloody minute!" he sputtered indignantly. "What did I do to deserve that! It was you that suggested that we travel together again, not me," he reminded him. Ralph scowled and went straight to what he thought was at the heart of Nifnaff's outburst. "You're still blaming me for that wizard, aren't you?" He shook his head. "You know that was an accident. If I could undo it, don't you think I would? You're blaming me as though I pushed him. I didn't push him; he fell because we had a stupid argument and he lost his footing."

Nifnaff knew that Ralph was right. Of course Ralph had not intended to hurt that old man! He knew that. The wizard's death was the end result of a rather bizarre set of circumstances that made less and less sense the more that he thought about it. Ralph was right about the other stuff as well. The fact was - and this was no great revelation to him either - he was being unfair to Ralph. Knowing this did not make him any more inclined to start being reasonable with him; not yet at least. "I will make a fire," he said sulkily, pulling himself back from the brink of an unbridgeable rift.

Ralph led his horse to a tree and attached a longer rope to her headgear which he tied to a sturdy branch. He took the saddle off and put it to one side, then waited long enough to be sure that she would have no trouble getting at the grass. He was not a lover of horses, and all he really knew about them was that one end attracted a few less flies than the other, but the mare was such a placid thing that he had quite forgotten to be afraid of her.

The horse was a gift from Roberin, along with the clothes on his back, his weapons, and a purse on his belt that bulged more healthily than it had when he arrived at Ithmar. One of the gifts that he had received was a lightly quilted gambeson. Somebody had painstakingly stitched the goats head emblem that was on his small buckler into its breast. The Illefed's badge was Roberin's to gift, and he had done so gladly. Ralph was stupidly proud of it. He found his fingers straying to the stitch work often. It connected him to Ithmar and to its old king for whom he had nothing but the highest regard, and in doing so, it connected him to Derain itself. The slight resemblance that the burn on his chest bore to the badge only served to strengthen his sense of rightful ownership.

The horse had belonged to the princess Miriam. Roberin had been concerned that Ralph would not be fully mended when he left the castle, and had insisted that he go and see his stable master for a horse. Ralph had done so reluctantly, and had chosen the least frightening looking horse there. That horse had turned out to be Miriam's. Knowing this, and knowing that Miriam was soon to be banished, he reasoned that she would most likely take the mare. Ralph could not imagine Miriam treating anyone or anything with much affection, and he was driven by compassion for the horse to ask Roberin if he could have her. Roberin had taken a certain satisfaction in agreeing to let him have the horse, and in later ensuring that his daughter found out who he had given it to.

Miriam was banished from Ithmar a few days after Ralph and Nifnaff left. She was told that if she should ever try to return, it would be to the bite of a sword on the back of her dainty little neck. Miriam did not doubt her father's sincerity, but she pushed her luck a little by asking that Ronl be released with her.

Roberin laughed at her request and told her that she was welcome to what was left of him, adding, "you'll find him waiting for you on the hangman's bough."

Miriam was led away speechless for once, and that was the last that the king saw or heard of his daughter until many years later.

Ralph watched Nifnaff blowing into a little pyramid of twigs. Each time he blew, it's smouldering heart glowed a little more brightly, until at last a few tiny tongues of flame curled around the twigs and took hold. He carefully put a few more twigs on top as the pyramid's glowing heart collapsed in on itself, then added a few bigger twigs and branches, until at last he had something that could credibly be called a fire. "Why do you want to return to your Earth so much?" he asked without looking up at Ralph. "Do you have family or a female there who are missing you?"

"No," Ralph told him. He thought about it then said, "it's my home. I fit in there. If things go wrong there, it's stuff that I understand. I mean, my first day here, I nearly got eaten by fairies! Can you believe it? But of course you can believe it, because this is your world."

Nifnaff stared at Ralph blankly.

Ralph sat down on what he took to be a rock and frowned. "Nothing here is ever quite what I expect it to be."

"Eff uff."

"What?" Ralph asked.

Nifnaff said, "what?"

"I said, what," Ralph told him.

"And I said gef off."

Ralph jumped up as the small rock that he was sat on moved. He looked down in surprise. "What the!" he exclaimed loudly as two eyes opened on the front of the rock and gave his shins a filthy look.

"That," Nifnaff said dryly, "is not what I expected either."

The creature - a Lowland troll - was buried up to its neck in a hole and had been partly covered over with leaves, presumably in the hope that no one would find it there. It took Ralph a while to dig it out. This was done without Nifnaff's help, who had made it clear from the outset that he did not like or trust Lowland trolls.

This was the first Lowland troll that Ralph had ever seen, and he was understandably curious. It was an odd looking creature, four or five inches broader across the shoulders than he was, and a little taller maybe, but rake thin and sinewy, with the cold uncaring stare of a feral cat. "It looks nothing like you," he told Nifnaff.

Nifnaff scowled at Ralph. "That is because it is a Lowland troll and I am a Mountain troll. It is short and ugly and I am neither." He gave Ralph a look that challenged him to say otherwise, then turned a suspicious eye on the troll. "What were you doing buried in that hole?" he asked, knowing full well the sort of mischief that Lowlands were capable of.

"Mindin' my own business," the troll answered irritably as it moved closer to the fire and rubbed its hands together.

Nifnaff glowered at the creature. "Would you like me to put you back in that hole so that you can mind it some more?' he asked pointedly.

"I had a bit of a dispute with some elves," the troll answered grudgingly, adding, "the buggers jumped me while I was asleep."

"You were caught stealing, you mean," Nifnaff said with a sneer.

Ethelthwaite shrugged dismissively. It was in keeping with his assumed disguise, so he let the Mountain troll's suspicions rest there.

Ralph was looking at the creature in a way that was always just enough to one side or the other so as not to be too direct. He knew enough basic anatomy to be sure that the creature was a male, but it was wearing a simple smock dress of sorts. Ralph would not normally have taken anything by this. Smocks were cheaper and easier to make than trousers, and were commonly worn in Derrian by men, but the troll's smock had been tailored, and it clung in a way that left Ralph, well, frankly a little unsettled! "I'm Ralph," he said, offering his name. He waited for the troll to respond in kind, but nothing was forthcoming and so he asked, "and you are?"
"None of your," Ethelthwaite started to say, trying to react as Daphne might have, then scowled at Nifnaff and said, "Daphne."

Ethelthwaite had spent the day buried in a hole. He had been unconscious for most of it. Given that he was still wearing a Lowland troll's body, it smacked of inevitability that he would have a run in with elves sooner or later, but he had not expected to be smacked over the head by that inevitability while he was sleeping! One might well imagine his surprise and suspicion, when who should come along as he fully regained his wits but Ralph and his furry sidekick. Curiosity and the need to get out of the hole decided him. It had been a simple thing to insinuate a need to stop and make camp into the troll's head.

Nifnaff poured water into a billycan and hung it over the fire on a metal pole between two forked branches that he had twisted into the ground. He opened a cloth bag and cut a few misshapen vegetables that they had foraged along the way into the can, then added some salt and a few freshly plucked herbs.

Ralph was a vegetarian. So was Nifnaff, and so the problem of cooking separate meals had never arisen. Nifnaff had no actual need to cook his food at all, and his stomach could tolerate plants that would have left Ralph writhing on the floor in pain, but he had tailored his eating habits to accommodate his travelling companion. The only area where Ralph had so far set aside his morals since arriving in Derrian, was in the matter of footwear and a few items of protective clothing for which he had found no natural native alternative. The balm on his conscience in that matter was that he had not bought any of those things, and much of it was secondhand.

Nifnaff waited until the water was bubbling, then crumbled up the last of their hard travel bread and dropped it in. Ralph leaned forward and sniffed the bubbling broth appreciatively. Maybe he had come to expect less from his food during his time on the road, but Nifnaff's ability to make a palatable meal out of a few foraged vegetables and a pinch of salt never ceased to amaze him.

"Where're you heading?" Ethelthwaite asked, eyeing the cooking stew hungrily.

"Brace," Nifnaff told him, surprising Ralph.

"Brace?" Ralph asked incredulously. "Aren't you forgetting something?"

Nifnaff tossed him a bowl. "I have been thinking," he said as he contemplated whether to feed the Lowland or not. He grimaced and tossed him a spare bowl. "And it bothers me that we managed to escape."

"Well it doesn't bother me!" Ralph told him. "We were lucky to get away."

Nifnaff shook his head. "I cannot believe now so easily what I had accepted in my haste then. You are not from here," he reminded Ralph. "You do not know about the wizards. They are many things, but stupid is not one of them."

"I'm coming with you," Ethelthwaite/Daphne said, interrupting Nifnaff.

Nifnaff shook his head. "You are not."

"I can't see the harm," Ralph cut in. "It's not like we've got to carry him."

They had barely gone five miles before Ethelthwaite started staggering with the effort of trying to keep up. Despite the implied strength of his assumed Lowland troll body, he was an old man still, and his recent trials had taken more out of him than he would care to admit, even to himself.

"If he cannot keep up I will leave him behind," Nifnaff said with a snarl in the Lowland's direction, adding, "I will not carry him."

"He can ride on my horse for a while," Ralph suggested, adding, "I can walk for a bit."

"He will steal your horse, and eat it," Nifnaff told him.

Ralph did not know whether Lowland trolls ate horses or not, but he could well believe that the creature would steal it given half a chance, so he climbed down from his saddle, and gripping the reins more tightly, said, "we'll just have to go a bit slower then."

Nifnaff shook his head in exasperation then stomped back to the Lowland troll. He lifted him roughly from the ground and threw him over his shoulder like a sack. "Do not fidget," he warned, "or I will put you down again, on your head."

It took them a few weeks to reach Brace's border again. What they saw when they got there was a far cry from what had greeted Ralph and Nifnaff the last time they were there. The linseed that had at first entertained then annoyed Ralph seemed listless, and there were large patches of open ground where the plants could no longer dig themselves in, either because the ground itself had become too hard or because the linseed no longer had the strength to. After a couple of halfhearted attempts, Ralph actually managed to catch one of the linseed plants. It squirmed in his grasp and he let it go, but not before seeing the fine peppering of tiny black aphids that were clinging to its stem and leaves. "They're being eaten by bugs," he told Nifnaff. He shook his head. "I don't get it."

Ethelthwaite kept his thoughts to himself, and Nifnaff who only knew the wizards through stories, could add nothing that would explain why they would allow this to happen.

Ethelthwaite felt as though he had been punched in the stomach. He had played in the linseed fields as a young student during his infrequent field trips there. To see it like this; it was difficult to hold his emotions in check, but to do otherwise would have invited curiosity from his travelling companions, and so he walked on in silence, inwardly seething that someone would have the audacity to attack them in such a direct manner.

Ralph could not shake the feeling that he had in some way caused this. Of course it was nonsense; he knew it was. The linseed was blighted by bugs, nothing more, but why had the wizards not done something about it? He stared ahead nervously and wondered what sort of reception they would receive when they reached the city this time. The only thing that stopped him turning his horse around there and then and riding away, was Nifnaff's unswayable belief that they had been deceived in some way the last time they were there.

That night another traveler joined them unexpectedly as they were sat sharing a meal by the gentle glow of a small fire. So silent and swift was his arrival that he seemed to bleed out of the darkness in front of them, catching even Nifnaff with his heightened night vision by surprise. Nifnaff would have made a grab for him but for Ethelthwaite's quick intervention. He stood warily, only half listening to the stream of assurances from Ethelthwaite that the stranger was a friend who meant them no harm.

Ralph saw the man's face in the flickering light and instantly recognised him. "Mr Wilkins," he said, recalling his name.

"Tumble to my friends," Tumble answered with a warm but brief smile in his direction. He turned to the Lowland troll and a meaningful look passed between them.

Ethelthwaite smiled apologetically at his two travelling companions. "Come," he said, taking hold of Tumble's elbow and leading him out of earshot. He returned a few minutes later alone and sat back down by the fire. "You won't find what you're looking for in Brace," he told them both, adding, "you've no cause to trust me, but if you come with me, I can make sure that you both get what you want."

Nifnaff stared hard at the Lowland troll across the small fire. He did not like or trust Daphne, but his natural inclination was to dislike and mistrust everyone until he got to know them better, so this was not in itself a reliable means upon which to decide whether to reject what he was saying. The fact that Daphne was a Lowland troll was however. "There are things that are not right about you," he told the Lowland.

Ethelthwaite met Nifnaff's stare solidly and shrugged his boney shoulders. "Have I tried to murder you in your sleep or rob you?"

"That is my point," Nifnaff answered dryly.

Ethelthwaite laughed. "Things are not always as they appear," he said, becoming serious again. "If they were, you wouldn't be going back to the city, would you?"

Ralph felt as though he was watching a mask slipping away. He did not trust Daphne any more than Nifnaff did, but Tumble's arrival and the conspiratorial manner of his meeting with Daphne, rather than increase his mistrust of him, resolved him to see how things would play out. He did not doubt that Nifnaff was right to be suspicious about Tumble, or about what had happened that day at the city wall. The more he thought about it, the more manufactured it felt to him. If that were true, if Nifnaff was right, then it seemed logical that Tumble Wilkins was also involved; and here Tumble was again, engaged in secretive business with a Lowland troll who had despite Nifnaff's animosity towards him, insisted on travelling with them to Brace. There were other things as well: the easy way that Tumble had submitted to Daphne's authority when he had been taken aside spoke volumes about the order of the relationship between the two. Whatever Daphne was, he was not what he seemed.

"Are you saying that if we go to the city we will not get home?" Ralph asked pointedly.

"Yes," Daphne answered simply.

"He cannot be trusted," Nifnaff warned again.

"I don't trust him," Ralph told Nifnaff, "but I trust you, and I do believe him when he says that the wizards wont help us," he said bitterly. "I want to know why we were given the runaround, and I've a sneaky suspicion that he knows."

The following morning Daphne surprised them by insisting that they continue their journey towards Brace for a short while. There were portals along the boulevards, that had been put in place centuries earlier against the eventuality that the wizards would need to evacuate the city and its surrounding settlements quickly. That had been during the time immediately after the war between the elves and the Lowlands, and the portals had thankfully never needed to be used that way.

The portals were hidden in plain view and could only be activated from the side facing towards the city. When Daphne stopped suddenly and cast his shifty eyes heavenward, so did Ralph and Nifnaff - stop that is - and when he turned and stomped back the way they had just come, saying that they had missed their turn, they reluctantly followed him. When they were no longer on the same road, but many miles away penned in by a wall of trees, they were less surprised than concerned.

It was not long before things again began to seem familiar - to Ralph at least. Ralph was shocked when he at last realised where they were. It felt like a lifetime ago when he had stood very close to this same spot, saying goodbye to Gemfelt and worrying that he might not survive the week on his own. So much had happened since then. He wondered if Gemfelt and his wife would be surprised or pleased to discover that he was still alive?

Just ahead was the village, sat in the middle of its clearing like a cluster of colourful boils. Ralph remembered his last night there, talking into the early hours about the differences between two worlds that were separated by more than just space. He felt as he examined the memory, that he had been a very different person then.

Daphne/Ethelthwaite grew more focused and resolute as they approached the village, driven by a purpose that he stubbornly refused to divulge to his two companions. Nifnaff did not know where they were, but he was ready to strangle that information out of Daphne. The only thing that had stopped him, was Ralph getting in the way and Daphne's hurried assurances.

"I know this place," Ralph told Nifnaff. "I have friends here."

As they entered the village they encountered several elves. They were on the most part surly and guarded, feigning disinterest where normally they would have been more openly inquisitive about strangers among them - especially a Lowland troll! Ralph thought that he recognised a couple of the elves, though none of them showed any sign that they recognised him.

Daphne/Ethelthwaite stopped at Gertru's house and knocked on the door. He waited a few moments then knocked again more loudly. There was a clunk as the bolt was withdrawn and the catch lifted, then the door opened a few inches.

"Yes?"

Ralph barely recognised the emaciated face that looked out at them, and it was a full thirty seconds before he realised who it was. "Northan?" Ralph asked in a concerned voice. He had not liked the elf particularly, but he and Gemfelt had helped him when others might have left him to die.

Ethelthwaite did not let the elf answer, though from the look on Northan's face, it was doubtful that he had recognised Ralph anyway. "Fetch your wife," he said impatiently.

Northan seemed to shrink into himself. "I, I," he stammered, suddenly very frightened. "See here, my Gert' don't like being disturbed from her reposing."

"Nonsense!" Ethelthwaite snapped. "Your wife knows full well that I'm here, and why. Now fetch her, or do I have to destroy this hovel around her ears?"

Nifnaff tapped Ralph's shoulder. Ralph turned his head and looked at what had taken Nifnaff's interest away from the odd exchange between Daphne and Northan. A group of armed elves had moved up quietly with the intention of catching them off guard, but there were indistinct shapes moving among them, yanking their weapons out of their hands or knocking them to the ground. Ralph thought that he could almost make out a leg here or an arm there, or what might have been a face turned their way, but these were fleeting impressions only.

Ralph looked back at Daphne, except that Daphne was not Daphne anymore. A shrewd looking little old man who Ralph instantly recognised as the dead wizard turned and winked at him. Ralph might have felt many things at discovering that the wizard was not dead: shock, anger, relief, curiosity; each and every one of these would have been justified, but his overriding feeling in that moment was curiosity.

Northan was yanked back inside with some force, his face in that split second before he disappeared showing more resignation than surprise. There was a loud thump and a pitiful whimper, then nothing. The door swung back slightly on its hinges and stopped. Beyond it was the silence of a held breath, and darkness.

Ralph took a step backwards, acting on something that might have been prescience or just fear, a moment before Gertru came bursting through the door like a charging bear. Ethelthwaite tried to get out of her way but was too slow. He staggered backwards and might have fallen over but for Ralph's quick intervention in catching him. Both men turned in time to see Gertru land squarely on her backside. She sat there dazed and confused, then tried to get up, made it half way and fell back down again.

Nifnaff unclenched his fist and shrugged his great shoulders. "I thought that she was going to attack me," he said simply.

"I thought much the same when I first met her," Ralph admitted.

Ethelthwaite looked down at Gertru as one might an unpleasant bug. "Tumble," he said without turning.

Ralph had not seen Tumble come up and stand next to him, and he jumped slightly.

"There's a Merlin gate in there," Ethelthwaite said, nodding at the door. "I blocked her from escaping through it, but it is still open. Take a few of your people through and bring back whoever you find lurking on the other side. And," he said, giving it further consideration, "you'd better take a witch with you just in case. I would rather there were no, misunderstandings."

Tumble nodded and gestured for a couple of his people to join him. "And you," he said, waving at a young witch.

Ethelthwaite turned his attention back to Gertru as Tumble and the others entered the house. She was sullen and watchful but not cowed. "You have an appointment with an inquisitor's stone in Brace," he told her as two of his people pulled her roughly to her feet. He turned to face Ralph and Nifnaff. "Now let's deal with you two."

"You lousy old git!" Ralph said angrily, cutting him off.

Ethelthwaite smiled, but his eyes turned as hard as flint. "Why," he asked, "because you found yourself in my world, or because you thought you'd killed me? I'll own the deception, but you weren't wholly innocent in how that came about," he reminded Ralph. "As for your being here?" He shrugged. "That wasn't my doing."

Ralph turned to Nifnaff for support, but Nifnaff was not about to ruin what might be his last chance to avoid a very long walk home. Ralph shot him a filthy look then turned back to the wizard, exasperated at how he was able to trivialise such a terrible deception. "I want to go home," he said, resisting the urge to say more.

Ethelthwaite frowned at him. "Is that what you want, or is that your anger talking?" he asked.

"I want to go home," Ralph repeated, almost pleading now despite being angry with the wizard.

Ethelthwaite looked almost disappointed as he shoved his hand into his pocket and pulled out a copper tipped walking stick that had the laws of physics run true, would have stuck out of the bottom of his trousers and made it impossible for him to bend his leg. He traced a rough circle with the tip just above the ground then stood back. "Step into the middle," he told Ralph as it turned milky white. "And do try to keep your hands at your sides."

Ralph did as he was told, albeit nervously. He was about to say goodbye to Nifnaff, but Nifnaff was no longer there. Nothing was there; then he was sat on a floral patterned settee with a cup and saucer in his hands, thinking that he had not had a chance to ask anyone to look after his horse.

"I'd offer you a penny for your thoughts," Edna God told him, "but I already know what they are. That's the thing about omniscience; it has its uses, but it can be a real bore at times." She sighed and gave his knee an affectionate pat. "Don't you go fretting yourself into a state now," she told him. "Things'll turn out as they will, which is how they're meant to." She leaned over and took the cup and saucer from his unresisting hand, the smell of her perfume and the warmth of her closeness filling his senses to the exclusion of everything else. "Easy tiger! Remember, I know what you're thinking." She watched him colour slightly and giggled. "Anyway, it's always nice having a little natter with you, but it's time that you were on your way."

Ralph stared at her as though seeing her for the first time. The turn of her full lips and the crinkling at the corners of her eyes when she smiled at him, the curve of her thigh within her yellow cotton dress as she leaned forward in her seat, the white of her neck as she brushed her auburn hair aside, and her eyes; Ralph wanted to fall into their sparkling depths and never surface again. "I'm Ralph," he said, trying to fill the uncomfortable silence that had grown between them. "And you are?"

"I'm many things, but you can call me Edna," she told him. "You won't remember that for very long I'm afraid." She saw the questions forming one behind the other and said, "yes," and, "because a question with an answer isn't a question anymore, and you humans do like your questions." There was a moment, a look that might have been consideration on her part, then she was gone: the room, the comfy settee, the vase of flowers on the small inlaid rosewood coffee table, all gone as though they had never existed, as though she had never existed.

An old lady in a thick winter coat and woolly hat tutted loudly. "Och!" she said in a slightly distilled Scottish accent, trying to look cross. "It's surely the cold that is making it such a wee thing, Janet. I've seen the like back in Achinduich when the local boys used to dare each other to go and swim nuddy in Loch Laro in the winter."

"Yes," her English friend agreed, suppressing a grin.

Both women went into fits of giggles and walked away, leaving Ralph stood there looking after them with a bemused look on his face.

It took Ralph a few seconds to realise that he was no longer in Derrian. Small and large details started to slot themselves quickly into place after that: cars and buses, acrid and loud to his unaccustomed senses as they crept along the busy street papping their horns impatiently, two pigeons squabbling over a chip on the pavement, pedestrians giving him a wide berth, his own naked reflection in the large shop window, the whoop of a siren as a police car pulled up against the curb. Ralph was home.

Printed in Great Britain
by Amazon